PRINCESS IN PLAID

AMY JARECKI

1

G race Eloise MacGalloway oft resented the swans who made Hyde Park's Serpentine Lake their home. She envied their freedom, their beauty, their elegance, their majesty. Grace had never beheld an unseemly swan. Their attractiveness was God-given. The birds had no need for finishing school, impeccable manners, alluring charm, or fine silks and brocades. They cared not a whit about using proper English and the pains to which a gentlewoman must go when seeking a husband—a man worthy of her station, no less.

But at long last, today Isidor Borowski had bestowed upon Grace the lofty title of princess. This very day, their esteemed wedding opened the London Season—touted as the most highly celebrated royal marriage of the decade. No expense was spared. All members of polite society were in attendance, filling St. Peter's Cathedral until there was standing room only. Flowers had been ordered from every hothouse within twenty miles of Town. The sanctuary came alive with her favorite scents of white gardenias and red roses, accented with sprigs of pink jasmine in exactly the right quantity to add a rich, slightly sensual fragrance.

The cost of Grace's wedding gown exceeded a thousand pounds and had taken the modiste three months to create. The ceremony passed in a blur. And with the whirlwind of excitement, Grace hardly had time to contemplate the proceedings as the Archbishop of Canterbury pronounced them husband and wife. Her heart soared to the skies. In this moment she accomplished all her life's goals. The pinnacle of her very existence!

Arm-in-arm, Princess Grace and Prince Isidor paraded out of the cathedral and continued into and into their gilt carriage, upholstered in red velvet. Tiny drops of snow danced upon the breeze as white ermine blankets were placed over their laps, warm bricks beneath their feet. A team of six white horses pulled their carriage through the streets of London where the newly espoused couple was cheered and welcomed by multitudes of British subjects, all elated with the news that one of the kingdom's daughters had married into the ancient Lithuanian Duchy of Samogitia.

As the carriage rolled through Hyde Park, they passed a bank of swans in the icy Serpentine. Grace smiled inwardly. At long last she knew what it was like to be as free and as beautiful as those majestic birds. Moreover, she was toasty warm, while she was quite certain they were not.

Henceforth, she would be a member of one of Europe's most powerful royal houses. Grace would be the mistress of no fewer than five Lithuanian estates including two castles and three country manors, the largest of which was near the seaside city of Klapedia. No longer would she need to prove her worth to the *ton* or feel pressured to dazzle London's elite. She now had risen to the top of the pecking order, not just in Britain, but in all of Christendom.

This moment was exactly why she had spent so many hours learning to dance with utmost charm and distinguished grace. This was why she had applied herself to every course of study with the potential to advance her status in society. This was the reason she had learned no fewer than four languages. Today's achievement was the very reason she strove for perfection in her every endeavor. After all, Grace had been born into a dukedom, albeit a Scottish seat. Though her mother was English, when attending Northbourne Seminary for Young Ladies Grace had been forced to prove herself at every turn. Even daughters of mere English barons thought themselves superior. Which was exactly why Grace had worked hard to affect an English accent and set her sights on the grandest prize—the very reason she had declined to accept ten proposals from perfectly decent, titled lords, even a duke.

Prince Isidor was the most eligible bachelor of Europe's elite, and Grace had now proven that the daughter of a Scottish duke had the wherewithal to marry His Highness.

The procession ended at the illustrious Carlton House where the Prince Regent himself generously had offered to host the wedding reception. Prince George might have bankrupted the kingdom when building Carlton House, though after the completion of the residence, no one could deny its spectacular opulence. And today, the regent himself had demonstrated the resilience behind England's purse. The meal consisted of eleven courses, after which, Grace and Isidor took their places in the entrance hall with its domed ceiling and Grecian marbles where they received felicitations from their guests.

Compliments bubbled like champagne with Grace's wedding gown receiving fervent adoration. Fitting royal tradition, the gown was silver as had been Princess Charlotte of Wales'. Though the bodice retained some features of a *robe de cour*, with layered sleeves and a train, the waistline was styled in the fashionable empire silhouette, sitting just below the bust. The modiste's use of silver thread on net with a silver tissue slip beneath gave the gown a dazzling, reflective, and majestic appearance. No detail was spared as silver thread was also used to embroider the skirt with shimmering shells and flowers. Grace's fair hair was simply arranged and crowned with a wreath of brilliant diamonds. She wore teardrop diamond earrings with a matching diamond pendant in a silver setting which had been an engagement gift from His Highness.

How positively regal Prince Isidor presented himself in his bright red military uniform capped by golden epaulets upon his shoulders and adorned with medals denoting his station. After the last of the guests had offered their congratulations, Lord Alder, the exceedingly handsome third son of an earl bowed to Grace. The man had all but attached himself to Isidor's side throughout the months of wedding preparations. "Would it be terribly impolite of me to invite your husband for one last cheroot before you set sail for the Baltic Sea?"

Grace's temper flared like flame to oil, though her schooled countenance maintained a calm and unfettered air. Nonetheless, the man's insolence was infuriating. How dare Alder—a mere third son—take her husband away to enjoy a cigar? This was her wedding, not his! Indeed it was exceedingly impolite for such a low-ranking gentleman to abscond with the groom...a prince, no less.

"Please, my dear," said Isidor, with a pronounced Lithuanian accent which made him all the more alluring. "Alder has become such a dear friend while I have been in England, it would be most thoughtless not to allow him to give me a proper send-off."

Engaging in a disagreement on their wedding day would be vulgar and unbecoming. And why not let Isidor enjoy a cigar especially since he had recited his vows so eloquently? As long as he didn't smoke the vile things in her presence. "Very well, but I shall miss you ever so. Please don't tarry overlong, my dear. Did you not just remind me that our ship is sailing promptly at six o'clock?"

"I shan't be away from your side but for a few moments, *širdelė*," he said, using the Lithuanian endearment for sweetheart. Aside from her native English, Grace was fluent in French, Italian, and German. In addition, after she'd attracted Isidor's attentions toward the end of last Season, her brother had engaged a Lithuanian tutor on her behalf. She might not exactly be fluent, but she now understood far more of the prince's conversations with his courtiers than her husband realized.

After Alder accompanied Isidor to the Rose Satin Room, Grace's brother Martin, the Duke of Dunscaby rescued her by offering his hand as well as a flute of champagne. "I do not believe Mama's eyes have been dry for a single minute this entire day."

Grace gave him a brilliant, practiced smile. "Oh, Marty, this has been the most fantastically wonderful experience of my life. I can hardly believe I am now Princess Grace. My children will be royal!"

As she dabbed the corners of her eyes, their mother approached along with a following of relatives —brothers, sisters, in-laws—in short, the whole brood of MacGalloways whom Grace adored (even though she oft feigned indifference). "I always said if any of my daughters were to marry into a royal house, it would be you, dear." Mama kissed Grace's cheek. "Where was that dashing husband of yours off to?"

"He stole away to enjoy one last cigar with Lord Alder." Honestly, Grace oughtn't blame him. Though a prince, Isidor had confided he was only able to tolerate grand affairs in small doses, a fact which made Grace his ideal partner. She had been trained to be a hostess extraordinaire. As soon as she arrived in Samogitia, she planned to take over the administration of her husband's social calendar. Though he wasn't yet madly in love with her, he soon would be because Grace had superb organizational skills. She had been born to run a grand estate. And at the risk of sounding excessively arrogant, she believed in her soul of souls she had been destined to become a princess, if not a queen.

"The bridal carriage has arrived, Your Highness," announced the steward.

"My, how the time has flown." Grace passed her glass to Modesty, the only one of her seven siblings who was younger. "I'd best fetch Isidor. He's in the Rose Satin Room."

"I can go," Marty offered.

"Oh, no. I'm his wife, now," Grace replied, heading off with a lightness in her step as if she were floating. It might be cold and snowing on this January day, but they had only a short carriage ride to the Pool of London where Isidor's ship was moored. They would spend their first night as husband and wife within the warmth of the royal suite. She could scarcely wait for her new life to begin. Perhaps she might conceive Isidor's heir this very eve!

As she approached, a resounding *thump* came from behind the closed doors of the Rose Satin Room. And then a horrendous moan.

Good heavens, has someone been hurt?

Grace hastened her step, threw open the doors, and stepped inside.

"Haaaaa—?" was the only sound that escaped her lips while the remainder of her question caught in her throat.

With Grace's attempted inhalation, her stays suddenly clamped around her ribcage, refusing to allow her to inhale.

Alder and Isidor were so absorbed by their *activity*, they took no notice of her arrival. Neither one had a cheroot in hand, nor was the stench of cigar smoke in the air.

A woman screamed most shrilly.

By the burning of her throat, Grace was quite certain the utterly unladylike, vile sound had come from the depths of her own very soul.

Only then did the two men glance up from their passionate entwinement. Passionate was the word for what she saw, was it not? Lewd? Inappropriate? Why were their breeches lowered? Why was Isidor mounting Alder like a horse? Grace attempted to blink. When her eyes remained wide open, she tried to look away but she was frozen in place, utterly shocked and appalled.

Martin barreled past Grace with their brother Gibb in his wake. "You bastard! I could have you hanged for sodomy!"

"Not likely, Dunscaby." Isidor smirked, pulling up

his falls and fumbling with the buttons. "I am not a British subject, nor am I answerable to your country's laws."

Grace swayed where she stood, clasping her hands over her heart. Her husband engaged in sodomy—the very man to whom she had just promised to be faithful? The man whom she planned to give her virginity this night?

What have I done to be dishonored in such a way?

"I canna allow this slight against my sister to pass. And on her wedding day, you immoral libertine!" Martin threw back his shoulders. "We shall duel."

Recovering enough of her wits to intervene, Grace pushed between her brother and husband. "No!" There had to be some explanation, yet for her life, she couldn't possibly imagine why two well-bred men would engage in such behavior only hours after one of them promised to love and cherish her as long as he should live.

Good heavens, if Marty were to be successful in his challenge, Isidor's life might be quite short. By this time tomorrow she could very well be a widow—or worse, Martin's son James might be named the new Duke of Dunscaby.

Still adjusting his clothing, Isidor had yet to meet her gaze. "My ship is sailing. No matter how much I'd enjoy shooting you, Duke, I haven't the time."

His expression deadly, Martin gripped Grace's shoulder and ushered her aside. "So, not only are you a sodomite, you are a coward. I do not take offences against my family or my family's reputation lightly."

"Nor do I," said Gibb, the second MacGalloway son and sea captain. He stepped beside his brother—the two composing a wall of kilted unity. "It will be dusk soon—plenty of time to shoot the wee bastard afore his ship weighs anchor."

"'Tis settled." Marty thrust his fists onto his hips. "Putney Heath. One hour."

Isidor grabbed Grace's elbow, his fingers painfully digging into her flesh. "Are you mad? If I ended your life this night, my wife would be unduly bereft. Come, my dear, we shall sail anon."

As Martin lunged forward, Grace twisted her arm from Isidor's grasp. "I refuse to go!" she heard herself shriek. For the love of molasses, this was no time to allow her temper to show. If she did not accompany Isidor to the ship, her life would be over. Suddenly, her new sense of freedom flew away as if on the wings of a swan—or a buzzard.

Gibb backed her toward the door, removing a pistol from inside his coat. "Our sister isna sailing anywhere until this matter is resolved, unless ye'd prefer a lead ball in your belly now and save us the ride to Putney Heath."

Isidor's lips thinned as he cast a scathing, hateful glare toward Grace. "One hour."

"Prepare to meet your end," seethed Martin while Gibb opened the door.

As soon as they stepped into the corridor, they were surrounded by a bevy of onlookers, the first of whom was the Prince Regent, standing beside their mother. "What on earth has happened?" he demanded.

Squeezing Marty's arm, Grace vehemently shook her head, willing the duke to hold his tongue. "You cannot possibly go through with this," she whispered into his ear. Everyone knew duels were illegal, though a gentleman's method of solving grave affronts to one's character or family. Not only that, her brother could be severely wounded or possibly killed.

Martin ignored her. "It was nothing but an exchange of words," he said loudly, obviously for the benefit of the crowd, attempting to downplay the gravity of the ordeal. "However, I do believe the festivities have ended for the day. Thank you all for coming."

The guests may have begun to disperse, but Mama stood rooted to the floor, her face growing redder with every passing second. "Martin MacGalloway, as duke you may be the head of the family, but I am not only your mother, I am the mother of the bride. I *demand* you explain yourself at once."

The Prince Regent cleared his throat. "I believe I have an inkling as to what may have transpired. If you will kindly join me in the privacy of my library."

Martin and Gibb exchanged dour frowns. "We havena much time."

"You *will* find the time to explain yourself," Mama said, lowering her voice and following Prinny.

Once behind the doors of the Carlton House library where no one was offered a seat, to Grace's horror, Martin relayed to the Prince Regent and their mother, of all people, how they had caught Isidor and Alder in the act of sodomy—a capital offence. Martin emphatically insisted upon the need to defend Grace's honor.

Mama received the news with an unseemly grimace of revulsion etching the dowager duchess' otherwise schooled features.

"You cannot challenge Isidor to a duel," Grace said, pleading and grasping her brother's arm. "It is far too dangerous. Think of Julia, of your children!"

Prinny smoothed his fingers down his pristine woolen lapels. "I could send for the City Marshal."

"What good would that do?" asked Martin. "Isidor said himself he is not a British subject. As a foreign envoy he has diplomatic immunity."

The Prince Regent's lips thinned. "Well then, I do agree, a gentleman's duel is the best way to erase this abominable offense to Princess Grace's honor."

The blood drained from her face. Dear God, in the past ten minutes her entire world had imploded. She was no more a princess than her capricious, red-headed sister, Modesty.

Martin snatched his pocket watch from his waist-coat and checked the time. "Once the duel is over we must address the subject of this farce of a marriage."

Prinny finally glanced at Grace. "I shall send word to the Archbishop of Canterbury at once pro-claiming my support for your petition of annulment."

"Annulment?" Mama asked as if the word consti-tuted blasphemy. She snapped open her fan and flapped it vigorously. "Heaven forbid."

Grace stumbled backward, collapsing onto a velvet settee, and burying her face in her hands. "I am utterly ruined."

"Your reputation can be salvaged," said Martin.

"How?" she asked, peering at His Grace through her fingers, her concern for him making it all the more difficult to breathe. "By losing a most-loved brother in a duel to a man who deceived me into a false mar-riage? You are a duke. Your life is far more important than mine. For the love of all that is holy, Martin, I've just estranged my husband—my only chance to live the life of which I've always dreamed. I cannot abide losing my brother as well."

Mama lowered herself onto the settee beside Grace and took her daughter's hand between two warm palms. "Family is nothing without honor. Mark my words, Martin will *not* fail."

THE MACGALLOWAY WOMEN gathered in the spacious drawing room of the ducal London town house. They comprised a party of seven somber, worried, unusually quiet ladies, including Grace, Mama, sisters Modesty and Charity, as well as sisters-in-law, Isabella, Eugenia, and Julia.

All five MacGalloway brothers as well as their brother-in-law, the Earl of Brixham, were presently riding for Putney Heath on the outskirts of Town. The wooded wasteland was a notorious meeting location where gentlemen settled grave disagreements by dueling either with swords or pistols. Though Martin was skilled in the art of fencing, he had stopped by the town house only long enough to collect his dueling pistols.

No matter how much Grace had pleaded with her brother to see reason, his decision had been made and he would defend her honor even at the expense of his own life. As a prince, Isidor was also well-trained in weaponry of all sorts. Indeed, Marty was fully aware of Isidor's skill with a musket. The men had gone hunting together at Stack Castle in the north of Scotland last summer and Isidor had shot his quota of grouse when no other man had come close.

When Grace had reminded the duke of the prince's hunting prowess, Martin had turned to Gibb and ordered him to shoot Isidor if Marty failed to do so.

The women huddled together, each with a needle in one hand, an embroidery hoop in another, though no one seemed to be sewing—especially not Modesty who sat in the window embrasure, her gaze focused on the cobbled street below. No one spoke. Julia, Martin's wife, used a handkerchief to dab her eyes. Charity, Grace's elder sister patted Julia's shoulder in silent commiseration.

Grace could only hang her head in shame. By morn she would be the laughingstock of the kingdom. It wasn't difficult to imagine what the morning's papers would report. Even though the family and the prince had not told a soul what had happened between Lord Alder and Prince Isidor, by morn, everyone would know a rift had occurred—one grave enough to incite a duel. Of course, gossip would spread as fast as a raindrop trickles down a windowpane.

As they waited, every tick from the mantle clock bore an ominous message. Someone would die this night, possibly many someones. Wars had erupted over less.

Grace couldn't think. Simply breathing brought a labored challenge. Her entire body had gone numb. Two hours ago, a housemaid had brought in a tray of sandwiches, none of which had been touched. Nor had the tea service. Nor had the duke's brandy sitting in a crystal decanter on the sideboard.

Grace jolted when the clock struck the hour of nine, it's clangorous chimes seeming to shake the entire chamber. Mama drew a stuttered inhalation. Certainly everyone was thinking the same—the duel was at dusk—four hours ago. Why had they not received word?

As the chimes faded into wretched silence, Modesty sprang from her seat and darted across the floor. "Riders are approaching!"

As the youngest clamored down the stairs, Grace clapped a hand over her heart as she exchanged distraught gazes with the remaining women.

Mama was the first to set her embroidery aside and slowly stand. "We shall all receive the news together."

Though Grace usually would be at the forefront of the procession, demanding answers as to what had happened, especially in matters concerning her, she held back—possibly for the first time in her life. Regardless of the news she was about to hear, someone was dead.

Because of her.

Because for some unknown reason, her bridegroom had rebuffed her. He'd turned her into a fool. His actions had clearly demonstrated Isidor's utter contempt for her person. If he harbored such hatred for her in his heart, why had the prince gone through with the wedding? Why had he proposed in the first place? He could have married any woman he wanted. Somewhere during their courtship, while he was showering her with flowers, jewelry, and sonnets, she must have displeased him.

How? What had she done to deserve such malice?

At the outset of last Season all the papers had named Lady Grace MacGalloway as the belle of the *ton*. They touted her as the most likely to marry well. At every ball she wore the most beautiful gown, danced every set. She was poised, polite, gracious, and (as the papers had reported) stunningly beautiful. Of course, all of her panache hadn't come easily. Grace had spent the entirety of her life preparing to become the wife of a prince or a duke or a marquess. Indeed, she could have settled for an earl or a well-to-do viscount and lived out her days in happiness. But no, she'd set her sights on a prince—on the greatest catch in all of Christendom. And for her ambition, she had been utterly, irrevocably ruined.

I am a bane to men. I shall spend the rest of my days humiliated and alone.

It was with a modicum of relief that Martin was the first through the door, albeit his expression grim. Nonetheless, their eldest brother was alive and apparently unscathed. The tension in the air eased as if the entire vestibule had released a pent-up breath. The duke was followed by his four younger brothers, Gibb, Philip, Andrew, and Frederick, as well as the imposing Earl of Brixham who at one time had been a boxer.

Before a word was uttered, Julia dashed to Martin's side while Grace's elder sister Charity went to Brixham, Lady Isabella to Gibb, and her newest sister-in-law, Lady Eugenia, fell into Andrew's arms.

With no man to comfort her, Grace stopped at the bottom of the stairs and stood beside her mother, again scarcely able to breathe. So this was it? A bride and a widow in the same day? "It is done, then?" she asked, her voice sounding raspy and haunted.

"Nay." Martin's lips pursed, his blue eyes darker than she'd ever seen them. "Isidor proved himself more cowardly than I could have possibly imagined."

"The sniveling bastard had no intention of facing Dunscaby in a duel," said Brixham.

Gibb, who owned a fleet of ships, drew his wife's hand to his lips and gently kissed her fingers. "Aye, when Isidor didna make an appearance at Putney Heath, we hastened to the Pool of London."

Grace doubled over as if she'd taken a knife to the solar plexus. Not only had she received the worst slight a bride could possibly imagine, she had been cast aside as if she were but a soiled serviette. "Do not tell me he tucked his tail and sailed without his wife? That despicable miscreant did not make one single attempt to fight for me-e-e-e?"

"Wheesht, sister," said Martin, pulling her into an embrace as she buried her tears in his shoulder. "After what you witnessed, that numpty's spineless disappearance is good riddance."

Gibb slammed his fist into his palm. "Och, I should have skelped him when I had the chance."

"I reckon the scoundrel will never show his face among polite society again. At least not in this kingdom," said Andrew.

Grace's heart shredded as she desperately tried to control her sobs. "Neither will I."

2

For most Scots, the Wars of Independence ended with the Battle of Culloden on the sixteenth of April in the Year of our Lord 1746. For Frasier Buchanan, however, it most decidedly had not. Regardless if Frasier had been born thirty-eight years after Culloden, he was now Chieftain of Clan Buchanan, still hiding at Druimliart in the Scottish Highlands where his kin had fled since that fateful day. The English had not only outlawed the wearing of clan tartan for twenty-six years, they had ruthlessly pursued the Buchanans, murdering many clansmen and women. His grandfather's lands had been seized, ancient artifacts collected over the centuries had been destroyed or stolen. Worse, the clan's wealth had been distributed among the Duke of Cumberland's closest allies. Aye, there was a reason the highlanders dubbed the bastard "Butcher Cumberland."

Nonetheless, the government troops only thought they had successfully expunged Clan Buchanan. The spirit of one of the oldest and most venerable clans in Scotland refused to die.

Frasier's kin had naught but to flee into the Highlands—to lands once owned by the Scottish king, once presided over by the Buchanan line. Though still officially considered "outlaws to the crown," the clan had survived, if not thrived. Now, seventy-three years on, those who had taken up arms at Culloden were no longer alive. And though Frasier and his clan had been outlawed for inciting a war, they were now largely forgotten if not ignored. The land upon which they settled was rocky, the soil poor, and snow covered the ground six to seven months of the year.

But this mountainous haven was the only home Frasier knew and, by God, he would defend it from anyone who dared threaten his kin.

Angus, Frasier's righthand man and brother-in-law hopped down from his pony and examined the spoor atop the snow. Angus was stout and built like a bull with a black beard and blacker eyes. "This is fresh —no more than an hour."

Frasier's gaze followed the tracks. "He's alone."

"And by the looks of those clouds, a storm's coming," said Blair, a good man and a better hunter.

Frasier cued his horse to walk on. "Then we'd best make haste if we want to fill the larder with fresh venison."

Together they tracked the deer through the glens and up the rigid mountains. The snow fell steadily, carried sideways by a brisk wind as they skirted along Loch Tulla's icy shores, lands owned by the Duke of Dunscaby, one of Clan Buchanan's closest allies—a powerful one. Thanks to Martin MacGalloway, Frasier could hunt these lands without fear of retribution, a fact which had helped keep the clan fed through the lean winter months when their herds of sheep and cattle were set free to forage.

The day was growing short by the time Angus

spotted a set of antlers through the wood. "Och, he's a bloody beauty, he is."

Frasier unsheathed his musket. "Haste ye afore we end up trapped in the snow freezing our ballocks all night."

"Willna be the first time," groused Ramsey, the fourth member of the hunting party, oldest, and most cantankerous.

"Blair and Ramsey—circle around the flanks," Frasier said, dismounting. "Angus and I will approach from the front."

"Leading him right into our sights, aye?" asked Blair.

"Nay," Frasier replied. "I'm no' aiming to miss." He rarely missed. Except for the last time, which the lads refused to stop blathering about.

He surged forward with Angus by his side as the wind and driving snow grew more intense. "What was that you said about freezing our ballocks?"

Frasier raised the flintlock to his shoulder and lined up the buck in his sights. "Och, mark me, I'll be sleeping in me own bed this night."

His finger caressed the trigger, the deer moving slowly, nibbling on branches, searching for any morsel of nourishment. With seven points on his rack, he was majestic, and powerful, and would provide well for the clan. The buck stopped, turning his head, and listening. Without hesitation, Frasier closed his finger on the trigger with a resultant, earsplitting crack.

The men gathered around the fallen deer, the snow now shin-deep, making the mountains eerily silent. Frasier brushed the accumulated flakes from his cloak. "We'd best tie him to the pack mule and hasten for home."

No sooner had the words left his lips when a thunderous tumult echoed between the hills—not a single crash like the falling of a tree but screeching as if from the iron rasped across iron, followed by a series of calamitous booms.

"What the bloody blazes is that?" asked Ramsey.

Frasier held up his palm, asking for silence. But the sounds that had been carried by the wind revealed nothing more. The falling snow was quick to silence the noise as if covering it in an icy tomb.

Blair pointed in the direction of the MacGalloway hunting lodge. "It came from yonder."

"Isna the London Season starting?" asked Angus. "His Grace wouldna be venturing this way—no' this time of year."

Frasier couldn't give a rat's arse if the Season had started or not, though the last newspaper he'd seen indicated that parliament was assembling at the end of January. As if the haughty, pretentious socialites were all the world cared about. The only peer worth his salt was the Duke of Dunscaby. Still, His Grace hadn't paid a visit to his hunting lodge in winter since he ascended to the dukedom.

After collecting the reins, Frasier remounted his horse. "It was most likely one of those giant sycamores falling, but I'll go have a wee peek. You men take care of the buck and I'll meet ye back at Druimliart."

Angus sheathed his dirk. "I'll go with ye."

"Nay, you're needed here more, else you'll prove Ramsey right and end up making camp in the snow. I'll just take a look over the ridge, then I'll head for home's hearth."

Throughout his lifetime, Frasier had seen his share of calamities, but as he crested the ridge, nothing could have prepared him for the disaster below. An upended carriage with three wheels slowly spinning sat at the bottom of the glen. Four horses, tangled among the wreckage, were unmoving, though a fifth horse wearing only a halter with a frayed rope attached stood motionless.

"Good God," he mumbled under his breath as he cued his horse to negotiate the steep slope, praying he'd find the carriage occupants alive, but knowing there was little chance for anyone to have survived.

What the devil was the duke thinking, attempting to pay a visit to his hunting lodge in the midst of a snowstorm? And why had he not attached skis at the first sign of snow? Or was this Dunscaby's steward? A brother, perhaps? It was perilous enough to come up here in winter on horseback, but bringing a carriage bordered on madness.

Frasier's sure-hooved steed trudged through the snow, snorting, the breath from his nostrils billowing with labored puffs of steam.

"Hello, the carriage!"

As expected, his call remained hauntingly unanswered.

The driver's body lay twenty paces away from the wreckage. A footman lay dead not far beyond. Two trunks had broken free of their bounds and were piled askew, covered by new snow.

"Dunscaby!" Frasier hollered, spotting the thrown wheel. By the way it hung precariously on the hill above, it must have been lost on the perilous hairpin turn.

After hopping down from his horse, Frasier trudged through the heavy snow—thigh deep in the ravine. He pounded on the carriage door before pulling it open. "Is anyone in here?"

Met with a riot of white petticoats and stockinged, female legs, he hoisted himself inside. "God on the bloody cross," he mumbled, looking into a vacant stare of a woman—one he didn't recognize, her neck broken.

From beneath her came a faint moan.

Frasier carefully moved the body aside, gasping at the lovely face he'd recognize anywhere. He gathered Lady Grace MacGalloway into his arms and cradled the unconscious woman to his chest. "What the devil are you doing here, m'lady?"

The last time he'd seen Her Ladyship had been in the summer at Stack Castle in the far north of Scotland where she'd accepted Prince Isidor's proposal of marriage. Indeed, the newspaper he'd seen had reported her marriage was to take place on the opening day of the Season. It was touted to be a huge fanfare, with the reception being hosted by the Prince Regent himself. But that was weeks ago, perhaps a month or more.

Moaning again, a stream of blood trickled from Her Ladyship's temple. Or was she a princess now? And if so, where was her husband? Frasier dabbed the gash with his handkerchief, then retrieved an ermine cloak from the tangle of cloth.

Frasier had more questions than answers, but if he didn't spirit Grace out of the glen forthwith, they both mightn't make it back to Druimliart alive. After wrapping Her Ladyship in her cloak and propping her beneath a tree, he made haste to place the dead on the back of the only surviving horse. With that done, he gathered bonny Grace into his arms, used the upended carriage as a mounting block, and headed for home.

3

A cool cloth dabbed Grace's forehead, making her wince.

"I ken it isna pleasant, but at least ye survived, m'lady," said a man, his deep bass barely louder than a whisper. She'd heard his voice somewhere before but was at a loss to place it. Though soothing, his tone did not resemble that of any of her five brothers, nor was it her brother-in-law's tenor. Lord knew her father had passed away so long ago, Grace hardly remembered the former duke let alone what he'd sounded like.

Regardless, she couldn't be dead because the man had just said she'd survived.

Survived?

"What happened?" Grace asked, though no sound escaped her parched lips. If only she could sink back into oblivion—back into the darkness where she'd been hiding since...

Where am I?

A few drops of something bitter moistened her lips. "Try to swallow a wee bit of tincture. It will soothe the pain," he said.

Was this man a physician? Is that how she knew him?

Unable to assuage her curiosity, Grace opened her eyes just enough to see through the fan of her lashes. Though a tad blurry, she recognized the chap—but from where? What was his name?

The man busied himself with stoppering a bottle and folding a cloth, setting both on a lone table in the small room with exposed stone walls—an exceedingly crude bedchamber. Across from the foot of the bed, coals smoldered in a tiny hearth with an ornately carved oaken mantle which was polished to a sheen and seemed quite out of place among such primitive furnishings.

Her healer appeared to be nothing like the dandies who paraded about London in their John Bull hats and finery. He wore no coat but tended her in shirtsleeves and a kilt belted low across his hips. Grace was no stranger to kilted men. After all, Highland dress was Martin's preferred costume, no matter how much Mama objected.

This man's hair was dark brown, almost black, and a shadow of thick stubble peppered his face. He wore his tresses unfashionably long, clubbed back, though a strand had escaped the leather thong and hung to the side of his face.

Only when he sat in the chair beside her bed did she manage to glimpse the piercing cobalt blue of his wide-set eyes. As recognition set in, Grace's breath stopped. Her eyes opened wider. She'd never seen Laird Frasier Buchanan up this close. True, the man was more rough-hewn than the Scottish Highlands—rugged and unpolished. He wasn't handsome when compared to a sophisticated gentleman like Prince Isidor. Buchanan was almost brutish. Fierce. Merely the chiseled contours of his face announced this was no man with whom to trifle.

Truly, whenever Grace had been in his presence, she had made a point to avoid him. He had a predatory presence that made her feel vulnerable, as if she were prey. Not that he had ever given her cause to suspect him of doing anything untoward. Her feelings had always been borne of intuition. He was not only a bachelor, his station was quite far beneath her rank, and as such, casting her attentions his way had always been dangerous.

Yet he was one of her brothers greatest allies. A rouge and a recluse. Grace had always kept her distance from this man because...

Why?

Because she did not care for the way he made her feel? The way his stare had warmed her skin? How she didn't quite feel in control whenever the man was in the same room?

Buchanan's gaze connected with hers, causing a moment of awkward intensity. "You're awake, m'lady," he said, his voice gentle, sending a shiver through her bones.

Grace moved her fingers to the sore spot on her head and hissed. "Where am I? What happened?"

"Ye are at Druimliart. Your carriage...ah..."

Her heart hammered with a memory of terror, of screaming, and falling.

There had been an accident. Though the snow had swiftly become exceedingly bad, the driver had insisted they keep going because they were nearly to the pull-off where they'd have to leave the carriage and ride the rest of the way to the lodge. But as they'd rounded a tight bend, the carriage careened down the slope, tossing Grace and her lady's maid about as if they were but rag dolls in an empty drum. "The driver lost control," she said, her voice haunted.

"The coach threw a wheel," Buchanan explained.

"And the others? Adele Sweeny, my maid? Rodney the footman? Our driver?"

"All perished. But one horse survived. The fifth." His Adam's apple shifted with his swallow. "My men chopped and burned through the icy ground in order to bury them."

"Good Lord, no!" Grace drew her hands over her face. Sweeny might have been recently promoted to lady's maid, but the lass was ever so helpful during Grace's first Season as well as throughout all the excitement leading up to the wedding. Tears stung her eyes, Sweeny couldn't be gone!

All dead? Why was I spared? I'm the one who is besmirched for the rest of my days. If anyone should have lost their life, it was me!

Buchanan sat in a rickety old chair that squeaked beneath his weight. "Och, I'm sorry. It was a good thing my men and I were nearby. We heard the clamor right after we felled a deer, else I'm afeared ye would have succumbed to the cold as well."

Succumbing to the cold wouldn't have been too horrible a death. It might have been far more welcomed than spending the rest of her life in misery...in purgatory. But Sweeny and Rodney had been with the family since they were children. And though Grace didn't know the driver well, his death was now on her shoulders. She was the one who had insisted upon traveling to the lodge for the duration of the Season because it was the only place she knew of where she could be utterly alone until Martin received a decision about the prospects of an annulment from the Archbishop of Canterbury.

Not wanting the laird to see her weep, Grace slid her fingers over her eyes. "You should have left me."

"You? The belle of the Season?" he said, his voice filled with disbelief. "I thought you were to marry Prince Isidor."

"I did marry him and then—" She bit her lip as she swiped away her tears and regarded Buchanan's confused expression. "It has been a fortnight, I'm surprised the entire kingdom isn't gossiping about my wedding reception by now."

In truth, Grace had been traveling ever since that fateful night. Whenever they stopped she checked the headlines, but the only one she'd seen had described all the pomp of the wedding. Bless her family for their efforts, Grace was growing more hopeful they had something to do with mitigating untoward rumors.

"News is slow making its way into the Highlands if it does at all. Ah..." He rubbed the back of his neck. "Were you to honeymoon at the lodge perchance?"

"Me?" She coughed out a rueful scoff. The last place on Earth she would ever consider taking a holiday was the medieval hunting lodge which all the men in her family happened to adore. Not Grace, however. The only reason she'd agreed with Marty to go to the lodge was because there she could hide—for the rest of her days if need be.

Buchannan arched a questioning eyebrow.

"No. Isidor and I were not honeymooning at the lodge." She pursed her lips and narrowed her eyes for added measure—her practiced expression was one that warned her questioner not to pursue the matter further. If the laird was unaware that her unconsummated marriage was about to be annulled, then so be it. He'd find out soon enough and then, like everyone else in the kingdom, he would see her as the utter failure she had become.

Buchanan waited, but when she volunteered

nothing further, His Lairdship bowed. "Verra well, Princess. Unless there is anything else you need, I shall leave you to sleep."

Grace nodded, the movement making her head throb. Perhaps she ought to have told him the marriage had been delayed...or she'd called it off. But lying wouldn't do. Though she was adept at withholding the truth, she hated uttering falsehoods. To avoid telling him that Martin was pursuing an annulment was not lying. It was simply keeping sensitive matters to herself. She was being shrewd. Aptly so. After all, though Buchanan had quite possibly saved her life, he did not need to know the reason for her visit to the Highlands.

Come morning, Grace would have the laird accompany her to the lodge, and then she doubted she'd see him again for months. Possibly years. Possibly never.

IT WASN'T unusual for the clan to be snowed in this time of year, but the blizzard last eve had surpassed anything Frasier had seen throughout the duration of his life in the Highlands. The snow was so deep it blocked doorways and climbed halfway up the thatch on the cottage roofs.

Druimliart consisted of twelve wee cottages situated haphazardly in a semblance of a horseshoe shape. Most homes faced the "courtyard" which in summer was a grassy lea with a large firepit in the middle. On the other side stood the hall where, on addition to containing the communal kitchens and larder, it was used for clan gatherings, evening meals, and for Frasier to conduct clan business.

It had taken him and his men the better part of the morning to shovel the courtyard to enable clan and kin to attend to their daily chores. While the other men set to their duties, Frasier and Angus continued clearing snow all the way down to the stables and over to the workshop where they tanned hides, wove wool, worked with a smithy's bellows, and had enough woodworking tools to make basic furniture and whatnot. In essence, Druimliart was a self-contained Highland settlement.

Frasier and his men ran three hundred head of cattle give-or-take. They kept a small flock of sheep for wool and meat. And of course they had the necessary livestock such as chickens and milk cows. They also raised some of the best Highland ponies in Scotland —all of which were sold in the wee village of Crieff, far enough away from nosy English magistrates who might choose to act upon old orders to exterminate members of Clan Buchanan. In an attempt to crush the Highland spirit, the 1746 English Act of Prescription had outlawed Highland traditions like wearing tartan kilts, carrying clan banners, bearing arms, and playing bagpipes. As supporters of Bonny Prince Charlie, Clan Buchanan had been outlawed by the English. The bastards put some to death and transported others. The few who remained were still hiding among lands no one wanted to till, living in this close-knit community much as their ancestors had done in centuries past.

The Duke of Cumberland's troops had razed Frasier's ancestral castle on the Isle of Clairinsh and had stolen anything of value. Had beheaded his grandfather in a public display at the Tower of London.

And now, this frigid Highland community was the only home Frasier knew. Of course, as laird he occupied the largest cottage, though it was by no means grand. As one entered the only door, to the left was the parlor with a table, benches, and a hearth that dueled as a hob. Straight ahead was a nook used for storage of his effects and to the right was the bedchamber, presently occupied by Princess Grace.

As Frasier cleared the snow from the workshop door, his sister, Fiona, hastened toward him, clutching a ragged fur-lined cloak about her shoulders. "That woman is impossible!" Fiona had married Angus and was Clan Buchanan's healer. She'd given Frasier the tincture late last night but couldn't attend the princess' bedside through the wee hours because Fiona had a young bairn of her own.

"Princess Grace is awake again?" Frasier asked.

"Unfortunately, aye. I prepared her breakfast with me own hands and she had the gall to accuse me of treating her like a convicted prisoner...providing her with stale bread, runny eggs, and serving them on an unwashed slab of wood to boot! You ken as well as I our wooden plates are of the finest quality."

A tic twitched in Frasier's jaw. He and Martin MacGalloway had been fast allies since boyhood. He'd been fostered by Martin's father. The closest Dunscaby estate was the ducal lodge where Frasier had visited many times and, though it was a medieval castle with few modern conveniences, it was colossal in comparison to Druimliart. Meals at the lodge were always served on fine china plates. There were servants' quarters and a great hall, a library, and more than one drawing room. And though Frasier wasn't exactly sure how many bedchambers were housed above stairs, he was fairly certain there were no fewer than seven.

When it suited him, Frasier had also been Martin's

guest at Stack Castle, which was quite possibly the most opulent fortress in all of Scotland. The mind boggled when considering its size—though the fortress had originally been built to defend the territory on the northeastern tip of Scotland's mainland. Stack had five hundred and twenty-one rooms and was surrounded by medieval curtain walls vast enough to enclose a small city. There were acres upon acres of land. The stables and outbuildings alone contained more square footage than all of Druimliart.

Such was the splendor to which Her Highness was accustomed. And that kind of grandeur was as foreign to Frasier's sister as the continent of Africa.

"Worse," Fiona continued. "The woman had the nerve to ask me to empty her chamber pot. For heaven's sakes, she treated me as if I were a servant!"

"Did you inform her that you are the clan's healer?"

"I didna manage to get that far."

"Oh?"

"After I told her to tend to her own damn chamber pot and dump it into the privy, she sacked me! I'm the laird's *sister*! I dunna care if that woman is the spawn of a duke, how dare she behave like a shrew?"

He tossed the shovel full of snow onto the mounting pile. "This sounds as if 'twas a wee misunderstanding."

"Och, ye dunna ken the half of it. Mistress High-and-Mighty demanded to see the housekeeper at once. I do no' care if she is royalty, no one can come into our home and act like a tyrant."

Frasier leaned on the handle of his shovel. "Princess Grace has gone through a terrible ordeal." Aside from having her carriage roll off a cliff, claiming the lives of everyone except Isidor's bride, there had to be a reason for a newly married Lithuanian royal to be travelling alone. Where was Prince Isidor? Where was Dunscaby for that matter? True, Parliament was in session, but Grace's unbidden presence made not a lick of sense.

"I dunna care what has happened. The woman is hideous," Fiona said, turning and making the hem of her cloak billow. The lass was not terribly unlike Grace—at least when it came to their temperaments.

"Och, she most likely doesna realize where she is," Frasier explained. "After all, she's never been to Druimliart afore. And I doubt she's ever awakened a day in her life when she wasna attended by a maid."

"Well, I have a bairn of me own to care for." Fiona glanced over her shoulder. "I've no time to spare for a spoilt woman who canna empty her own chamber pot."

"Not to worry." Frasier tried the latch on the work-shop. Finding it frozen shut, he bore down and forced it open. "She'll only be here a day or two. All we need is a wee bit of fine weather and the snow ought to tamp down enough for me to take her to her brother's hunting lodge. Until then, I would appreciate your help." In truth, they needed a miracle. It was not quite mid-February and the melt wouldn't begin until the end of March.

"I beg your pardon?" Fiona pointed her finger beneath her brother's nose, her eyes fierce. "I'll no' go near your cottage until the Queen of Sheba takes her leave. Moreover, by the way she behaves, I doubt there is a Buchanan woman who will tolerate her."

"Och, give me a chance to have a word with the lass. As I said afore, I'm certain there has merely been a misunderstanding."

Frasier trudged back to his cottage where upon

opening his door, he found the princess limping from one end of the cottage, through his storage area, and stopping at the entrance to the bedchamber. She faced him and jammed her fists onto her hips, appearing none too steady and definitely unamused. "Laird Buchanan, have you put me in the servants' quarters?"

He removed his bonnet and pushed his fingers over his clubbed hair. "Ye ought to still be abed, Princess. Ye suffered quite a nasty fall and ye're swaying like a tree in a gale."

Why was she limping? He'd given her legs a quick check—very quick, however. Even for Frasier Buchanan it was improper to run his hands over a woman's legs, especially a woman as untouchable as Grace MacGalloway. "Have ye any injuries aside from the gash to your head?"

Reaching up, the princess dabbed the wound and hissed, her expression shifting from piqued to uncertain. "Is it awfully unsightly?"

He leaned in and examined the scab that had formed overnight. "'Tis healing already," he said, glancing away. He'd best hide the mirror until her bruising faded—but presently with all the snow, there was no place to stow it. "I noticed your limp. Have you a sore knee? Ankle perchance?"

"Ankle."

"May I have wee peek?"

Her delicate chin ticked upward. "Absolutely not."

"Of course, how thoughtless of me. I'll fetch the healer."

"Pardon me, sir, but you have not answered my question. Why have you, a man of esteemed rank taken me to the servants' quarters of all places? Or is this a *barn*?"

Barn? Of course his cottage wasn't remotely close

to containing the comforts to which Princess Grace was accustomed, but it was a far cry from a bloody barn. "Och, ye dunna understand."

"What, exactly? That I have been absconded from my carriage and taken to a hovel?"

Dear God, he loved a woman with a solid backbone. Even with the enormous bruise on her forehead spreading under her eye, she was stunning—crystal blue eyes, tresses shimmering like honey, and an unflappable air as if she knew every man had been born to worship her. Even Martin had trouble saying no to his sister. Worse, her present incensed state made Grace all the more alluring.

Damnation!

If she hadn't just insulted him, Frasier might opt to spend the day admiring her beauty. But he refused to allow himself to be enchanted. Aye, he knew all too well what Her-Damned-Highness expected.

Last summer Frasier had attended the Duke of Dunscaby's house party in hopes of finding a wife—a young woman with a sizable dowry who could help him expand Druimliart and turn his *hovel* into a livable house. But as soon as he'd set eyes upon Lady Grace, all other lassies had paled in comparison. Every time Martin's sister had walked into any room, she had taken Frasier's attention captive where it had remained throughout the duration of the sennight. Needless to say, he hadn't found the heiress he desired. Mayhap he never would.

When he didn't immediately reply, she threw back her shoulders and again tipped up her chin, looking as regal as a queen. "Do not mistake me, I am grateful for your gallantry, my larid, but I cannot abide these quarters. I must insist you take me to my brother's lodge immediately."

"Och, ye ken I would like nothing better than to see you home, but I'm afeard that is impossible."

"So you are refusing to be a gentleman and assist a stranded woman—lady, no less, when she has suffered a hideous ordeal?"

"Whether or no' I am a gentleman has little to do with it," he said, a tad less gentlemanly. "Unless you want to trudge five miles through six feet of snow. However, I doubt you would make it more than fifty paces afore succumbing to the bitter cold."

"Six feet?" she asked incredulously, marching past him and opening the door.

It took but two ticks of the mantle clock before Her Highness slammed it closed. Though she did not turn around. She stood facing the timbers, slowly rubbing her outer arms, her back trembling as if she might start to cry.

"I wish I were a wealthy man like your brother, but my lot in life is far different—far cruder than anything you could possibly imagine."

When she finally faced him, the anguish straining those lovely features made her appear older than her years. Grace's gaze met his but only for a moment, then she looked beyond Frasier's shoulder, her lips parting as if she'd recognized something. She hobbled past him and fingered the fine black doublet he had hanging on a peg. "You wore this when you visited Stack Castle last summer."

Good God, as far as he knew, Grace hadn't glanced his way once during the entire week. "Aye, my sister made it. Fiona, the lass who brought your breakfast."

Grace dropped the sleeve. "She's your *sister*?"

Frasier nodded. "And the clan's healer."

"Oh, dear." The princess bit the corner of her

mouth, looking worried, and adorable. "I was awfully cross with her."

Frasier mirrored the princess' expression. "So she said."

Grace shifted her gaze to the parlor and then to the bedchamber. "I take it these are not your servants' quarters," she said, without a note of haughtiness.

"We have no servants."

"None?" she asked, tossing her bonny head as if she didn't believe him. "However can you manage?"

"Take my word for it, the greater part of the populous manages to eke by without housekeepers, footmen, butlers, cooks, and lady's maids."

"You haven't a cook?" she asked, sounding far too English for a lass born in Scotland.

"No' exactly. The clansmen and women do meet in the hall for the evening meal most every night, which is prepared by the wives who have a talent with wooden spoons, but I wouldna ever refer to them as servants. At Druimliart everyone is equal."

"*Everyone?* I thought you were a laird?"

"By birth I am. I lead the clan, but I dunna reckon I'm the overlord of these hardworking folk. I stand shoulder to shoulder with each and every man and do my part—solve grievances when need be."

She almost smiled, tapping her fingers to her bow-shaped lips. "Good heavens, your little Druimliart sounds positively medieval."

"Mayhap because it is." He offered his elbow. "Allow me to help you back to bed, then I'll fetch Fiona to have a wee peek at your ankle."

4

"Princess?" called the woman as she opened the door. It was Fiona, the healer, the laird's sister, whom Grace had insulted by not-so-nicely demanding she remove the chamber pot.

Normally when someone came to call, especially a person to whom Grace owed an apology, she would offer them tea and biscuits. She would pour from a porcelain teapot with her own hand. She would compliment the caller's frock or how she'd styled her hair. But how did one compliment a woman who wore a tattered tartan arisaid belted around her waist and draped over her head?

Furthermore, Grace now loathed to be called Princess. Only weeks ago, she could hardly wait for someone to refer to her thus, but now the title had become tainted by ugliness, by shame. If by some divine miracle, she were able to obtain an annulment, her marriage to Isidor would become null and void, and she would be free to revert to the courtesy title of Lady.

Except Grace was filled with misgivings even if she did have the Prince Regent and the Duke of Dunscaby petitioning on her behalf. She'd been married in England where women had few legal rights if any. She didn't know much about the annulment process except that obtaining them was exceedingly difficult if not impossible. She had indeed garnered rumors at finishing school as well as from the *ton's* gossips—nonconsummation was not sufficient to obtain annulment unless the husband or wife had a proven condition that precluded them from engaging in the marital act.

Perhaps the fact that Isidor was now residing in Lithuania without his bride might be cause enough? Dear, oh dear, I pray Martin comes up with something irrefutable.

Even if Martin was successful, who knew how long she would have to wait for the whole unseemly process to play out?

How does one tell an Archbishop about happening upon a prince in the arms of another man? I certainly have never heard gossip of a sodomite in conjunction with an annulment. Might Isidor's sexual indecency be grounds enough?

Most of all, by no means could Grace seek a divorce. It didn't matter that divorces were outlandishly expensive. Wives had no rights whatsoever. Petitions must originate with the husband—and then the groom could only seek a divorce because his wife had committed adultery.

Which she had not.

If Isidor dared to fabricate a story of unfaithfulness against Grace and file such a petition with the English courts, she would be scandalized beyond measure. She would be barred from court and ostracized from polite society. She'd be forced into exile, living in some remote outpost, never to show her face in society again. Even in Scotland she'd be outed by the social elite.

Heaven's stars I'm going to drive myself mad with worry. Regardless of what happens, my life is over.

"Princess?" Fiona called again.

Grace shook her head, snapping herself away from her woes and swinging her feet over the side of the bed. "In here."

"Frasier asked me to tend your ankle." Fiona stepped into the bedchamber her jaw set as if she were ready to mince words. "Why didna ye tell me it was ailing and save me a return trip?"

"I beg your pardon?" Grace asked before she checked herself. She had resolved to make every attempt to appreciate the kindnesses of Clan Buchanan, including Frasier's sharp-tongued sister.

The woman frowned. "I have a wee bairn at home, mind ye, and havena time to be traipsing back and forth tending folk who are nae seriously ill."

"Forgive me. I should have mentioned it before." Grace drew in a deep breath, to cool her ire. "Had I known you were the healer, I most definitely would have done so. But as I recall you did not mention you were skilled in the healing arts."

Fiona set her basket on the bed. "Humph."

"May I ask you a favor?"

"Och, now 'tis favors ye want?"

"A very small request, that is." When Fiona crossed her arms with aghast disdain, Grace was not dissuaded. "All I ask of you is to please refrain from referring to me as Princess."

"Then what shall I call ye? Miss High-and-Mighty?"

Goodness, it wasn't easy to warm to the woman, but Grace was not going to be at Druimliart for more than a few days. At finishing school, she had become quite adept at ignoring those who annoyed her which had become her way of avoiding fits of rage (definitely unbecoming and in no way acceptable when in the public eye). Nonetheless, asking the laird's sister to call her by any title at all seemed oddly pretentious. "Grace will be sufficient, thank you."

"Humph," Fiona repeated, pointing to Grace's eye. "Och, that looks worse now than it did this morning."

She shifted her fingers to her hairline. "You're referring to the gash at my temple?"

"Nay, I am talking about your blackened eye. 'Tis as dark as the sky at twilight."

As Grace patted the sensitive skin beneath her lower lashes, she slid off the bed and hobbled to the washstand, its mirror speckled with dark spots where the silver backing had been eaten away. Even through the warped reflection, her left eye was purple and revolting.

"Oh, my heavens, I look as unseemly as a corpse. Why did you not mention it before?"

"Mayhap 'cause ye dunna belong here," Fiona said dryly.

Do not belong?

Those three words made Grace want to scream. Made every muscle in her body tense. Made every breath short and strained.

Grace had been the recipient of such a statement many times before. It wasn't easy being the sister of a Scottish duke when attending an *English* finishing school. During her first year, the other girls had treated her as if she were a doormat. But Grace hadn't been about to roll over and let those snotty hellions push her into the shadows occupied by wallflowers. She made it her quest to excel at everything, which had initially earned her a rival or two. But, she had also made it her quest to find ways in which she could make herself invaluable to her classmates, and thus by her third and final year, she had won their favor and had become one of the elite, both in culmination of friends and in academic achievement.

Fiona nodded to Grace's skirts. "I havena all day, let me see the wee damages."

"If you must." Grace returned to the bed and tugged up her hem enough to reveal the swelling.

"Good heavens, that's the size of an overgrown turnip. Why the devil have you been walking on it?"

"Well, I haven't exactly gone far—" She pursed her lips together to prevent herself from saying more. Since they were snowed in, there was no place to go outside, and this entire cottage was far smaller than her bedchamber at Stack Castle. "So, do you recommend I rest it?"

"Let us have a better look first."

Rather mercilessly, Fiona moved Grace's foot up, down, and side to side, each time asking if the movement hurt. It did, of course, because who wouldn't feel pain when a sadist was twisting one's ankle in unnatural angles, but she refused to cry out or gasp or show weakness of any sort.

Fiona dropped Grace's foot and brushed off her hands. "I reckon 'tis badly bruised, mayhap twisted."

"So then, I'm fit enough to walk to the privy?" Grace asked, the corners of her mouth turning up ever so slightly.

"Aye."

Spreading her palms, Grace looked from side to side. "Which is?"

"Out the door, turn left, and left again."

"Thank you."

Fiona tugged down Grace's skirt and then snatched up her basket, adding yet another audible harumph. "You may no' like being here, but at least ye'll be on your way soon."

"Yes," she whispered...on her way to where? To what? Not that she wanted to remain at Druimliart, but presently her future was utterly bleak. "I beg your pardon, but can you tell me why Laird Frasier's clothes and weapons are in the...ah..." What should she call the crude storage area? Entryway? Doorway? "*Vestibule?*"

Fiona's eyebrows pinched together. "Ye dunna ken?"

"What, exactly?"

"This is Frasier's cottage. Me brother has given up his verra own bed for Your Highness' comfort, and I'll reckon ye havena an ounce of gratitude for him."

"Oh no, Mistress Fiona, that is where you are grossly mistaken." Grace's mind boggled. The laird himself lived in this hovel? Frasier ought to be enjoying the comforts of a manse...ought to have at least a butler, a cook, and a maid. He mightn't be wealthy, but Martin saw Buchanan as one of his greatest allies. That a dear friend of the duke lived in such primitive conditions was incomprehensible. "I am very grateful to His Lairdship. He has been most kind."

Turning on her heel, Fiona smirked over her shoulder. "Most kind," she said affecting an awful English accent. "Ye certainly ken how to be charming when it suits ye."

Grace resisted the urge to grab the Bible off the table and throw it at the woman. Regardless of whether she had asked Fiona not to refer to her as a princess, she still expected a modicum of respect. And aside from her first year at Northbourne Seminary for Young Ladies, no one had *ever* spoken to her with such rudeness. For heaven's sake, she'd merely mistaken the woman for a servant. Given the fact that Fiona was dressed like a peasant, Grace surely ought to be forgiven so such a minor misstep. After all, the lass had brought in food as if she were a maid...served on a trencher, no less, the sausages looking as if they had been singed over an open fire, and the eggs were hardly cooked at all.

Worse, His Lairdship had given up his bed for Grace's comfort. Did these people not have guest chambers? Guest cottages? But then again, over the years Grace had learned a few things about Clan Buchanan. They had been aggressively pursued after the '45. At the time, most of Frasier's kin had fled to the continent, or to America, even Australia—all but the handful of stalwart outcasts who had fled to this remote outpost in the Highlands. And that was how Martin and Frasier became allies—their friendship had started as boys. Nonetheless, who would bother to look for them up here where the snow was abominable, especially after over seventy years had passed? For goodness sakes, the playing of bagpipes and the wearing of clan tartans had been reinstated before Grace was born.

With nothing to do in this godforsaken cottage except to read the Bible by the light of an odoriferous tallow candle, Grace donned her cloak and lumbered outside, ever so glad not to be seen by any members of the *ton*, especially with her unseemly eye.

The icy air stung her cheeks and made her eyes water. She drew her cloak tighter about her body as she crossed the slippery ice toward an open firepit. Situated around this frozen courtyard was a haphazard collection of ramshackle cottages with thatched roofs, all covered with thick blankets of snow from peak to ground.

Adjacent to His Lairdship's cottage was a larger building into which a woman carrying a basket hastened, looking down, clutching her cloak closed at her throat. Was that the hall to which Buchanan had referred? The place where the clan gathered to take their evening meals?

Grace resisted the urge to pop her head inside to see if it had any creature comforts. The most medieval hall in her family's collection of castles was the one at the lodge with its stone, tapestry-clad walls. It boasted a solid oak table that sat eighteen in exquisitely carved sixteenth century chairs. At one end there was a hearth so large an average woman could stand upright without hitting her head. Though judging by the state of the laird's cottage, Grace held no illusion that the Buchanan's hall might contain an iota of splendor. Most likely the rafters were bare and the tables were lined with benches over which the women must gracelessly climb in order to sit.

A man hastened through the courtyard, his head bowed against the wind, his arms wrapped tightly around his coat.

Grace stepped toward him. "Excuse me, sir. Might you be able to tell me where to find His Lairdship?"

The man stopped, regarding her as if she'd flown down from Mars. "Och, is it Frasier ye're looking for?"

"Yes," she said, tugging her hood across her bruised eye. "He rescued me from my overturned carriage and I'd like to speak with him."

"Everyone kens who ye are, Princess." Holy macaroons, was she to suffer that awful title throughout the duration of her stay? The fellow pointed down a small hill beyond which one could see the top of a roof with a tendril of smoke blowing sideways from its chimney. "Frasier's most likely down at the workshop."

"Thank you. Ah, what—"

The man tipped his hat and started off. "Good day, miss...ah...m'lady...er...your majesty."

"Please just call me—" He disappeared into the hall before she had a chance to finish. What did she prefer to be called? She'd told Fiona to call her Grace and had hoped doing so would help make up for confusing the lass with a servant.

Perhaps everyone here ought to call her Grace? After all, in a few days she'd never see any of these people again. And they were a world away from polite society. Who would care? The only person who came to mind was Mama who was in London with Martin doing what she could to hold together the vestiges of Grace's reputation by telling everyone tall tales about letters received from Lithuania and how happily the newlywed princess was faring in her new home.

Her decision made, she stumbled her way down to the workshop, the hinges of the door screeching as she stepped inside finding nothing like she'd ever seen before. The room was cluttered, yet tidy. Her eyes stung with layers upon layers of overpowering smells. There were dozens of tools, all neatly hanging on the walls or placed on shelves as if they were in the exact spot where they belonged. At one end hung sheets of leather, ready to be tooled into shoes or saddle bags. Perhaps someone was skilled enough to make saddles? There were sheepskins, a loom, and woven cloth. As Grace blinked her eyes to adjust to the light, she spotted Frasier bent over a table, using a sanding stone, so absorbed in his work he hadn't noticed her arrival.

He was a large man. Far more attractive than she had formerly thought—possibly because as a woman being introduced to the marriage mart, he was not a good catch. During her Season she could not afford to find a man like Frasier Buchanan handsome. True, when other girls swooned over the penniless Baronet of Sleat with his dashing good looks, Grace hadn't given that man an opportunity to sign her dance card. But now, everything had changed.

"Good afternoon, Buchanan. What are you working on?" she asked, truly curious.

He glanced up, the stool tipping over as he hastened to his feet and held up a spindle. "Blair's wife Moira gave birth to a wee lassie a few days past. I'm building a cradle."

"Now? After the babe was born? Why not before?"

Frasier righted the stool. "'Cause 'tis bad luck," he said, sanding again.

Grace watched his hands—nicked with thin white scars as if he often sparred. Though they were twice the size as hers, Frasier had the long fingers of an artist. His nails were clean and cut short. He sanded a bit and blew off the dust, his thick lips forming the shape of a kiss as he exhaled a puff of air. Grace's own mouth puckered as kissing came to mind. Were Frasier's lips soft or rough and rugged like the man?

Isidor had kissed her twice before. The prince's kisses were not necessarily pleasant, his mouth a bit too slack, but she hadn't married the man based on the way he kissed. Grace had received a number of kisses during her Season, all of which made her wonder why other girls always attributed so much significance to the act. One of her friends had claimed to swoon after receiving a kiss from the Earl of Sandwich.

Swoon?

Hardly.

Isidor had gone so far as to stick his tongue into

her mouth, the experience devoid of emotion, akin to being examined by a dentist. Perhaps now she knew why. Her *husband* preferred to be affectionate with Lord Alder. Yes, she understood that such affection between men was illegal, but honestly, she only wished that if Isidor preferred kissing Alder, he would not have proposed to her. In Grace's opinion, she had been misled and lied to, which caused her far more consternation than a man who loved another man.

Before she retreated into a state of self-pity, Grace picked up one of the spindles and ran her fingers over the wood, feeling no roughness at all. "This workmanship is exquisite."

"'Tis passable, I suppose."

"Passable? It is as smooth as silk."

"Perhaps, but I havena the tools to make some of the more detailed pieces—carved works, such as filigrees and things I'm certain to which ye're accustomed."

"I don't know. Good craftmanship is more important in my book. Not everything needs to be à la Louis XIV."

"Surprising admission coming from the likes of you."

"Likes of me?" She batted her eyelashes, not intending to flirt, but unable to stop herself. "My laird, it sounds as if you've prejudged me."

"Does it? I do recall a certain Lady Grace dazzling a prince last summer—always dressed in the finest, manners impeccable, her beauty unsurpassed. I would imagine a woman like you has very expensive tastes."

Grace did have expensive tastes, thanks to Mama. Thanks to her friends as well. And why should she not?

She replaced the spindle and tapped the unfinished base of the cradle, making it rock. "I'm certain you hardly noticed me at Stack Castle. As I recall you were keen for the shooting, am I wrong?"

Buchanan's eyes turned dark before he shifted his gaze back to his work. "I always enjoy hunting with your brothers."

"And they with you." Moving beside him, she examined the finished cradle pieces he had neatly lined up on the table. "Did you carve the hearth's mantle in my bedchamber?"

A tad of color flashed on the back of his neck. "Aye."

"'Tis beautiful. I say, the carved oak was the first thing that drew my attention." *Aside from your eyes.*

"Thank you," he said accepting the compliment, though he didn't appear to be proud. He turned the spindle between his fingertips and gazed down the length of it. "I'm surprised to see you up and about so soon after your ordeal. Was Fiona unkind?"

Grace stood taller, her way of making herself aloof as well as to keep tears at bay. Yes, Fiona's words had cut her deeply, but she wasn't about to let Buchanan know how deeply. "Your sister was efficient. Quite forthright with her opinions as well."

He stopped sanding and eyed her. "Och, what did she say?"

"She made it clear that I do not belong here." Grace released a breath, the puffs billowing about her showed how cold it was inside. "I happen to agree with Fiona and came to ask if you perchance have a set of sled skis to attach to a wagon? I want to go home —I mean to say to the lodge. I need a bath. I need my trousseau, and most especially, I need to not be sleeping in your bed!"

He stood, putting his tools aside. "I've never had much use for skis, m'lady. We're oft snowed in at this time of year and it suits us fine."

"Well it doesn't suit me. I'd like to pray over my servants'—ah—*companions'* graves and then be on my way."

"Forgive me," he said, donning his bonnet and swinging a heavy woolen cloak over his kilt. "I should have offered to take you to their gravesites sooner. However, no matter how much you want to go home, unless you have a direct line of communication with Our Father, I'm afeared ye're as trapped as the rest of us."

"Well then, I must insist you find somewhere else for me to sleep. I will not put a man out of his home."

His Lairdship offered his elbow as they stepped outside. "Och, I wasna out of me home."

She leaned on him heavily as the smooth leather bottoms of her boots slipped on the snow and ice. "Do not tell me you haven't slept."

"My rest is none of your concern."

"Well, I'm making it my concern. No one can go overlong without a good night's sleep."

"I'm touched that you're so concerned about my welfare, m'lady."

"Do not patronize me."

"Me? I would never deign to patronize Princess Grace MacGalloway."

She glanced up at him, the corners of her lips tight. "I thought I asked you not to call me Princess."

"Aye, but ye didna explain why. After all, you married Isidor, did you not?"

"Wheesht," Grace said. Though she was a Scottish born woman, she rarely used her homeland's figures of speech. However, presently, it felt right. The word told him to mind his own affairs and keep his nose out of hers.

Buchanan said nothing further as he led her around the back of the settlement, which was situated in a glen between two steep, wooded slopes. Though much of Scotland had been deforested, it wasn't unusual to see woodlands in the Highlands. Even the ducal lodge was tucked away amongst the trees.

In a clearing they stopped beside a patch of charred ground that was free of snow. There were three body-sized mounds of black earth, one beside the other, each with a wooden cross made from tree limbs and tied together with leather thongs.

The sight of the stark reality of their deaths made her curl over as if she'd received a blow to the solar plexus. Her nose dripped as her eyes welled. She should have put up a sterner argument. She should have insisted Brigham turn the carriage around and head back to the boarding house at Crianlarich.

"We had to burn through the icy ground," Frasier whispered.

No matter that she was wrapped in an ermine cloak, her hood pulled low over her brow, ice pulsed through her veins. "Sweeny...ah...*Adele*," her voice trembled as tears finally broke through her ironclad armor. "You were such an angel. Why were you taken and not me?"

Her shoulders shook as she reached inside her sleeve for a handkerchief that was no longer there. "Rodney, you were so kind and gallant."

Frasier handed her a worn, yet clean handkerchief. "M'lady."

"And you, Brigham. I told you to stop at the inn in Crieff, but you assured me that you had ferried the duke up that awful, winding, rutted road many times, and I wasn't to worry." She curled over and sobbed. "I should have worried. It was snowing and windy and c-c-cold!"

Frasier slid his strong arm about her shoulders and drew her against his side. Grace shouldn't have allowed it, but the warmth of a caring soul was far more appealing that propriety. Weeping, she pivoted and buried her face against his broad shoulder. "What will become of me?"

5

"*What will become of me?*"

Frasier could scarcely believe his ears. The woman in his arms was a jewel—irresistible to any man, beautiful, intelligent, refined, and she possessed a backbone which Frasier had always admired as unbreakable. Last Season she had refused at least ten proposals from very respectable peers—powerful men. Her brother had told him that any one of her suitors would have made an excellent match, however Her Ladyship proved shrewd and patient, setting her sights on the most eligible bachelor in Europe.

But now, her words chilled Frasier to the bone. Something awful had happened for certain. Aye, Lady Grace was truly bereft at the loss of her servants, but it didn't take a seer to realize their deaths weren't the only disastrous calamity she had endured. He held her close, smoothing his palm around her back while she wept as if her own kin had been lost deep in that ravine.

He pressed his lips to her forehead, kissing her over and over again, whispering comforting words.

"Everything will work out in the end..."

"I know how much it hurts, *mo leannan*..."

"'Tis all right. Let out all the anguish…"

"I shall be here always…"

"Dunna cry, *mo chridhe*."

"Ye are a fine woman and no matter what, ye always will be starlight to my soul…"

Frasier's lips trailed from the lass' temple to her cheek, to her ear, along her jaw. Until finally, ever so gently, he brushed his lips across her quivering mouth.

"You cannot fathom the depth of my humiliation," she said, pushing him away, yet without enough force to actually make him step back.

"Help me to understand," he said, cupping her beautiful cheek in his palm and kissing her bruised eye.

"No." A furrow formed between her brows as she shoved him more forcefully this time. "I am hideous!"

Did she feel that she looked unseemly because of her bruised eye? Or did her self-loathing run deeper? Frasier guessed the latter. Regardless of what she believed, Grace was not remotely close to being hideous.

Her Ladyship turned back toward the graves and mumbled a litany of prayers, crossing herself repeatedly. Frasier felt compelled to follow her every gesture though living in the Highlands, he rarely ever made it to the kirk.

As she fell silent, together they stood beside the graves while time seemed endless around them. Perhaps an entire hour passed, mayhap more. Her Ladyship would burst into tears and fight to control herself, each time Frasier reaching out to console, but drawing his hands away before his fingertips brushed the soft ermine of her cloak. Earlier, he had overstepped. Lady Grace was married. She was his greatest's ally's sister. The woman outranked him on so many levels, he did not have the right to kneel and kiss her impractical traveling boots.

When it seemed the last of her tears had subsided, Grace drew in a deep breath. "I am ruined," she said as if it were an unadulterated truth.

Rather than deny her statement as false, he simply replied yet again, "Please help me to understand."

"I suppose the news will eventually arrive in Druimliart."

"Aye, it always does, sooner or later."

She faced him, her eyes swollen and red, the one with the purple bruise more so. "My brother trusts you as much as he trusts his own kin. Though I have no cause to doubt his convictions, I must ask for your discretion."

"Of course." He spread his palms indicating the wintery clearing surrounding them. "If you havena noticed, I am most likely Scotland's most forthright keeper of secrets."

She almost smiled, albeit despair reflected in her bonny eyes. "Martin is pursuing an annulment on my behalf and he is doing so with the Prince Regent's blessing."

Good God, whatever had transpired, it must have been horrendously scandalous for the Duke of Dunscaby to be compelled to take such drastic steps—steps that might indeed result in Her Ladyship's expulsion from polite society for the rest of her days. "Och, this news is grave. I am so verra sorry."

"As am I."

"May I ask what happened?"

Color blossomed in her cheeks as she bowed her head. "I cannot speak of it."

"Of course no'. You must have suffered a calamitous ordeal if the Prince Regent was involved."

"It was awful. So unbearable, Martin challenged Isidor to a duel. That was when my husband showed his true colors and fled to Lithuania like a coward." Her Ladyship's shoulders shook as she buried her face in Frasier's handkerchief. "A-a-and he discarded me as if I were nothing but a worn glove. He never loved me."

Such words did not surprise Frasier in the slightest. Women of Grace's ilk seldom married for love. "Did Isidor declare his affections?"

"Yes...once. The day he proposed." She balled her fists as an anguished cry erupted from the depths of her soul. "He lied to me! By his actions, he forced me to flee London. He forced me into exile, and I doubt I'll ever be able to show my face in Town again!"

With Frasier's next blink, Grace fell into his arms, erupting in a renewed bout of mournful sobs. God save his soft heart, he could not help but console the woman. He repeated his words of endearment, applying light kisses, stroking her back, finding new phrases of encouragement.

Of course, everything he did was merely meant to make her feel better. He in no manner was feeling affection for his closest ally's sister. He hardly noticed the lush contours of her feminine body molding to him through her thick ermine cloak. Nor was Frasier moved by the alluring scent of lavender, delicate enough to bring a hardened highlander to his knees.

He kissed her tears, the saltiness spreading across his tongue. Frasier's gaze dipping to her beautiful mouth—those delicate lips reminding him of precious rosebuds. As Grace opened those brilliant blue eyes, she held him captive with a single look, hesitating at first, then tipping her chin upward. Their lips joined as if pulled by a magnetic force, as if they were both helpless to draw away. Grace's mouth was so supple and sweet, so full of curiosity, eagerly receptive. She tasted of honey and apples. And, God save him, of woman.

This lass did not deserve to be cast aside by a pompous prince, who Frasier had already deemed as brimming with self-importance. Isidor never did deserve Lady Grace's affections. Perhaps all of polite society imagined she was filled with as much pride as her bridegroom, but Frasier knew better. He'd known her when she was climbing trees with her brothers and playing King of the Rock with her kin on the shores of Loch Tulla. All his life he'd watched her bloom from a dainty wee bairn into the beauty she had become.

Yes, though Frasier never left Scotland, he had been to Dunscaby's castle in the northeast several times where he observed as Lady Grace commanded every ballroom and dazzled every man who set eyes on her. He didn't begrudge her for becoming what everyone expected of such a highborn lass—for fulfilling the Dowager Duchess' greatest dreams. But as the seasons passed, Frasier understood more of the lassie's character beneath all the pomp necessary to survive among London's elite. He did not begrudge her, though he had done his best to ignore her.

Now the lass was vulnerable and alone. Her dreams had shattered. And presently preying upon her moment of weakness, he was kissing her...

God bless it! I must stop!

It took a herculean act of self-control to end the kiss and draw away. They were both panting as if they'd run a footrace, Her Ladyship's eyes wide, the crystal blue barely discernable for the size of her pupils.

"Forgive me," he said gruffly.

She tapped her fingers to her lips as mortification filled her eyes. "You are not at fault. I should not have thrown myself at you."

"Then we shan't speak of it again."

"No." She stepped back, clutching the collar of her cloak closed. "We most definitely must not."

The dinner bell clanged—thank God.

Frasier offered his elbow. "Allow me to escort you to the hall. 'Tis time ye met Clan Buchanan, m'lady."

GRACE COVERED HER AWFUL VISAGE. "Please, I look a fright. I would prefer it if I were to meet your kin after my blackened eye fades."

"Och, even with the bruising ye are far bonnier than any woman I've ever seen."

Why, oh why did his words soothe her melancholy so very much? Grace had been given far more eloquent compliments in London's ballrooms, but this man had a way of making her feel truly beautiful, even when she was hideous. "Then I think you must be addled in the mind. Either that or biased."

"I'm not."

She limped as she tried to keep up with Frasier's broad strides. "Pardon me, but your sister is lovely."

"Mayhap, but she's no' you."

Grace attributed the warmth spreading throughout her body to the fact the wind had eased. If she were being honest with herself, she might have admitted to developing a slight infatuation with Buchanan because of his heroic gallantry, but her fondness would soon pass. After all, he lived in a hovel, had no servants, and was as removed as far as he possibly could be from everything Grace held dear. "Well, that's very kind of you to say, sir. However, I would still rather take the evening meal in the sanctity of my...*your* cottage."

He stopped and thrust his fists onto his hips, towering over her, his dark eyebrows slanted inward with his imposing stare. "Ye mean to snub Clan Buchanan's Highland hospitality?"

Now he'd gone and thrown down the gauntlet. There was no chance for Grace to refuse any offer of hospitality from a highlander. Mere Lowlanders knew it simply wasn't done even if one was not looking her best. Even if one desperately needed a bath. Even if one was on the verge of becoming the laughingstock of polite society.

Grace pressed her lips together. "Of course, not."

As they continued to the hall, she did her best to hide her limp and took the opportunity to broach the subject of their sleeping arrangements once again. "I should very much prefer it if you would find me a different place to sleep."

"Why? Isna my bed comfortable?"

The man could be maddening. First he played the "Highland hospitality" card, and now he was trying to goad her into denying the ease of his feather mattress. "Comfort has nothing to do with the fact that I have posed an inconvenience to you, sir. Surely there is somewhere else I can stay?"

She reflected inwardly. A month ago, she would have thought nothing of inconveniencing the Buchanan Laird. But something had changed. Perhaps it was the blow to the head she'd suffered. Perhaps it was the humiliation of finding her newly wedded husband in the arms of Lord Alder. Perhaps it was something deep down which hadn't yet boiled to the surface.

"Och, most every family has wee ones. The lot of them sleep in boxbeds on account their cottages consist of only one room—and the snoring can be awfully difficult to tolerate. Ye could share a bed with the Widow Alice, but she's eighty and suffers from flatulence," he added, grinning and regarding her out of the corner of his eye. Was the laird teasing her?

Of course, he was. Grace had five brothers all of whom teased her mercilessly upon occasion. "You are horrible."

He snorted. "I'm merely honest."

"Is there truly no other place for me to stay?"

"Och, why worry?" he asked as snow began to fall in flakes the size of silver sovereigns. "In a sennight or two, I'll take you to the lodge and you'll forget all about your stay at Druimliart."

Grace highly doubted she'd forget a single moment of her stay here. First of all, today she had wept in the highlander's brawny arms not once but twice. And then he'd kissed her...also twice, though the second kiss had been nothing like the kisses she'd received while being courted. Not a single prior kiss had affected every fiber of her being. After experiencing the melting of her bones, could she even call those brief encounters kisses?

Frasier's kiss hadn't been brief in the slightest. He'd taken his time as if he were exploring the landscape of her mouth. As if he'd longed to kiss her for his entire life, which he most definitely could not have done. Buchanan had visited her family's estates on many occasions and their interactions had always been nothing but cordial and succinct. The man hardly glanced her way, at least until she awoke in his bed.

Ever since, it had been quite difficult not to look at him. And he was oft staring at her. Who knew a man so rugged with such bold features could be indescribably beautiful? Alas, he was right. She would be leaving soon, and until then, she mustn't think about how he kissed, or his alluring intensely blue eyes, or how a man with such hard features could have a mouth so soothingly soft it could lull her into mindless submission.

The interlude had been a mistake. A moment of weakness and they had agreed never to mention it again, thank the stars.

"Are you ready?" Frasier asked, brushing the freshly fallen snow off the door's latch.

"Should I not have prepared?" Of course, at home she would have dressed for dinner. Sweeny would have helped pick out a dinner gown, then would have expertly pinned up Grace's hair. Poor Sweeny. Her heart squeezed. She should have been kinder to her lady's maid. She should have complimented her talents more often. And now Grace would never have the opportunity to do so. "Perhaps I should have bathed?" she said.

"Not necessary."

"You do bathe in winter, do you not?" Goodness, how gauche of her to ask such a personal question. Never in all her days would she have considered verbalizing such an inquisition, though she would have thought it and worse. Her mind must be addled by the mountain air...*or the kisses.* "I—ah—was not referring to you singularly, but you meaning the general populous."

Dear Lord, the man's grin was devilish enough to

melt the snow on the very ground. "Aye, bathing isna taboo in winter though 'tis a wee bit chilly."

In truth, she was hoping he'd tell her where to find a bathhouse, or a copper tub. Instead, he opened the door and provided no further information. Exactly how did one bathe when there were no footmen to tote pails of water? No maids to infuse her bath with sweet smelling salts and oils?

I suppose a washstand and bowl would have to suffice.

So very barbaric.

Just as Grace had imagined, the hall was devoid of embellishment. There was a substantial hearth at one end inside which hung a myriad of cast-iron cooking pots. "Have you no hob?" she asked.

"Would ye like to tote one up the mountain?" he asked rather sardonically. "I reckon it might come in handy."

Why couldn't she keep her mouth shut? Of course, they didn't have a hob. Those cast-iron stoves had to be heavier than a barouche.

Everyone fell silent as Frasier led the way inside and gestured toward her with an upturned palm. "This is Lady Grace, the Duke of Dunscaby's sister. She is our guest until the path along Loch Tulla clears enough for a horse to navigate her shores." He looked at Fiona and arched his eyebrows. "We are all to make her feel welcome and anyone who does no' will answer to me."

His sister brushed a lock of chestnut hair away from her face and glanced to the man beside her, mumbling something imperceptible.

Grace curtsied and affected her most affable smile. "Thank you for your kindness. I am truly grateful to be a recipient of your generous hospitality."

As she rose, Frasier's palm pressed against the

small of her back, urging her forward. There were four tables placed in a square and, as she'd predicted, everyone sat shoulder-to-shoulder on long benches. Moreover, at least a half dozen children darted about like untamed hellions. Above, the rafters made of whole logs were bare and an enormous iron candelabra hung from the center beam, looking as medieval as anything Grace had ever seen.

Frasier led her to the bench with its back to the hearth where there was a space wide enough for him —definitely not for both of them.

At least so Grace believed. She lifted her skirts only as high as was necessary to climb over the seat while Buchanan followed. Once they were settled, her entire left side squished flush against his. The older man to her right also brushed shoulders. He offered a grin full of crooked teeth. "Good evening, m'lady. I'm Ramsey."

"Pleased to make your acquaintance," she said, trying to scoot closer to Frasier, but to no avail. If she tried any harder, she'd end up in his lap.

Scandalous!

"I thought you were supposed to be a wee princess," Ramsey said.

"I prefer Lady Grace, thank you," she replied with enough vinegar to elude the subject and discourage the man from pursuing the matter further.

A toddler tugged on Grace's sleeve. "Up." If she thought there was enough room for her small frame to fit on the cramped bench, she was sorely mistaken.

"Well, hello, darling," Grace said before giving Frasier a look. "Do you always allow children to dine with the adults?"

"Aye. 'Tis only natural to have the clan all together. The rules of your class never made a lick of sense to me." With a great deal of jostling, Frasier twisted round and gave the child a kiss on her cheek. "Now run along to your Ma, wee Cadha."

"Mead?" asked Ramsey, raising a flagon.

Grace nodded. "My thanks." *Mead?* Now she knew she had stepped back in time. Though there were also pitchers of ale on the table, she couldn't ever recall being offered a glass of mead during an evening meal. She sipped, expecting the libation to be sweet, but it was spiced and somewhat dry.

"Is something amiss?" asked Frasier, using a fork to place a slice of meat on her plate.

Unable to shift away, Grace had no option but to ease her tense muscles and let her leg slacken. The sensation brought with it a fluttering throughout her insides—something she must endeavor to quell. "No. I've just never enjoyed mead with my dinner."

"'Tis excellent with roast lamb," said Ramsey, passing her a dish of mint jelly.

"I see you're quite the connoisseur," Grace mused, giving the jelly to Frasier, then taking another sip from her tankard and deciding she liked mead.

"I reckon I ought to be." He drew in a deep breath and thumped his chest with an air of importance. "I'm the bloody bastard who brewed it."

"Are you the clan's master brewer?" Grace asked, ignoring the man's vulgar tongue. She busied herself by putting a couple of potatoes onto her plate from a central bowl, then poured on a bit of gravy. "I am duly impressed."

"How are you feeling after your ordeal?" asked a woman. "On the mend, I hope?"

"Your eye looks awfully sore," said another who had a kind face and who now held Cadha on her lap.

"Please forgive me." Grace shifted her gaze to her

plate, her cheeks burning. "I fear the bruise is rather unseemly."

"We've all had our lumps and bumps, that's for certain," said Ramsey.

"Aye, but we all still manage to do our part," said Fiona with an edge to her tone. It obviously would take some time to win the laird's sister's favor. "I was up and about two days after Magnus was born."

Grace swirled a bite of her lamb in gravy. How a woman of Fiona's ilk could give birth and two days hence expect to be washing and cooking and tending the sick was beyond her imagination.

Not surprisingly, Fiona initiated a conversation about the chores everyone, including the children, were expected to do each day. From the way things bounced across the table, Grace garnered individuals specialized in something like spinning, weaving, or hunting. Then there were the more mundane chores that were done en masse, such as cooking and washing up. The laundry was done every Saturday, and once a month a few got together for making tallow candles, which they were planning tomorrow.

Fiona caught Grace's eye. "Ye said ye canna abide the stench of tallow, *m'lady*." She uttered the address with a sardonic inflection in her tone.

Grace imagined herself sliding under the table and hiding for the rest of her stay. She had complained about the smell of the candle before she fully understood how poverty-stricken these people were. Nonetheless, she would counter Fiona's rudeness as a lady ought. "I apologize. I've never had the *privilege* of breathing in the scent of burning animal fat in my travels before I arrived here." Grace took another sip of mead which had been topped up by Ramsey more than once. She regarded the man. "Since you have access to honey for your mead, do you not also have beeswax?"

"Aye, but beeswax candles are only used in the hall —for the chandelier so we dunna end up with fat drippings all over the floor."

"And our heads," said one of the children.

Grace looked up, ever so glad not to have smelly animal fat oozing onto her wooden plate. "I see. Very prudent of you."

Dessert was a simple affair of stewed spiced apples, but in truth, Grace was surprised when they served more than one course.

"What are your talents?" asked a woman who Grace had learned was named Senoaid, who was in charge of the meal preparation.

"Mine?" Grace's face heated as if she were suddenly ashamed of her many accomplishments. She most certainly wasn't adept at cooking or weaving or spinning wool. "I fear I am not nearly as skilled as the likes of you."

"I would disagree," said Frasier. "You are educated, and I recall ye sing quite well. And dunna ye speak French?"

"All ladies must be musical, and at finishing school languages happened to come easily to me." Grace took a bite of the apple dessert. "I do quite enjoy embroidery."

"What did ye do with all that education?" asked Fiona.

"I'm afraid nothing as of yet," she said, her stomach beginning to roil. Since the day Grace was born, she had been destined to become the wife of a peer. How could she tell these people she'd spent years learning to be the mistress of a grand house? Of course, she had studied languages and figures, but most importantly she had learned to host parties and manage servants. To plan menus with innumerous courses. To be graceful and light on her feet. To speak and act with impeccable manners. As the head-mistress at Northbourne often said: *use sense and judgment that affords members of polite society undeniable superiority over all the rest of creation.*

It didn't escape her notice when a handful of women cleared the table with the help of a few of the older children.

When everyone stood and started moving tables and benches against the walls, Frasier offered his hand. "'Tis Saturday. We usually dance the night afore the Sabbath."

Grace allowed him to help her climb over the bench. "I did not realize you were so religious. Does a minister visit Druimliart."

"Nay. The dancing was started by me ma. The Bible in my cottage was hers as well."

It took but minutes to push the tables and benches against the walls while Blair produced a drum and the Widow Alice placed a fiddle beneath her chin. Some of the younger children darted about the hall in a game of chase, while many of the adults and older children kicked up their heels to traditional country dances like reels and jigs.

Grace was all too happy to sit against the wall (for the first time in her life) and enjoy the festivities. More than one clansman invited her to dance but she declined, excusing herself because she might reinjure her ankle.

Everyone in the hall began to cheer when Frasier and Angus appeared. Side by side they marched forward, each holding two great swords with blades held high. They bowed and placed their weapons in the shape of a cross on the ground.

The drumbeat sped as the men danced, their kilts swishing with every leap, and flicking up just enough for Grace to catch sight of Frasier's well-muscled thighs. Indeed, she'd considered him physically powerful, but now, in comparison with the man dancing beside him, Frasier was nothing short of imposing, magnificent, commanding.

Even his predatory gaze commanded her attention, her very breath. Unable to look away, Grace admired how the highlanders embarked on a contest of wills, the current between them nearly palpable. His expertly placed footwork displayed the physique of a man in his prime, powerful and deft. With every jump, Frasier grew stronger, his grin growing broader while the candlelight flickered above, turning his skin deliciously golden.

His words continually replayed in her mind, *"No matter what, ye are always starlight to my soul."* Of all the endearments he had uttered up there on the hill, this one struck her the deepest. This one she wanted to put into a locket and cherish for the rest of her days.

The music stopped and the connection of their gazes was broken when Frasier bowed. Grace quickly looked away, catching Fiona's disapproving frown. The man's sister was right to be irked, possibly judging her. Grace was still a married woman. She could no sooner set her sights on Buchanan now than she could before she'd accepted Isidor's proposal.

She did not belong here. That had been made clear.

Grace gathered her cloak and slipped away.

6

Frasier stirred the pot of porridge, then hung a kettle of water over the fire. Sausages sizzled on the round griddle also suspended from a hook inside the stone fireplace. The sound of rustling came from the bedchamber, a sure sign Her Ladyship was awake.

Last night after she'd abruptly left the hall, he'd debated as to where he'd sleep for the night. But given the cold, there weren't many options and though he trusted his men, the idea of leaving Grace alone did not bode well. The first eve after he'd brought her to Druimliart, he'd dozed in a chair beside her bed. Last night if he hadn't slept, he'd not be able to function today. So, he opted to stay in the hall and enjoyed a few tots with Ramsey, waiting long enough for the lady to fall asleep before he slipped into his cottage and fashioned himself a pallet near the parlor's hearth.

The door to the bedchamber opened but by the time Frasier turned around to wish her a good morn, Grace had slipped outside. He gave the porridge one last stir before following the lass. She proved to be a step ahead of him again as the door opened, bringing with it a flurry of icy snow.

"Oh, my. You're here?" she said, chamber pot in hand, her bruise now showing a hint of yellow around her eye. "I cannot believe how much it snowed last night. If this continues, I fear I shall pose an imposition upon you forever."

He reached for the chamber pot but she moved it out of reach. "I should have emptied that for you."

"Absolutely not." She headed back into the bedchamber, her limp not as pronounced as it had been the day before. "When in Rome and whatnot."

Frasier leaned against the doorjamb. "But you are my guest. I canna expect you to serve yourself."

She set the pot under the washstand and cleansed her hands in the bowl. "After listening to all the chores done by each and every member of your clan, I'm afraid I feel rather like a laggard. And I most certainly do not wish to be a burden. Perhaps it is good for one's character to learn some of the skills needed by the..."

"Lower class?" he ventured.

She dried her hands on the cloth hanging to the side of the bowl. "Your words, not mine."

"Perhaps you forget I've been to Stack Castle as well as to the lodge." The sausages crackled and he stepped toward the beckoning sound. "I ken the comforts to which you are accustomed."

Grace followed him into the parlor. She gazed over his shoulder, observing his every movement as he used a fork to move the sausages to a plate.

"Good heavens, how did you learn to cook? Especially on this primitive equipment."

He took the canister of tea leaves off the mantle then added three spoons to the kettle now that the water was steaming. "Mind you, your brother and I have cooked on an open fire many times when we've been hunting in the mountains."

"Marty? He hasn't used a spoon to stir porridge in his entire life let alone cooked a sausage."

"He only wants you to think he doesna ken how to cook. Duke or nay, he manages to survive in the wilds."

"I shall have to tease him about that at my very next opportunity." She continued to watch intently as Frasier used a folded cloth to remove the hot kettle from the fire. "Is that how you make tea?"

"Aye. 'Tis merely hot water and a few spoons of leaves."

Grace tsked her tongue. "Who knew? By the way the maids fuss, you'd think it would take a master brewer to produce a flavorful drop."

"I suppose a good brew is all in the leaves. These I purchased in Inverness when passing through. Tea is quite dear, ye ken."

"Is it?" Grace pursed her lips as if she didn't quite believe him. Ladies of her ilk imbibed a great deal of tea and he imagined few knew the cost. "But you are able to afford it?" she asked.

"There are some comforts I choose not to do without," he said, placing the kettle atop a woven mat so not to scorch the table.

"I'm glad of it. A man like you ought to enjoy a great many of life's luxuries, and I daresay tea is trivial when compared to man's vices." She took a turn around the room, stopping at Frasier's pallet. "Someone slept here."

He spooned the porridge into wooden bowls. "Aye."

"You?" she asked as if flabbergasted.

"'Tis a mite warmer in here than out in the stables."

"You wouldn't dare sleep in the stables in this cold. You'd be a frozen corpse by morn."

He handed her the plate of sausages and took the bowls to the table. "Would you prefer it if I bedded down with Fiona and her brood?"

"Perhaps they'd give you their boxbed," she said looking at the plate, biting her lip, then placing it in the center of the table.

Frasier grinned, already today the princess had not only taken care of her chamber pot, she had served food with her own hands. "Highly unlikely."

"Having you sleep here is rather untoward...*scandalous*."

"No' exactly. You're in the bedchamber and I'm out here on a pallet." He gestured to the bench, encouraging her to sit. "And we are completely isolated from society."

She reached for the kettle, but when she struggled to lift the heavy cast iron, Frasier slipped it from her grasp. Her Ladyship might be accustomed to serving tea, but she did so with a silver or porcelain teapot not a sooty cast-iron kettle that had been suspended over a fire. "But people will talk. They always talk."

"Since you must be referring to Clan Buchanan, the lot of us ken better than to gossip. Even if my kin had somewhere to spread rumors, they would have to answer to me."

Grace huffed. "If any of my brothers discovered you were sleeping with only a single door between us, they would challenge you to a duel. And I..."

Frasier sat opposite, picking up his spoon. "You...?"

Her gaze slid from his eyes to his mouth. "Could not bear it!"

Unable to help himself, he scraped his teeth over his bottom lip. Was she thinking of their kisses? Lord knew he'd not been able to cast them from his every thought. "I rather doubt it would come to that."

"Oh?" She picked up her cup and took a sip of tea, making her lips moist and nearly too tempting not to kiss. "Please do explain."

Frasier growled under his breath and took a bite of sausage. He mustn't kiss her again. He was no cad, but he had taken advantage of the lass at a time of weakness and he would not do so again. "First of all, your brother and I are fast allies. The Duke of Dunscaby kens I'd never cross him."

"Perhaps Martin might actually listen to what you have to say before he shoots you." She chuckled, a mischievous glint sparkling in her blue eyes. "But you said, 'first of all.' What else will redeem you?"

"Several things really. I reckon your prince didna ever pull you from a wrecked carriage in the midst of a blizzard."

"No."

"Well then, that has to account for something." He sipped his tea. "Furthermore, you are married now, which changes things a great deal."

"I think not." She delicately plucked a sausage with her fork and put it onto the plate beside her porridge. "Unless you believe it is up to my husband to defend my virtue."

"Nay. You told me the marriage is to be annulled."

"The key phrase is *to be*. The transaction has not been executed, or if it has I have not received word. If and until I do, I am still married."

Grumbling under his breath, Frasier shoveled a bit of porridge into his mouth. She was another man's wife, even if that person had forsaken her. She was right to remain careful. "Then I give you my word, I shall not importune you..." He thought twice about saying more.

She again looked to his lips, a blush spreading across her lovely face. "You have a condition to your continued honorable, polite, and well-mannered behavior?"

"No' exactly." His thoughts in this moment were not entirely honorable, nor terribly polite. If only he could pull her into his arms and kiss her again—show her what it was like to have a man truly worship her. But more than that, with every fiber of his body he wanted to be her protector. That she had been upset and humiliated by a man who promised to love her infused him with rage. "It doesna take a seer to ken Isidor hurt you deeply and for that he ought to be skelped. I would take great satisfaction in being the man to make the scoundrel pay."

She took a dainty bite of porridge, then thoughtfully rested her spoon beside her bowl. When Grace looked at him, her eyes were brimming, her lips forming a tight, well-controlled smile. "I do believe that is the most chivalrous thing a man has ever said to me, my laird."

AFTER THREE DAYS, Druimliart was still snowed in and Grace was about to lose her mind from utter boredom. At the moment, she had no embroidery, no music, no friends to call upon, and no charity that needed her as a benefactor. Idleness sent her mind running amok, fixating on either the horror of discovering Isidor with Lord Alder, or diving into the depts of guilt and melancholy at the loss of her servants.

She blamed herself, of course, even though the decision to go into hiding had been unanimous. After Martin and her brothers had returned from Putney Heath, Mama and the duke took her into the library where they discussed the precariousness of her circumstances. There it was decided that Grace would take her trunks and wait for an answer from the Bishop of Canterbury while remaining out of sight at the lodge. To prevent any further chance of scandal, she had departed London that very night.

And now she was not at the lodge, but biding her time in a tiny cottage with snow piled all the way to the top of the sloped roof. She broke her fast with Frasier in the mornings before he'd disappear to do whatever lairds did in the midst of winter, leaving her alone in the chilly cottage. No one had come to call, though she did go to the hall for the evening meals regardless of how out of place she felt. As a matter of course, she chose not to sit beside Frasier lest everyone suspect her of being a woman of easy virtue. For the last two nights, she sat beside the Widow Alice, who not only suffered from excessive flatulence, she was incredibly hard of hearing, which made the meals rather tedious. But at least the widow didn't prejudge Grace as a laggard. In fact, the woman rarely spoke.

Since the novelty of Grace's presence had worn thin, at mealtimes she was largely ignored and the conversation seldom included her. It was as if she were an island in a sea of people with whom she had nothing in common. Even His Lairdship seldom glanced her way, especially after their entirely inappropriate interlude at the gravesites. He most likely thought her a harlot after the way she'd behaved, throwing herself into his arms.

But heaven help her, she was filled with melancholy. This was not how Grace had envisioned her married life. In fact, she'd never dreamed of spending time in a backward village in the Highlands, let alone Scotland. Grace had always longed for the excitement of the *ton*, attending balls or the theater, shopping along the Pall Mall and taking coffee on the Strand. She missed her friends from finishing school, though those dearest to her had all accepted marriage proposals last Season and were now happily running their own homes.

She also missed her family, especially planning recitals, summer house parties, and soirees with Mama. She even missed her sister Modesty. At one point Grace could barely endure being in the same room with the outspoken imp, but presently, engaging Modesty in a conversation of any sort would be better than pacing Laird Buchanan's primitive cottage with nothing to say and nowhere to go. How people lived in hovels such as his was beyond her. For goodness sakes, the servants at her brother's many estates all lived in more comfortable accommodations than His Lairdship.

Did they not?

She didn't often inspect the servants' quarters. Grace scoffed. That wasn't exactly true. She had never inspected the servants' quarters, though she had wandered up to the women's accommodations a time or two when she was a child. The rooms were neatly appointed as she recalled, if not a tad cramped.

Grace should be running her own home now, in charge of dozens upon dozens of servants. If only things had not crumbled about her feet on her wedding day, she would be meeting with dignitaries, speaking many of the languages of the Continent, planning her first ball, establishing the menus and making sure that in addition to Isidor's favorite fare, they served hers as well.

Alas, here she was without her trousseau, without a single change of clothes, captive with a clan of highlanders who lived as if they were still in the Middle Ages.

Well, at least Fiona had stopped sniping at her. Actually, Frasier's sister hadn't said much at all. The word snub came to mind, because at dinner for the past three nights, Fiona hadn't even glanced at Grace, nor had she enquired as to the state of Grace's ankle, or her megrim.

Fortunately, the bruising around her eye was much improved. If Grace had her toilette, she would be able to powder the unseemly discoloring, but such comforts were not to be had until the snow melted enough to return to the lodge...where her exile would begin in earnest.

For the first time in her life Grace was emptying her own chamber pot, acting as if it were no bother whatsoever. What was it she had told Buchanan?

When in Rome...

At least she was trying to convince herself that if the majority of the human race took care of such things, she ought to do so as well. She had also had to fetch some wood for the fire yesterday when Frasier was out, which had given her an odd sense of accomplishment. At home, if the fire needed tending, she would ring for a servant to do it. Though in truth, Dunscaby servants were so well trained, the fire was always glowing with warm coals. On chilly mornings a maid would slip into Grace's bedchamber and stoke the fire before she awoke.

Never ever had she thought about the maid who was as quiet as a mouse. At what hour did she arise?

How old was she? What was her name? What were her quarters like? Were they comfortable? Were they warm during the long winter nights?

Why hadn't Grace cared?

But mostly, why did she care ever so much now?

She groaned as she donned her cloak. *This is what happens when a woman is bored out of her mind.*

After all, she had no embroidery, there was no one to call upon and no one had come to call. There were no soirees or recitals to plan. There were no dress fittings. She couldn't practice pianoforte, not that she had a talent for it. For goodness sakes, she wasn't even able to dress for dinner.

Grace stepped outside without a plan. The air was bitterly cold and froze her cheeks, her breath billowing about her head in one ominous grey cloud.

Since remaining out of doors was impossible, she darted into the hall. The sound of happy chatter ceased as soon as the door closed behind her. While the women stopped their work, Cadha toddled across the floor to Grace then raised her arms. "Up."

"Good morning, sweeting, what have you been up to today?" she asked, lifting and resting the child onto her hip.

The little one squirmed, making Grace tighten her grip. "Da-cing!"

"Is that so? I love to dance."

"What about cooking?" asked Seonaid, one of the wives who did a great deal of work preparing the evening meals.

Grace looked to the hearth with its cast-iron pots and griddles—where Fiona happened to be sitting on a stool, turning a row of chickens with a hand crank. "I do have a number of recipes that I assembled for my trousseau." Recipes she had intended to share with Isidor's cook.

"Can you make bannocks?" Seonaid asked.

"I could try. If you have a recipe."

"I do," said the woman, pointing to her head. "In here. Passed down from me ma."

Grace placed Cadha back onto her feet. "I see."

"She doesna ken how to do anything aside from be a lady," said Fiona, as if being a lady was objectionable.

A number of retorts came to the tip of Grace's tongue, like speaking fluently with dignitaries from the Holy Roman Empire, or her ability to embroider animals and make them appear life-like. She once embroidered a great tit with its brilliant blues and yellows, and everyone marveled at how real it appeared, as if they could reach out and pet the bird. Her embroidered flowers were equally as impressive. She was equipped to plan a menu for a king. She had the training to run the household of a vast castle. And she knew the difference between pompadour and rose—which she doubted a single woman living at Druimliart could distinguish. Furthermore, Grace had met Queen Charlotte who deigned to sit in the front pew at her wedding beside Mama.

But if Grace uttered a single word of that which riffled through her mind, she would be considered boastful. So, she stood a bit taller. "Bannocks are made with flour, lard, milk, and a bit of salt, are they not?" She only knew this because she loved the flat cakes and had added them to her book of recipes, which was in one of her trunks presently at the bottom of the ravine.

"Aye," said Seonaid. "We use oat flour—coarsely ground. A bit of barley as well."

"That's what gives them substance," said Lena, smiling. She was Cadha's mother and seemed to be the warmest of the three.

In no time, Grace found herself with a pestle in hand, grinding oats and barely until she had blisters on her palm.

Seonaid leaned over the bowl, inspecting her work. "Now mix it with a bit of lard, a pinch or two of salt, and milk."

"How much of each do I use?" Grace asked.

"A dollop of lard, and three parts flour to one part milk."

"Just dunna make it too moist," said Lena. "Cut in the lard, then add enough milk to hold the dough together."

"Very well." *What in heaven's name does she mean by cut in the lard?*

They all stared as she took a knife from the chopping block and repeatedly sliced the fat into the mixture. No one uttered a word when she added more water. And by the time Grace had managed to get the dough looking like something Cook at Newhailes might throw to the chickens, she'd had to grind more oats with her tender fingers, but eventually, Seonaid said the mixture ought to suffice.

"Now to cook the bannocks," she said, casting a sidewise smirk at Fiona. "Ye have enough there for two dozen or so—that'll do for this evening's meal."

Except by the time Grace spooned the dough onto the griddle to make a patty, the women had disappeared—gone to their cottages to do whatever women who had families did before they served the evening meal. She burnt the first. Her fingers were so sore, she dropped the second into the fire, and the third fell apart in crumbles. If it weren't for Lena returning and helping Grace salvage the remainder of the dough, there would have been no bannocks served whatsoever.

"Is it awfully different up here in the mountains?" asked Lena, adding a bit more milk to the batter and stirring.

Grace watched as the woman wielded the spoon in a blur, making the lumps disappear. "Yes. It is like nothing I've ever known."

"It must be wonderful to be born into a life of privilege."

"I suppose so. Honestly I'd never really given it much thought until I came here."

Lena efficiently dropped three dollops onto the griddle. "Och, this is the only home I've ever known—havena been more than a handful of miles away from Druimliart."

"Truly? Have you seen the lodge—my brother's castle? I believe it isn't far from here."

"Aye, from a distance. Ye can see it from the top of Black Mount."

"Oh, yes. I've been up there. From the acme, one can gaze out over Loch Tulla with a great view of the castle's turrets."

The woman smiled wistfully. "It looks like it ought to be in a fairytale."

"The castle's very old—one of my brother's oldest estates."

"Ye mean to say he has more than one?" Lena asked, taking the spatula and flipping each one over.

Grace waggled her eyebrows. "Most dukes do."

"Why? Who needs more than one castle?"

"That is a very good question." Grace took the spatula and put the cooked bannocks onto a plate. "I suppose in my world, families merge to make their holdings larger, so they have more land, and more power."

"That hardly seems fair."

"Perhaps you're right." Grace took the bowl and spoon. "I ought to be able to cook the rest. I wouldn't want Seonaid and Fiona complaining that I cannot do my part."

"They shouldna be goading ye at all. Ye're a guest here."

"That may be so, but at best I am an uninvited guest."

They chatted together while Grace cooked, ever so relieved that the lass came back to help. When she removed the last bannock from the griddle, Lena pointed to Grace's woolen traveling gown, now covered in flour. "Ye'd best go brush off afore the meal is served."

She cringed, having never been so out of sorts. "If only I had a change of clothes."

7

When Grace entered the hall, Frasier had to look twice. Not that she didn't steal his breath away, but this evening she resembled nothing like the glamorous debutante who had dazzled everyone at the house party last summer. Nothing akin to the polished woman who always had not a hair out of place, whose costume was forever at the height of fashion. Was Her Ladyship's blue traveling dress faded or had it been powdered? Though she held her head with an aristocratic air, wisps of blonde hair had escaped her usually tidy chignon, giving her a somewhat disheveled appearance as if she might have just awakened from a late afternoon nap. Either that or she had rolled up her sleeves and taken a turn with the washing?

Moreover, rather than her usual schooled expression of unflappability, she smiled and nodded at him as she headed toward Alice.

Dear God if he hadn't been attracted to Lady Grace before, there was no chance he'd be able to ignore the woman now. Frasier beckoned the lass with a wave of his hand. "What have you been up to today, m'lady?" he asked, standing and offering her a seat beside him.

She glanced at Alice who had yet to notice Her Ladyship's arrival, then Grace made her way toward him. "I've been making bannocks."

"You?" he blurted with disbelief before he checked himself.

"Certainly." She showed him a blister on her palm that had burst and looked quite tender. "I have proof."

He took her hand and stooped to kiss it. Halfway down, he thought better of any sort of public display. If he dared kiss even her hand in front of clan and kin, they'd start gossiping for certain. And he'd sworn to Grace that the Buchanans did not gossip, which was only partly true. They didn't go around Scotland gossiping, but they prattled amongst themselves like a gaggle of squawking geese. "That looks awfully sore. Ye'd best ask Fiona for a salve."

Grace's smile fell. "If I had my effects, I'd be able to apply a salve from my own medicine chest."

"Are you a healer as well?" asked Ramsey.

"Oh no, but all young ladies who attend Northbourne Seminary are required to study the administration of home remedies as well as herbal lore."

Frasier glanced at his sister out of the corner of his eye who happened to have her head together with Seonaid. Did that pair have something to do with Grace's blisters? "Ye ken there is no need for you to work yourself to the bone."

"I do so appreciate your hospitality, but all this idleness has been driving me mad."

"Are nae you always idle?" asked Fiona who'd obviously turned her ear toward the conversation. "I would think with servants to do everything for you, your days would be verra idle."

"Not whenever my mother is nearby." Grace took a

bannock and set it on her plate. "And she is *always* nearby."

Frasier took one as well, slathering it with butter. As he bit into the oatcake, his teeth stuck. The pastry seemed to have hardened like fired clay. With effort he managed to sink his teeth all the way through the damnable thing, but chewing was akin to grinding his teeth against a mixture of leather and sand. He forced himself to swallow the bite, chasing it with a healthy swig of ale.

"You've made bannocks afore?" he asked, coughing.

"No," she said, her eyes bright as she bit into hers and drew it away from her mouth. The lass hadn't even made teeth marks in the crust. Grace appeared to shrink as she curled forward and shook her head. "Oh dear. I'm afraid I've found yet another thing at which I'm not terribly talented."

"These are awful," said Seonaid, tossing her bannock back onto her plate.

"You wasted our oats and barley!" Fiona sniped. "I said it afore and I'll say it again, ye dunna belong here."

"*Haud yer wheesht*, the lot of ye!" Frasier pounded his fist onto the table, making the silverware and glasses rattle. "Lady Grace didna have to offer to help. She did so out of the kindness of her heart. Look at the lassie's hands—she's blistered. Did any of ye offer to instruct her?"

"I told her the ingredients," said Seonaid as if she actually had helped, which Frasier highly doubted.

Everyone else looked to their laps, even the men.

"Well, did ye?" Frasier demanded.

"I helped her cook them after I gave Cadha a bath," said Lena. "I reckon I'm to blame. They *looked* good enough to eat. I didna realize they'd be hard as stone."

"'Tis not your fault," Grace said. "You were very kind, and I truly appreciated having your help, but the bannocks are awful because I cannot cook."

"If ye cannae cook, what can ye do?" asked Fiona.

Grace opened her mouth to reply, but Frasier held up his hand and cut in. "I told ye to *haud yer wheesht* and I meant it. This woman may no' have the same skills as the lot of ye, but she has talents ye canna even dream about."

Fiona crossed her arms. "She thinks she's above us."

"I do not!" Grace said, her back ramrod straight.

Frasier wanted to hurl one of the bannocks at his sister's head and tell her that Her Ladyship was so far above them not a one had a right to kiss her toes, but that would be received about as well as a poke in the eye with a blunt stick. Then he remembered the embroidery he'd seen of the bird. "I'll tell ye all now this woman creates miracles with a needle and thread."

"I beg your pardon, my laird." Her Ladyship nudged his arm and scoffed. "I do no such thing!"

"I disagree. I have seen Lady Grace's work with my own eyes," said Frasier. "Mounted on the wall in the parlor at Stack Castle is a great tit sitting on a tree limb and the wee bird looks so real, for a moment I thought it was going to fly away. I've never seen such detail in an embroidered piece."

"You should have seen my wedding dress," Grace mumbled, her words hardly perceptible, but Frasier heard them. He didn't doubt her wedding dress was a work of art, but it had doubtless been made by a modiste. Though Her Ladyship had a great many talents, the fact that none of them were practical in a

Highland village like Druimliart was neither here nor there. The lass must have her due respect. Just because she couldn't cook, or wash laundry, or spin wool into yarn had no bearing on her worth or charm. Hell, Frasier had no idea how to spin wool.

"I will no' tolerate another insulting word toward Lady Grace. How many times do I have to tell the lot of ye that she is our guest? Do we no' pride ourselves on our hospitality? How many opportunities do we have to entertain a highborn woman such as the Duke of Dunscaby's sister?" He glared at the women who'd prepared this evening's meal. "If there were oats and barley wasted, lassies, the error is yours. Not Her Ladyship's."

"I am sorry. I truly do not wish for anyone to be chastised for my misdeed. I-I wrongfully thought I might be able to help." With a strangled sob, Grace climbed off the bench and dashed out the door.

Frasier pushed to his feet, sweeping his glare across the faces of his kin until he homed in on Fiona. "I willna stand for this! That woman's brother is my greatest ally. He is the man who is helping me search for the Buchanan treasure. Do ye no' want to hold the Horn of Bannockburn given to the seventh laird by the great Robert the Bruce? Are ye so blinded by self-importance to jeopardize the relationship I have spent decades forming? I have never in my life been so ashamed of the lot of ye!"

～

FACEDOWN ON THE BED, Grace wept quietly into the pillow. What had she done to make the world turn against her? A few weeks ago, she had been the darling of the *ton*. She dreamed only of becoming a princess. She had planned to dazzle Lithuania just as she had dazzled London.

But all of a sudden, she was a laughingstock. She had become an embarrassment to her family, a barnacle on her brother's side. Worse, she had survived a harrowing carriage accident that had claimed the lives of everyone else—good people who should have lived long lives, who were kind and talented. Sweeny never once complained about all of Grace's petty demands:

"...this dress is too long. Take it up now!"

"...my stays are too loose. Tie them again!"

"...I do not care for the way you styled my hair. Do it again and make sure there are no flyaways this time!"

And Rodney was always eager to help. Even the footman could brew a kettle of tea. Sweeny certainly could. And Brigham was a very good driver. He was always concerned about the horses and careful not to drive them too hard.

Why had Grace been spared and not the others? Why had Frasier come to her rescue? If he had left her at the bottom of the ravine, she would have perished by dawn for certain. But the powers that be saw fit to extend her torture and bring her to Druimliart where she was not a darling. Here, she was seen as a talentless laggard, scoffed at for trying to be helpful. She never should have left the cottage this afternoon.

A woeful cry screeched from her throat. "I want to go home!"

She missed her mother and her family. She missed waking up to a warm fire in the hearth. She missed dressing for dinner. She even missed dancing lessons with Modesty.

After a long while, she must have cried herself to

sleep because she startled awake when a soft knock sounded on the door.

"Lady Grace?" asked a deep voice—*Buchanan*.

Why did merely the sound of his whisper set her insides to flitting about? Grace's ridiculous feelings had absolutely no business confusing her with whimsical fancies. She rolled to her side and hugged the pillow. His Lairdship most likely was counting the hours until he could move back into his bedchamber. "I do not wish to be disturbed," she said, fully aware she was sounding snobbish, but not caring a whit. At home she could utter the same words and not feel an iota of guilt. Why did she feel so abominably horrid now?

"You left without eating. I've brought you some tea and bread with a bit of cheese."

Her stomach growled. "I am not hungry."

A moment of silence ensued before Buchanan cleared his throat. "I'm afraid I willna take no for an answer. If ye dunna come out here, I'll have no choice but to enter directly."

Groaning, she rolled off the bed then opened the door. "My horse is still in the stables is she not?"

"Aye," he said, holding a tray with a proper teapot and teacups. "And she's as stubborn as ye are."

"It has not snowed for two days. If you would point me in the right direction, I think I would like to travel to the lodge on the morrow."

One corner of Frasier's mouth ticked up. "What if it snows tonight?"

Grace expected him to argue—to say it was still unsafe or at least to insist he send along an escort. Heaven forbid she end up lost and perish. "It will not."

"Och, lassie, 'tis snowing as we speak."

She shoved a rogue lock of hair away from her face. "Dear God, must my every plan be thwarted?"

"Ye ken as well as I, Scottish weather in February is bad one day and worse the next. Our only saving grace is it will soon be March." When the annoying strand of hair fell back over her eye, he balanced the tray in one hand and gently tucked it behind her ear. "I've been remiss when it comes to you."

"How so?" she asked.

With an incline of his head, Frazier led her into the parlor and set the tray on the table. "I should have realized...so...so verra much about you."

She dipped her chin and gave him a questioning look.

"I ken ye lost your lady's maid, and ken how difficult it must be to manage without her."

Grace gave a nod. If he only knew how difficult it was to tie one's own stays. She'd had to switch the laces to the front. Her hair was in a state of disaster, and now she'd soiled her only gown.

"Furthermore, your dress, though well-tailored and verra becoming, isna exactly practical."

"Practical?" she asked as if the word were foreign. No modiste had ever presented her with an item of clothing and referred to it as practical.

But that was exactly what Frasier did. He offered her an arisaid along with a well-starched shift. "These were my ma's finest." He gestured to a half-barrel that had been moved in front of the hearth. "I thought ye might like to put them on after your bath."

Grace's arms dropped to her sides as she looked longingly at the tub. "Is the water warm?"

"The kettle has been boiled. I just didna want to add it until you were ready. The water cools fast in winter."

She accepted the parcel of clothing. "Thank you for your thoughtfulness, my laird."

He pulled a tin box down from the shelf then removed a bar of soap from within. Would ye like me to send Lena to help with your hair?

Though Lena had been kind, Grace was reluctant to ask any woman from Clan Buchanan to assist her. And if she'd learned nothing from her foray to Druimliart, it was that all her life she had been relying far too heavily on the assistance of others. Though Mama had always said it was important to allow servants to serve because it was not only their duty, it gave them a sense of purpose, the dowager had never emphasized how important it was to be self-sufficient. Indeed, it was a privilege to have servants, but if Martin actually knew how to fend for himself when hunting, Grace ought to be able to dress herself and manage her hair. "Have you a comb?"

"Aye." He handed her the box. "Use whatever you need."

Inside was a razor, sharpening strop, a shaving brush, a toothbrush and tooth powder, a comb, a brush, an assortment of leather thongs similar to what Frasier used to club back his hair. But what she found truly curious was the razor's handle. She leaned closer to inspect the inlaid rubies and garnets, then gently pulled the piece out. "This is a work of art."

Frasier slid it from her grasp. "You may use anything but this."

"Is it an heirloom?"

"Aye."

"But I thought your clan lost everything of value in the '45."

"Verra little remains. Butcher Cumberland saw to that." Frazier held up the razor. "This was my grandfather's. He left it with his valet afore they took him into custody—afore the Butcher beheaded him."

She shivered. Her stomach turning over. "I'm so sorry."

He slid the keepsake into his sporran. "Aye, well, it isna your fault. I just wonder—"

"What?"

"Were you not born at Newhailes?"

"I was. 'Tis Mama's favorite manor house."

"What I dunna understand is that you were born in Scotland like the rest of your siblings and they all sound like Scots, but no' you."

Grace's face grew overwarm. "You may recall my mother is English."

"Aye."

"Well, upon her urging I attended Northbourne Seminary for Young Ladies in the Cotswolds, which happens to be the finest finishing school in all of Great Britain."

"I kent that as well."

"As I thought, but what I assume you do not know is that I was treated horribly by the other girls until I learned to conform—until I spoke as they did, acted as they did."

"I see."

"Do you? Have you any idea how difficult it is for a Scottish woman to be accepted into London society? How difficult it is for a young Scottish lass to find a suitable husband among all the dandies, even if said lass is the sister of a duke?"

"But it wasna for you, was it? No' in the end. You had ten marriage proposals."

"Eleven if you count Isidor. And do you know why?"

An easy grin spread across his full lips. "Because ye are the bonniest woman in all the world?"

"No." She blinked at the compliment but swiftly disregarded it. Frasier couldn't really believe such an audacious statement—surely he was merely trying to be kind. "My success was because I learned to talk like an English noblewoman and behave like a lady. I learned to become attractive to the opposite sex—to bat my eyelashes and make riveting conversation. To dance like a nymph and sing like a lark—but only at private recitals, mind you."

"I ken all that, but dunna ye ken how beautiful ye are?" When Grace chose not to reply, he shifted his lips to her ear and whispered, "Whenever ye are in a room, you are the brightest shining star."

As he swept his lips across her cheek, Grace shivered in anticipation of another kiss from the laird who had imparted such passion in her time of sorrow. Who had spoken so softly, and with such care. Heaven help her, she still ached for him. She didn't know a great deal about the marital act, aside from the requirement on the wife's part to submit. Also, on the eve of her wedding after Mama had left Grace's bedchamber, Charity slipped inside, offering a few tips from a married sister. That conversation had revealed far more about what to expect than any text. Charity had said the *act* did require the discarding of clothes. The man would lie with his wife and there would be pain the first time. Her elder sister had grinned bashfully, turning as red as the scarlet drapes as she admitted, "...subsequent couplings have the potential to be most enjoyable."

Glancing to the buttons of her pelisse, she unfastened the top one, feeling ever so daring. Frasier's lips parted as he watched her unbutton the next. Grace's breath labored as she released another.

Frasier covered her fingers with his rough, powerful hand. "Och, if ye dunna stop, I'm likely to do something both of us will regret."

"Will we?" she challenged, taking a step closer.

"Aye," he rasped.

She glanced down at the three undone buttons, which merely revealed the Prussian-blue traveling gown beneath. "Are you certain?"

Frasier closed his eyes and groaned. "Bloody hell, m'lady. I canna take advantage of you."

She wanted to turn and flee, but presently she had nowhere to run. "Why not?"

"Because ye are married."

"Married and alone," she whispered, her heart squeezing.

"Not to mention, your brother would skewer me if I importuned you."

She slid her finger around the clan pin at his shoulder, the subtle flirtation daring him to kiss her. "What if I do not consider myself importuned?"

Frasier grasped her shoulders and pulled her into a tight embrace, his lips caressing her hair, her ear, her cheek, her neck...but never her mouth. When he pulled away, his eyes were wild and nearly black. "I canna take advantage of ye because ye are wounded. Because ye are in hiding and sooner or later you must return to your kin—to the life ye were meant to lead."

He backed away and thrust his hand toward the fire. "I'd best add the water afore I break my promise."

She knew what he meant, of course. They had agreed their kiss had been a mistake. But would she ever experience such a thrill again in all her days? Most likely, it was a memory she would have to lock away and cherish—a secret she would carry with her and dream about on dreary days.

Grace thanked him before he added the hot water to the tub and then took his leave. As she lowered herself into the warmth, she audibly sighed. This might be the crudest bath in which she'd ever immersed herself. However, after all that had transpired since her wedding day, merely bathing in a wooden half barrel was the most soothing experience imaginable. Especially while nibbling fresh bread and cheese, and sipping warm tea.

8

W hen Grace emerged from the bedchamber the following morning wearing the arisaid belted at her waist and draped over her shoulders like a Highland lass, she walked into the parlor with her head held high. She had even plaited her hair in a rope which hung down her back. Smiling broadly, her gaze swept across the parlor but Frazier was nowhere to be seen. The bath barrel had been removed. A pot of oats simmered on the grille over the fire and a kettle was suspended from the hook above the fireplace.

Though a tad disappointed not to be able to show off her new attire, she ladled the oats into a bowl then used a folded cloth to remove the kettle, albeit with both hands, the thing was quite heavy. Just as Frasier had done, she added tea leaves, making a mental note to send him a tin of tea as a thank you gift just as soon as she rejoined civilization.

Why hadn't she been aware of the high cost of tea before? Truly, there were many things she had taken for granted, like flowers in winter, and ices, and carriages, and all the outrageously lavish gowns for which her brother paid. And, of course, she had never thought twice about the duke's hundreds of servants from scullery maids to Giles, the elderly butler who'd always traveled with the family.

Was her character unduly shallow because she had accepted the servants' presence as if it were the natural progression of things for them to be born into a life of servitude and she into a life of privilege? After finishing her porridge, she washed the bowl in the basin, pondering her upbringing as well as her family. She compared herself to Fiona and found it all but impossible to find any parallels. She compared Martin to Frasier. They were fast allies, and though Frasier was a laird, Scottish lairds were lower in the pecking order than barons. The divide between the amenities enjoyed by the two men was akin to comparing the duke's most extravagant town coach pulled by a team of six matched horses to a hay wagon pulled by a mule.

Honestly, Grace could draw no lines of equity between them either. True, she had known of a great many gentlemen as well as peers who had squandered their fortunes. But all of them were reckless spendthrifts, or the sons of reckless spendthrifts. Buchanan was neither. And what she truly did not understand was why, after seventy-odd years had passed, was he still hiding?

She pulled a cup down from the shelf when a knock came at the door. "M'lady, 'tis Lena. May I come in for a moment?"

I actually have a caller?

Grace smiled, skipping to the door and feeling completely unabashed about doing so. After all, there was no one to see or criticize her display of exuberance. She opened it and beckoned the lass inside. "How wonderful your timing is. I was just about to enjoy a cup of tea. I would be ever so delighted if you would join me."

"Tea?" Clutching a basket, Lena's round face turned scarlet. "Och, m'lady. 'Tis I who should be delighted."

"Excellent." Grace gestured to the bench at the table. "Please do have a seat."

"Ye're ever so kind," Lena said, sliding onto the bench and setting her basket atop the table.

Grace took a second cup from the shelf and set to pouring from the heavy kettle. "It is quite thoughtful of you to come to call."

"Aye, well, I got to thinking last night and...ah...I dunna want to be improper..."

"Oh?" Grace was not swayed. At last she had made an ally. "I'll have you know I spend a great deal of time making calls to all manner of ladies when I am home. It is what we women do. Why would you think you're being improper?"

"'Tis no' about the call so much, but I have an idea. Though I'm no' so certain it will be well-received on account of Frasier saying ye're a guest and all."

"How will you know unless you ask?" Grace served the tea, offering Lena a small pitcher of milk. "Tell me what is on your mind."

Lena glanced to her basket. "Well, I thought that since ye are skilled at embroidery, ye might deign to give your hand a try at mending."

"Mending?"

"Nothing overly difficult. A few busted seams. A torn hem."

A sennight ago, Grace would have chastised the lass with a few choice words. But only yesterday she had gone to the hall asking to help. She was so out of sorts in this place that time had forgotten. *How difficult could mending be? There isn't an embroidery stitch I do not know, surely I ought to be able to fix a torn seam.*

She selected the top garment—a linen shift—and held it up.

Lena charged her tea with milk, then took a sip. "That one has a hole under the arm."

"I see." Examining the torn seam, Grace fit the two halves together and decided it most certainly would be a simple task. "Have you a needle and thread?"

The lass grinned. "In the basket."

Grace threaded the needle and set to work. "Is the man you sit with at meals your husband?" she asked, ignoring her tea.

"Aye—Davy MacIan is his name."

Grace worked swiftly with exacting stitches. "A MacIan? How did you two meet?"

"At the Highland games at Rannoch Moor. The Buchanans go every summer—clans like the MacIans, the MacIntoshes, and the MacDonalds generally attend as well. I reckon 'tis the time of year most love matches take place."

Though Grace had been to a number of Highland games over the years, she asked Lena to describe the events that were endemic to Scotland from the caber toss and the stone put to the sword dance and the *ceilidh* always held on the last eve. Listening to the lass calmed her while she worked. At home, she would oft spend winter afternoons embroidering in the ladies' parlor with Mama and her sisters where they never lacked for conversation—especially once Modesty left the nursery.

"Do you enjoy dancing?" Grace asked after Lena described last summer's *ceilidh* at Rannoch Moor.

"Och aye, who doesna like to dance?"

"I, for one, dearly love to dance," she said, tying off

the thread and finding a pair of shears in the basket with which to snip it.

"Then we ought to have a *ceilidh* whilst ye're here."

"Oh, no. I'm certain I will not be here long enough to organize such an event."

"Och, all we need is a fiddle and a drum. Ramsey always does the calling. We could push the tables against the wall and kick up our heels this night."

"Tonight? Do people not need time to prepare? Tell me, if a Buchanan *ceilidh* is so easy to organize, what do you call your Saturday night flings?"

"There's no' much difference, but I reckon we ought to have a celebration of some sort afore ye haste away."

"Well, if this weather keeps up, I shan't be hastily going anywhere."

Grace started on the next garment. A man's shirt with a frayed cuff. She studied the damage for a moment, trying to decide what stitch would work and opted for feather couching because it would both cover up the fray as well as embellish the cuff.

Lena went on to talk about how well each of the Buchanan clan members danced. Not surprisingly, the lass said Frasier was quite accomplished, which Grace already knew because she had seen him in action on more than one occasion, though she couldn't recall His Lairdship ever signing her dance card. Evidently, Seonaid had a little trouble with distinguishing right from left because when the caller said to turn to the right, it was a toss up as to which way the woman would go.

"Where did Buchanan learn to dance?" Grace asked, feigning indifference, though she whipped her needle faster—hardly a sign indicating her sudden rapid heartbeat. Grace prided herself in her ability to hide her true feelings—at least when she desired to do so. She had so many questions about the man, yet for some reason there hadn't been many opportunities to ask him.

"Ye dunna ken?"

"I'm afraid I know very little about His Lairdship."

"For heaven's sakes, Frasier's da sent him to foster with your da when he was fifteen. I reckon 'tis why the laird and your brother get on so well."

"Truly? Fifteen?" Grace's hand stilled. Frasier and Martin were the same age—fourteen years older than she. She still would have been in leading strings at the time. "Do you know how long Buchanan was with my father?"

"Not certain. Two or three years? Long enough to become a proficient dancer, that's for certain."

Interesting. Grace was unaware that the amicability between their families spanned generations. But the MacGalloways had supported the government during the Jacobite wars. Or had they? She didn't recall. Perhaps they had escaped the ordeal because there wasn't a man of fighting age in the family at the time? What she did know was the family supported the crown now, and Martin presided over the strongest dukedom in Scotland.

"Fancy that," Grace mused, thinking back to her father. It had been seven years since he'd succumbed to a fatal bout of dropsy. She'd been only thirteen years of age when he died. Her father had always been a stern man, at least whenever he actually graced the nursery with his presence. And when he did, the nursemaid insisted the children remain silent and stand as if they were balancing books on their heads. The only way for one of her father's daughters to win his favor was to be perfectly behaved and stunningly beautiful, which Grace had learned far earlier than Charity or Modesty. Nonetheless, that the former duke had taken young Buchanan under his wing was difficult to fathom.

Lena picked up the shift and studied Grace's repair. "My heavens, this needlework is sturdier than the original seam."

"Is it too much?" Grace asked, biting her bottom lip. Her lady's maid had always done any mending necessary, and Grace was ashamed to admit she had never bothered to question Sweeny's work.

"Nay. 'Tis perfect. I ought to get at least another two or three years out of this." Lena craned her neck to better see the cuff in Grace's hand, then ran her finger over the stitching. "This is astonishing. If I hadn't kent the sleeve was frayed, I'd reckon this was a new shirt for certain."

"Do you really like it?"

"Aye. And so will Davy."

Grace plunged her needle into the muslin cloth. "I say, since I'm a failure at being a princess, mayhap I can become a seamstress."

"I beg your pardon?" Lena gaped. "Did ye say failure? Ye are so refined and have such polished manners, ye certainly are no' a failure in me eyes!"

Focusing on the mending, Grace berated herself for allow such a faux pas. She oughtn't have said anything at all.

Lena, placed a gentle hand on her arm. "Tell me, is that the reason ye dunna want anyone calling ye Princess?"

Grace swallowed against the sudden thickening of her throat. How could she have been so careless as to mention anything about the reason for her exile. "Forgive me. I was jesting."

"So why are ye here and no' with your prince?"

Oh dear, had she now opened Pandora's box? She whipped a few more stitches before saying, "I'm afraid it is a very long and convoluted story."

Lena straightened and folded her hands. "Cadha is with her da, so I've no place else to be at the moment. I'd like to ken what happened. We all would."

"I cannot utter it." Grace's hand stilled. If only she could confide in Lena, or anyone for that matter. But the memory was still too raw. Perhaps she'd never be able to speak of it.

Then again, why not share a little something?

She took a small sip of tea, followed by an enormous sigh. "All I can say is that I found Isidor in the arms of another on my wedding day. My brother happened to be with me at the time."

"The duke?"

"Aye...*yes*," Grace corrected herself. Since changing her accent at finishing school, she rarely slipped anymore. "My brother is helping me to obtain an annulment."

"Oh, my lands. How devastating for ye." Lena pressed her fingers to her lips. "No wonder ye have gone into hiding, m'lady."

Grace tied off her work before placing her hand atop the other woman's shoulder. "I'd be truly grateful if you would keep this between us. 'Tis a delicate matter to say the least. I haven't even told Buchanan all of it."

Lena's lips pursed. "I willna tell a soul...except..."

"Hmm?"

"Well, everyone is awfully curious as to why ye're no' with your husband. 'Tis ever so *unusual* especially since ye are newly wed. May I at least tell them the prince turned out to be a scoundrel?"

Unable to hold in her scoff, Grace tossed the shirt at her newfound friend. "I think that is a very apt descriptor for the bast—*ahem*—the man."

FRASIER LAY ATOP HIS PALLET, reading by the light of a tallow candle while sleep escaped him. In truth, sleep had been fleeting at best since Lady Grace had been occupying his bedchamber. For the past fortnight the woman had been resting her head upon his pillow, her skin caressed by his very own bed linens.

Damnation, if only he could trade places with his bloody linens. If only he could provide her with the comfort imparted by his woolen blankets. If only he could hold her in his arms and protect her from knaves akin to her mishappen prince. So, the bastard had been found in the arms of another woman on the eve of his wedding night—aye, thanks to Lena, now all the clansmen and women kent the truth.

If only Frasier had been there, he never would have let the slippery eel escape. He would have taken the blackguard outside and shown him what happens to men who cross him...well, not exactly him, perhaps his kin. Hell, Grace's family was close enough to kin. He loved Martin MacGalloway like a brother, but the duke was too much of a gentleman, far too embroiled in the ways of polite society for the likes of Frasier. His Grace had challenged the prince to a duel in good faith—a mistake that had given the miserable fiend the opportunity to tuck tail and flee like a bloody chicken-livered cur.

Clearly the prince was a dishonest maggot, a lying charlatan who thought nothing of humiliating Lady Grace on what should have been the most important day of the young lassie's life. Instead, her world shattered as he embroiled the poor woman in a hellacious scandal.

Lady Grace had been bred to be worshiped—to be the wife of a man with the means to shower her with anything she desired. She was born to be the princess she had become. Frasier had never met a woman who possessed as much charm, who was socially as polished, who always could turn every head when she entered a room, both male and female, mind you.

Grace was a diamond who glittered more brightly than any other woman Frasier had ever beheld. Even when she was a child, she was radiantly beautiful. That Isidor callously disregarded her honor was unthinkable. That Isidor could cast aside the catch of the decade for a salacious romp only hours after he had recited wedding vows.

Dear God, Frasier would be forever content if such a woman would look upon him with the same affection she'd afforded her prince. For the past fortnight it burned to watch the woman slip into the bedchamber and close the door, bidding him goodnight as if he were one of her brothers. Every night he had lain awake, his heart yearning, his mind unable to think of anything but her. What would it be like to hold her in his arms, to adore her as she deserved to be adored?

The snow had most likely packed down enough to escort Lady Grace down the mountain to the lodge. It also might have already melted at the lower altitude but Frasier hadn't mentioned it yet, mainly because there was still plenty of snow at Druimliart and that's what mattered most. Of course his decision had nothing to do with Lady Grace's company.

Over the past several days, half the clanswomen had brought their mending to the cottage. Frasier ought to be appalled to see Grace subjected to such menial labor, but Her Ladyship insisted upon setting herself to the task. And from what Frasier had observed, she seemed to enjoy the labor. She sewed tirelessly, often adding embellishments that delighted the ladies, at least those who brought her their mending.

Fiona and Seonaid had not done so. Frasier didn't even try to understand the opposite sex, especially his sister. Women held grudges far longer than any man he knew. Hell, if he had a bone to pick with a lad, they'd settle their differences in the sparring ring and that would be the end of it.

A resounding thud came from the bedchamber, making Frasier nearly drop his book. He held very still for a moment while a great deal of mumbling came from the other side of the door. "Lady Grace, are you well?" he asked as he stood and moved into the vestibule.

"Yes, fine," she replied, her voice caressing him as if his heart had been brushed by a feather. "I'm sorry if I woke you."

He placed his palm on the door as if he could feel her presence through the timbers. "Och, I'm still awake, lass." Biting his bottom lip, he hung his head. He shouldn't speak so informally to her.

"It seems sleep is eluding us both," she said, her voice clear as if she were standing but inches away. Perhaps she was.

"Would you care a round of hazard?" he asked, nearly kicking himself. Of course a woman of Her Ladyship's ilk would not want to play a gambling game.

As the door cracked open, the candlelight within radiated above her head, making her tresses glow like sun-kissed wheat. Frazier's breath stopped.

She blinked like a blue-eyed doe. "Upon what shall we wager?"

His mouth dropped open. "Forgive me. I'm afraid I wasna thinking clearly when I asked a lady to take a turn at throwing the dice."

"Do not be silly." She pulled the door wide and walked through, still wearing the arisaid he'd given her. "I've played hazard in the gaming rooms at Almack's. Goodness, I would think you of all people at Druimliart would realize games are oft played at balls and house parties."

He stared as she moved through to the parlor, her long braid swishing across wonderfully sculpted hips. "Almack's as well? I would think your dance card would be so full, a woman like you wouldna have time for the card tables."

"You flatter me." She glanced at him over her shoulder, her eyes dark, sad, and filled with something else—something that stirred his blood.

He gulped, following. "I merely speak true. After all, at the few balls we've attended together you were always surrounded by men and woman alike. No mere laird such as I had a wee opportunity to sign your dance card."

She lowered her chin and looked up at him shyly, her lips slightly curled upward at the corners. It had to be the most seductive expression he'd ever beheld. "No laird such as you deigned to ask, sir."

Frasier chuckled, as he forced himself to shift his gaze away from her enticing blue eyes. He busied himself with collecting the cup of dice from the shelf. "Och, ye ken as well as I you were destined to grace the halls of a stately home, no' some hovel like my wee cottage."

"I hardly see what that has to do with a quadrille."

Frasier didn't reply as he watched her climb over the rickety old bench. God's stones, even his furniture was beneath her. How did one reply to a woman he had spent years going out of his way to avoid? How did one reply when his tactics had failed to put a casing of iron around his heart? How did one reply when she continually commanded his attention?

With no answers to his questions, he took a seat on the bench across. "Shall we roll to see who will be the caster?"

She pushed the cup containing the dice toward him. "I shall defer to you, oh rescuer of damsels."

Chuckling, he picked it up and rattled the two dice within. "What shall we wager?"

Gesturing to her arisaid, she bit her bottom lip. "Considering the fact that most of my worldly possessions are most likely encased in ice at the bottom of the ravine, I haven't much to wager with."

Frasier gestured from one wall to another. "Ye ken my treasure is long lost."

"Your family's treasure?" she asked.

"Aye."

She smoothed her fingers over the table's aged oak. "Yes, I am aware, everything was lost in the '45? Correct?"

He nodded. "Stolen is more apt." Then he again shook the cup, determined not to let the memory of his clan's misfortune cloud his mood. "The wager shall be a dance."

"If I lose? But I quite like dancing."

He did as well—but he'd never had the pleasure of dancing with the partner he wanted. "The winner chooses the dance."

"What about music?"

"The loser hums." Frasier would win either way. If

he won, he would listen to her hum a waltz. If she won, the poor lass would have to suffer him butchering whatever tune she chose. He winked. "What say you, oh rescued damsel?"

A slow grin spread across her lips. Such a simple expression. But one of Lady Grace's smiles brought more complexity than he ever could have imagined—especially when the object of her attention was him. He adored having her gaze meet his eyes. Though his heart hammered so loudly, he would be surprised if she didn't remark on it. What would he do if she called him out? Admit his infatuation? Admit to how long he'd admired her? Reach across the table, cup her lovely face between his palms and kiss her? Aye, and then to pull the woman onto his lap and kiss her until dawn?

Instead of acting on any one of his desires, he rattled the dice. "I call six as main."

"Six?" she said, her voice like sin, her expression tempting as a she-devil.

He cast the dice onto the table, unable to look away from those alluring blue eyes.

"My," she said, those delicate brows arching. "It appears as if luck is with me this night."

He glanced down—a measly three. "I do believe *you* need no luck, m'lady."

"Perhaps that might have been true at one point, but presently I am in dire need of a great deal of luck. I'm afraid I require a miracle."

"Because of the annulment?"

"Yes, and because of the possibility of so many things going wrong. I fear not even Martin will be able to negotiate me out of this disaster."

"If anyone is able, it is your brother." Frasier stood

and bowed. "However, presently, we have a dance to share. What is your fancy?"

She took his hand and allowed him to pull her to her feet. "What would you say to a waltz? Too scandalous?"

"Waltz?" he croaked, the palms of his hands beginning to perspire. Dear God, rarely in his life had he been so nervous as to cause his hands to sweat.

"Would you prefer a quadrille?"

He drew her into his arms rather more powerfully than he'd intended. "Waltz."

She grinned again, face turned up to him, looking more tempting than a freshly baked apple tart. "You must hum."

"Hmm?"

"Sing."

"I'm afraid I'm a wee bit lacking in musical talent. Perhaps you ought to put some wool in your ears."

"Absolutely not," she said, taking his hand as if she were a queen. "You shall sing for me sure and clear."

Frasier gulped and managed a simple three-beat tune. It wasn't Mozart, but the Gaelic ditty was enough to set the tempo.

Grace followed his lead as if she were as malleable as clay. "You have a pleasant voice."

Not only was she a proficient dancer, the lass was quite good at telling tall tales. Chuckling with the tune, Frasier picked up the pace, making her eyes flash wide.

"Mmm," she said, not missing a step. "I do enjoy a challenge ever so much."

If he weren't humming, he'd compliment her footwork, but instead, he nodded.

"Lena mentioned you fostered with my father."

He blinked—had she not remembered? But then

again, Her Ladyship had been but a bairn during the time he spent at Stack Castle learning to become a gentleman, learning how to understand books of accounts and all the duties necessary for clan leadership. "You were not aware?" he asked as he stopped, still holding her in his arms.

"How could I have been?"

"Dunna ken. I suppose I assumed it would have been mentioned a time or two. After all, I'm oft a guest of your brother. Our friendship was greatly strengthened during those years."

"I wish I'd been old enough to..." She glanced aside.

He strengthened his grip ever so slightly. "Please tell me what you were about to say."

"I suppose I would have liked to have made friends with you as well."

Warmth seeped through to his soul. "Truly?" he whispered, trying to remember why he needed to keep this woman at arm's length, why he wasn't kissing her right now.

A lovely shade of pink flushed her cheeks—bonny enough to erase every well-mannered thought which was preventing him from tasting her lips. "Forgive me. I suppose I'm being too forward."

Frasier clamped his jaw shut. She wasn't being forward, she was being sweet and lovely and *desirable*. Lady Grace should not be his arms—in his cottage—dancing a waltz. Furthermore, Druimliart was no place for a highborn maid—matron—princess—lady.

Hell, whatever her title, I should not be holding her breasts so tightly to my chest.

His heart thundered as he resumed the dance, fighting an internal battle. How could he ever release her? How could he convince her to stay?

Somewhere in the middle of his musings, they stopped dancing. Grace lifted her chin, the lids of her eyes slightly lowered as she stared at his lips. The glow from the hearth's fire danced shadows across her shimmering face. Heaven help him, he wanted to ravish her.

"Your singing is far better than you give yourself credit for." Her eyes flickered up to his, reflecting amusement.

"Thank you," he rasped.

He collected her dainty hands between his rough fingers, raised them to his mouth, and kissed her knuckles. The lady's sleeve slipped to her elbow, revealing a pathway of flawless skin along her forearm. Merely the scent of her pulled on his heartstrings. Dear God, he'd never wanted anything in his life as much as he wanted Grace MacGalloway. Yearning consumed him as he trailed kisses from her wrist to her elbow.

Then the lady's throaty sigh sent him undone. Made him harder than the hilt of his dirk. "I want to kiss you, just once more," he growled, because this time he would taste her and commit it to memory, treasure her wiles in his heart and lock her away forever.

Grace's breath quickened as she gave a single nod. Taking her hands, he urged them around his hips. With one more step, he pressed his body against hers, molded to her form as if God Almighty had made them a matched pair.

Slowly, he dipped his chin and brushed his mouth across hers, stroking the parting of her lips with his tongue until she opened for him. Sighing into her mouth, Frasier closed his eyes and kissed her, taking his time, familiarizing himself with the suppleness of her breasts, the small arc of her waist, the womanly flare of her hips.

It took no time for passion's grip to move him while together their entwined bodies rubbed from side to side. Grace returned his kiss with fervent licks and swirls of her tongue. The desire growing, surging, pushing Frasier to the very precipice of losing control.

Heaven help him, if he didn't stop now he'd whisk the woman into his arms and haul her into the bedchamber. His breath turned ragged as he pulled away. Grace's eyes glazed, her cheeks red with lust. She quickly dropped her hands and cast her gaze downward. "Please forgive me. I'm afraid I lost all vestiges of restraint."

Frasier caressed her cheek. "Och, lass, 'tis I who must be forgiven. Ye are far too tempting to resist."

She didn't look up. "We mustn't forget the fact I am married."

His gut clenched—what he wouldn't do to reverse the course of time. "Aye." He took a step away and bowed. "Then I will bid you sleep well, m'lady."

As Grace headed for the bedchamber, a pounding came at the door. "Frasier! Moira's wee bairn is burning with fever!"

9

Without stopping to don her cloak, Grace hastened after Frasier and Fiona, the babe's cries resounding on the icy breeze as soon as she stepped outside.

"I applied a leech to the bairn's leg and gave her a teaspoon of willow bark tea. For hours I've been applying cool cloths to the wee one's forehead, but Aggie willna stop crying."

Blair stood in front of the cottage door, wringing his hands, the high-pitched shrieks now louder. "I dunna ken what else to do."

Frasier marched up to the man and clapped him on the shoulder. "Fiona kens best. Mayhap we need to let the fever run its course."

Blair's gaze shifted to Grace and narrowed. "There's no need for ye to fash yerself, m'lady."

With an uptick of her chin, Grace refused to flinch. "I may be of assistance. I do not have my medicine bundle on hand, but I'm from a family of eight children."

"Och, I dunna see how ye can help," said Fiona. "Me ma trained me in the healing arts. I ken what I am on about."

"Except this situation has become dire, has it not?" asked Grace with an edge to her voice.

The lass pursed her lips, but it was Frasier who gestured inside. "Why not let Her Ladyship have a wee peek at Aggie?"

With a huff, Fiona marched inside while Blair gave a nod. "Thank you, m'lady."

Grace squeezed Frasier's wrist. "I'm not sure if I can do anything beyond what Fiona has already done, though I did study herbal lore and healing at finishing school."

Inside, Moira held the fussy baby. The air was thick with woodsmoke and burned the eyes.

"You have bad air," Grace said, propping the door open, then taking a dish cloth, and flapping it, trying to urge the smoke outside.

"What are you doing?" Fiona demanded. "'Tis freezing out there."

"Then find a cloth and help me, curse it all!"

In no time, all four adults were flapping cloths to clear the smoke while baby Aggie lay in the cradle Frasier had made, shrieking like a banshee.

"How long ago did you give her the willow bark tea?" Grace asked, blinking, relieved their efforts were beginning to help—at least her eyes had stopped stinging.

"Three, four hours ago," said Moira.

"Then give her another spoon."

Fiona threw her arms out wide. "'Tis too soon!"

"Is the babe still fevered?" Grace asked, receiving a curt nod. "Then do as I say."

As Fiona reached for the vial, Grace spotted a wooden tub in the corner. She tapped Frasier's elbow. "Can you please fill the bath with snow?" she whispered before turning to Moira. "Have you an ewer of clean water?"

Moira pulled the babe into her arms, trying to calm her enough to administer the tincture. "Aye. I always keep water by the hearth and at the washstand."

Grace found the ewer by the hearth half full just as Frasier returned with the snow. "What shall I do with this?" he asked.

"Here," she said, gesturing to the floor near the hearth. He hefted the half-barrel into place, then Grace poured in the water.

"What the blazes are you doing?" Fiona demanded while Moira turned away as if to protect her child from the daft woman.

Grace dipped her fingers in the icy soup. "When my sister Modesty was a babe, she ran a high fever. My parents sent for the physician who did everything from bleeding to giving her tinctures akin to your tea. When that did not work, he put her in an ice bath."

"God no! Ye'll kill her," Fiona shrieked above Aggie's wails.

Moira stepped beside her husband. "You are not putting my wee bairn in freezing water. She'll perish for certain."

"I promise you, the cold will not kill her." The corners of Grace's lips tightened as she looked each person in the eyes. "But Aggie could succumb to the fever before this night's end unless we try. I give you my word, I've seen this tactic used by the most heralded physician in Edinburgh."

Fiona shook her head.

Grace held out her arms. "I cannot promise this will work, but I assure you it shan't make your bairn worse."

"If Lady Modesty endured the ice bath, then so

can our Aggie," said Frasier, asserting himself with his fists on his kilted hips. "Go on, Moira, allow Lady Grace to give it a go."

After a moment's hesitation, the mother holding the hysterical, flailing child gave a single nod. Grace took Aggie and held her head securely, dunking the babe including her hands and arms in the icy water. The poor infant's cries soared to new heights as she kicked and thrashed with surprising strength. Gnashing her teeth, Grace held on for dear life.

"Easy, Aggie," she cooed, taking deep breaths in an effort to keep herself calm, hoping to pass a modicum of tranquility to the child.

"Enough!" Moira shouted, the mother on the verge of hysteria. "Canna ye see ye're freezing her half to death?"

"Bring me a drying cloth," Grace commanded, trying to purchase a few moments longer, even though her fingers were nearly numb.

When Moira held out the cloth, Grace gladly deposited the babe into her mother's arms. She used the back of her wrist to test Aggie's forehead for fever, but she didn't have enough feeling to be able to tell.

After the babe was dry, Fiona stepped in with a spoonful of tincture and dribbled it on Aggie's tongue. Only then did Grace realize the wee one had stopped crying. "Is she still fevered?" she asked.

Moira pressed her cheek to her daughter's. "She's cooler for certain."

"Aye, but her fever can shoot back up," Fiona warned. "The cold bath may have only masked it for the time being."

"Correct," Grace agreed.

The healer shook her spoon. "We will need to

keep a watchful eye on the bairn throughout the night."

"Then as her parents we shall," said Blair, taking the babe from his wife's arms. "Thank you, m'lady, Fiona. I dunna ken what we would have done without you both."

FRASIER FOUND Her Ladyship sitting in a chair by the hearth, studiously focused upon tatting a row of lace around the edge of a mob cap. Her every stitch tiny, her hand weaving through the thread in a blur. He stood for a moment watching her fingers work, imagining what it would be like to have the bonny lass here smiling at him whenever he walked in the door. To be able to hold her, to love her, and, dare he think it, to have a family with her.

As if she sensed his thoughts, she smiled now, looking up from her work. With all the mending the women had brought in, he hadn't once heard her complain. "Is all well, m'laird?"

Alas, he would do anything to avoid what he was about to say. "Aye...*ah*...I reckon the snow has finally cleared enough to safely take you to the lodge." He wanted to add if she still wished to go, but of course she did. She'd been talking about leaving ever since she'd arrived at Druimliart.

Her smile fell for a moment as she looked down and made another stitch. "Oh?"

"Aye, Lena hasna stopped badgering me about hosting a *ceilidh*. Normally we wait until Beltane, but given the circumstances, I thought we ought to present you with a proper Highland send off."

"That is very thoughtful of you—and Lena." Grace bit her bottom lip. "What of the others?"

"How many garments have you mended?"

She held up the mob cap. "I've lost count. But I have enjoyed the work much more than I ever dreamed possible. It gives me a sense of accomplishment to know I've done something to help others aside from being a benefactor for the various charitable organizations supported by my family."

He smiled at that. He should have known of her philanthropy. There were still so many things he didn't know about the lass. Sure, they had been acquainted since she was in leading strings but before the past few weeks, Frasier had only admired Grace from afar. Which was exactly where he needed to continue to admire her. She wasn't only married, she was the sister of his friend, not to mention her family was the most powerful in Scotland. The sooner he could take her back to the lodge the better it would be for them both. Neither one of them could afford another romantic misstep.

Nonetheless, Lady Grace did not belong at the lodge either. It was draughty and *medieval*. And if she didn't belong in Lithuania, she needed to reside at one of the dukedom's many, comfortable estates with a host of servants to wait upon her. She should not ever, not for one day have to hide herself in an old castle nestled in the remote Highlands.

"I ken it wasna easy to come here, but ye found ways to endear yourself to the clan. Even Fiona has finally forgiven you for asking her to empty the chamber pot."

Her Ladyship chuckled. "Thank goodness Aggie responded well to the ice bath."

"That and Fiona's tincture. As Blair said, we owe a

debt of gratitude to you both." Frasier stepped nearer and bowed. "My lady, I would be ever so grateful if you would attend tonight's *ceilidh* as my esteemed guest. After all, we are holding it in your honor."

A lovely blush blossomed in her cheeks. "How can I resist such a gallant invitation?"

"You canna." Unable to help himself, he brushed a lock of hair away from her face, his breath catching when she blessed him with a lovely smile. If only he could ask her to stay. If only he could fix her woes.

But Frasier had grave problems of his own. Even when he was fostering with the MacGalloways, he had made it his life's quest to clear his clan name and recover their stolen treasure. Over the years he and Martin had made numerous enquiries as to what had happened to all that had been seized by the Duke of Cumberland. It was tedious business as with every lead they uncovered, they were hindered by a number of dead ends.

Perhaps the gold and jewels were gone forever, but the Horn of Bannockburn had to be out there somewhere and Frasier aimed to find it. The relic had been given to his ancestor, Sir Maurice Buchanan by Robert the Bruce after Scotland won the battle by the same name. The horn which called the troops into battle was priceless. Aye, it was but a carved piece of ram's horn, ornamented with a handful of precious stones, but it was a symbol of clan pride, of their rich history. The Horn of Bannockburn proved that Clan Buchanan was not only one of the oldest, long-lived clans in Scotland, it undisputedly heralded Frasier's place among Scotland's chieftains.

His father had told him it was Frasier's destiny to reinstate the Buchanan's good name. It was the main reason the old chief had sent him to foster with His

Grace, the former Duke of Dunscaby. Frasier learned the ways of the aristocracy because his father had dreamed that in his son's lifetime the day of reckoning would come. Clan Buchanan would see the orders of tyranny against them expunged and again be recognized by the crown. Unfortunately, Da had no words of advice as to how Frasier might go about clearing their name. And of late he had realized his father might have been more dreamer than strategist.

Lady Grace's gentle touch drew him from his reverie. Her fingers were warm and invigorating as if she possessed the ability to caress his soul. "I sense you are miles away, my laird."

He gathered her fingers and kissed the back of her hand. "Och, ye ought to call me Frasier. Everyone else does," he said, avoiding her question and forcing himself to release her. The lass had far too many worries of her own.

"May I ask you a question?"

"Aye."

"Why, after three and seventy years are you still hiding in the Highlands?"

Because there was still an order to shoot any Buchanan on sight. Because this was the only home he knew. Because he needed to recover his kin's lost treasure however he must. "We are a clan exiled," he finally replied, his father's dreams ever so far away. "Where else would we go?"

10

G race affected an unflappable expression of
serenity while she sat beside Frasier at the high
table, not that it was really a high table akin to the
great halls of medieval times. Though it wasn't even
atop a dais, she had dubbed it so because this Highland village seemed to be lost in time. Even though
His Lairdship treated everyone as an equal, to any
stranger who might pass by there would be no question as to who was in command. But that is not why
Grace presently maintained a schooled countenance.

She was quite enjoying the intimacy beneath the
table, the length of her thigh flush against Buchanan's.
As he cut his roast lamb, his shoulder brushed hers in
familiar closeness. Grace's insides warred between the
comfort of his warmth together with the grim reality
that her short time there had come to an end. Frasier's
warmth, his nearness, his casual friendliness had become most dear. It seemed as if she'd been there all
winter, but it had only been a mere nineteen days
since the carriage had slipped off the cliff.

Who knew how much her ideology would change
in less than three sennights? When Grace first arrived,
she'd considered herself superior to these people. She

didn't understand how they could possibly be happy living in such rudimentary accommodations so far away from civilization, relying on themselves as if they didn't need the rest of the world beyond. But those of Clan Buchanan seemed content. Happy to rise in the morning and work their fingers to the bone, falling into bed every night.

Grace might not be bred for such a life, but during her time here, she'd gained an understanding of their lot. And with her reflection came respect.

"You haven't touched your meal," Frasier said, his shoulder pressing hers.

She picked up her fork. "I've a great deal on my mind," she said, her gaze shifting to his lips, the bottom fuller than the top. His tongue slipped out and moistened them, causing her to draw in a staggered breath.

If only she could kiss him right now—shift onto his lap and wrap her arms around his neck. If only she weren't deeply embroiled in scandal, or married, or a princess. If only she were a Highland maid born into a simple family.

Grace swallowed her urges and cut a bite, slipping it into her mouth. How wayward her thoughts had become. Though as a woman scorned by her estranged husband, could she not allow her mind to wander a tad? By this time on the morrow she would be alone. Of course, as soon as she reached the lodge, she would have to send word to Martin and inform him of the wrecked carriage as well as the grievous loss of their servants. Most likely he'd send their brother Philip to her aid. Philip's estate was but a two-day ride from the lodge.

Perhaps I ought to write to Philip as well. That would certainly save time.

Though the idea of returning to her calamitous life was dreadful, it must be done. Perhaps Martin had already obtained an annulment on her behalf?

Perhaps he had not.

Regardless of what had transpired in London, Grace needed to pick up the pieces of her life. She could no sooner ask Frasier to embroil himself in such a disaster as he could ask her to stay in his tiny cottage. Her life was a shambles. No matter if he was an outcast, the laird deserved a woman who was not tainted. A woman he could marry, with whom he could have a family.

Grace doubted she would ever marry again.

Who would want her? A ruined woman who had been spurned on her wedding day?

As the tables were cleared at the end of the meal, the Widow Alice with her fiddle and Blair with his drum took their places while the tables were pushed toward the walls to make room for the dancing. Even the high table was shoved back and, as they sat on the bench facing the floor, Frasier tapped her elbow and inclined his lips to her ear. "I ken ye have a great deal on your mind, lass. Why no' let it go for one night—just kick up your heels and forget about what lies beyond the mountains."

"Quite right," she said, sitting taller. "My father said no one ever accomplished anything by feeling sorry for herself."

"That's the spirit, lass."

A swarm of butterflies flitted through her stomach. Why did the laird sound so irresistible when he referred to her as lass? She had been around men with Highland burrs all her life, but Frasier's was a tad more pronounced, his voice deeper, his rugged looks unbearably alluring.

Davy came past, offering mugs of mead while clansmen, women, and children gathered for a reel. Grace sipped the honeyed ale, her foot tapping to the beat. The Buchanans were an exuberant lot, though not a one possessed enough polish to make an appearance in a London ballroom. Nonetheless, the laughter made up for anything this whooping crowd lacked in technique. The men swung the ladies by the crooks of their arms, the floor thundering as they stomped their feet.

Oh how the Almack's patronesses would be appalled!

Of course, Grace had been taught not to make a sound, dancing like a feather while wearing tiny slippers. She had been trained to ensure her every move was practiced, balletic, and elegant.

Who knew how much I had been missing?

Kenny, a gawky lad of about thirteen years of age, appeared in front of Grace, his arms crossed, his shoulders hunched, and his face apple red. "Um...I...um..." He raked his fingers through his hair.

"Och, lad, if ye have something to say, out with it," Frasier said.

The boy stared at his toes, his color spreading to his neck. "W-w-would ye dance with me, m'lady?"

"How very kind of you to ask, sir," she said as if she were speaking to a knight. "Though I'm not certain I am able to match the Buchanan vigor."

Frasier gave her a gentle nudge. "Ye are by far more polished than anyone in all of Britain. Go on, kick up your heels and enjoy yourself."

Kenny grabbed Grace's hand and tugged her out to the floor with such exuberance, she was forced to break into a run. The dancers were lining up for another foot-stomping reel. "If ye dunna ken the steps, just listen to Ramsey, ye canna go wrong when he's doing the calling."

Grace moved into the women's line as the dancers took their places. "Thank you. I shall."

The boy proved himself indeed full of vigor as he looped his arm through hers and skipped in a circle with youthful gusto. It was all Grace could do to keep up with the lad, but keep up she did, stomping her feet just as boisterously as everyone else.

FRASIER LEANED BACK and rested his elbow on the table while he savored his tankard of mead. Kenny whirled Grace through the reel as if he were charging into battle, the lad's footwork awkwardly ahead of the beat dictated by Blair's drum. Such was youth.

Before Her Ladyship came to Druimliart, he never would have guessed she would put up with such ruckus from a wee whelp, but Grace threw back her head and laughed. Nonetheless, her footwork remained in time with the music. When Kenny locked her arm so forcefully she stumbled, Frasier nearly came off his seat, ready to intercede and rescue the woman. But she recovered with a snappy pirouette, taking the lad's arm, her smile not faltering.

Dear God, the woman was having fun. When she'd first arrived, she'd insisted she didn't fit in, but tonight, wearing his mother's arisaid, she looked like a Buchanan. He would have liked to believe he had something to do with her transformation.

But did I?

More than anything, it was reassuring to watch her enjoying herself. Lord knew she needed a respite from her woes. Oddly, Grace's presence here had given him a renewed sense of power, of purpose, of courage. It meant ever so much for the lady to accept him as he was, accept him as a man in exile, who's family fortune had been plundered, who now lived in modest poverty.

Frasier finished the dregs of his mead as he watched her among the others, a sparkling ruby among stones of milky quartz. Aye, because of her refined elegance, no one could help but stare at her. She was both out of place, and exactly where she ought to be.

When the reel had nearly come to an end, he stood and sauntered around the hall to where Kenny was still regaling her with gawky antics. As the song ended and the dancers applauded, Frasier tapped the lad on the shoulder. "I believe the next dance is mine, laddie."

The boy's face fell, but after a stern frown from Frasier, he bowed and kissed the lady's hand, evidently completely recovered from his prior bout of bashfulness.

"Perhaps we can dance again," she said, earning a toothy grin. With a soft chuckle, she curtsied to Frasier. "Goodness, that young man is as spirited as a colt."

He took his place in the men's line and bowed. "He certainly is. I shall endeavor to at least keep time with the music, m'lady."

Ramsey's voice boomed over the crowd. "A strathspey!"

Frasier gave a wink. "This ought to give you a wee chance to catch your breath."

Grace acknowledged his remark with an uptick of her chin, her crystal blue eyes sparkling with the reflection of the candlelight overhead. "Have you forgotten I am accustomed to dancing into the wee hours, my laird?"

As the music began, Ramsey insisted the corners take a turn, blast him, Frasier didn't want to skip in a circle with Seonaid, he wanted Grace all to himself. Damnation, the minutes were ticking too quickly and soon, he'd never be able to hold the lass in his arms again.

Frasier's disappointment was short lived when Seonaid danced to her partner allowing him to turn and grasp Grace's small hands. They were soft and supple though he couldn't help but notice a wee callous had arisen on her pointer finger.

Again recalling how diligently she had worked, his chest filled with admiration as together they sashayed in a circle.

"What?" she asked as her gaze shifted to his.

"Bonny lass." Was all he had time to say before Ramsey demanded he release her hands and the dancers return to their respective cues.

She blessed him with a radiant smile before she had to again lock elbows with the corner. Frasier obediently followed along, taking Seonaid for a turn while watching Her Ladyship out of the corner of his eye. He much preferred their dancing four nights ago, waltzing in the privacy of his cottage, the woman in his arms, her body scandalously close, her gaze only on him.

When again, they joined hands and sashayed, he tightened his grip and drew her closer than necessary. If anyone was staring, let them. Frasier could see only Grace's face, her smile, the vivid blue of her eyes, the rose of exertion in her cheeks. Ramsey's orders became but a whisper, the music thrumming through his blood. And as he tugged Grace even closer for the spin, the intoxicating scent that was all her own drew him in like a bee to honeysuckle. The music disappeared. Time stilled. Frasier stood motionless, gazing into the most fathomless eyes he'd ever beheld—eyes alive with fire, with want, yet guarded with hurt too deep to measure.

Frasier's gut twisted. He prided himself in his ability to solve his kin's problems. But Her Ladyship's affairs were something only her brother and the Archbishop of Canterbury could fix.

God save the bishop would do the right thing.

Only when Grace took a step away and dipped into a curtsey, did Frasier realize the strathspey had ended. He bowed, throwing his shoulders back when he straightened. Had anyone noticed the lapse of time? Had anyone noticed how he'd stared? How he'd lost himself in the woman's gaze?

It was almost a relief when Davy asked Her Ladyship for the next dance. Frasier would be taking Grace to the lodge in the morning. On the morrow she would return to her privileged life and her time at Druimliart would be but a passing memory.

Raising his tankard of mead, Angus smirked as Frasier returned to the table. "Ye've got eyes for the wee lassie."

"What the blazes are ye talking about?" he asked, dropping onto the bench.

"Och, ye ken as well as I ye've fallen in love with the sassenach."

"She's no' a sassenach—born in Scotland. Mayhap the Lowlands, but Scotland all the same." Frasier grabbed the pitcher and poured himself another drink. "Lady Grace is leaving on the morrow and I doubt the lot of us will ever see her again."

"Bloody shame, that," said Angus, smirking into his cup.

"Wheesht. 'Tis for the best."

Angus snorted. "Now I ken you're telling tall tales."

Frasier shot his brother-in-law a seething scowl. Aye, he'd pay a thousand pounds to have her stay. But Frasier didn't have a thousand pounds to his name. He knew the life to which the *princess* was accustomed and she would never find a modicum of comfort at Druimliart. Certainly, she passed the time with trivial mending, but she would soon grow bored of the tiresome labor. The passion between them had been nothing but a pair of lonely souls reaching for each other in a time of need. Grace could not hide forever. She must face her lot.

Truly, Frasier had best face his as well. He needed a woman—a wife. Mayhap once the Season was over and the gentry returned to their country estates, he might attend a house party or two and continue with his search for a bride. He ought to resume his quest to find his kin's treasure as well.

As he continued with his musings, the doors to the hall burst open, bringing with it a rush of cold air and a screeching stop to the music.

Martin MacGalloway, the Duke of Dunscaby marched inside, his eyes ablaze. His Grace first homed in on Frazier, but at the sound of his sister's gasp, his gaze immediately shot to her. "Grace! Thank God ye're alive!"

11

"I have armies of people searching the Highlands," Martin said. After they moved to the laird's cottage, the duke turned a glass of whisky between his fingertips as he sat across the table from Grace and Frasier. "A fortnight ago Mr. MacIain found the wreckage and sent word that he suspected the worst. Since no bodies were found, I feared the lot of you may have tried to make it down the mountain in the midst of the blizzard and succumbed to exposure."

Grace should have known the snow had melted down below. Though she'd never wintered at the lodge, snow always melted within a fortnight or two at Newhailes. Here she had been biding her time for nineteen days while her family thought her dead. She should have taken her horse and set out for the lodge as soon as the skies cleared.

"Forgive me," said Frasier. "I didna reckon the snow at the castle would melt so quickly."

"'Tis still icy, but if I were snowed in up here, I might have thought the same." Martin took a sip of the amber liquid, his gaze focused on Buchanan. "Why did ye bring my sister up here rather than take her to the lodge?"

Grace looked to the man beside her. Goodness, how daft of her not to have asked the same question as soon as she opened her eyes.

"As ye're aware, I pulled her out of the carriage during a blizzard," Frasier said, shoving an errant lock of hair out of his eyes. "I sent the lads back to Druimliart with a fallen stag whilst I rode off to see what caused the noise. The princess was unconscious when I found her. I only thought to take her to safety—to where I kent there was a healer. I suppose if I'd tried to make it to the lodge, we would have been trapped there as well. Moreover, my kin would have sent out a rescue party blizzard or nay."

Martin's eyes narrowed as he focused on the laird for a moment before he let out a huff and shifted his focus to his sister. "Och, you gave us all a terrible fright. Come morn I'll send word to our mother. Tell her of Buchanan's rescue."

Grace's trepidation eased as Frasier's leg nudged hers beneath the table. "I'll wager Mama is worried half out of her wits."

"Aye. When the messenger came, she swooned so, she required a wee whiff of smelling salts. Then once she gathered her wits, she insisted on traveling up here with me. Only when I convinced her that I could reach the Highlands much faster on horseback, did she see reason and remain in London with Julia and Modesty."

Frasier removed the stopper from a flagon and topped up his whisky as well as Martin's. "It is still too icy for a carriage. Ye were wise to dissuade your mother, else she might have ended up at the bottom of the ravine as well."

Martin growled under his breath. "Damnation,

Grace, I never should have allowed you to come up here."

He was right, of course. Her journey had led to the loss of the lives of three souls even if Martin and Mama had encouraged her to await word from the Archbishop of Canterbury at the lodge. "We cannot sit here and ruminate over what might have been," she replied, unable to imagine spending the past nineteen days anywhere else. So much had changed in such a short amount of time. For once she had actually been forced to tend to her own needs without relying on servants. And destiny must have led the man sitting beside her to her rescue. She hadn't ever given herself leave to take notice of him before, but he'd made her feel safe, made her feel wanted when it seemed her worth had fallen into an abyss of nothingness.

Though Frasier had offered her a tot of whisky, she had refused. But now that Martin brought with him the reality of her woes, she stood and took a glass from the shelf. "I believe I would like to taste your liquor, if not simply to see what you men find so enjoyable about it."

"Ye willna like it," said Martin, though he did not try to dissuade her.

She said nothing, but returned from the table and poured a drop for herself, the two men gaping at her wide-eyed as she took the smallest of sips. The spirit burned a stream down the length of her throat. Her eyes watered as she tried not to cough, but her efforts were of no avail. As delicately as possible she tapped her fingers to her lips. "Ahem."

"Well?" asked Frasier.

"I say, it is quite potent."

Martin's lips curled in a smug grin. "Dunna tell me I didna warn you."

Ignoring him, Grace slid back onto the bench beside Frasier. "Have you perchance received word from the Archbishop?"

Her brother's gaze darkened with his nod. "We shall discuss his reply on the morrow."

Every muscle in Grace's body clenched. "Please, I won't be able to sleep if you do not tell me this very moment!"

"Would ye like me to leave you pair alone?" Frasier asked.

As Martin started to agree, Grace raised her palm. "No. His Lairdship is aware of what transpired, and I trust him." Truly, she trusted him with her life.

"All of it?" asked the duke.

"*Most* of the details." She gulped and looked at Frasier. "You assumed I found the prince in the arms of another woman. But the truth of the matter was—"

"The scoundrel was engaged in the act of sodomy with Lord Alder," Martin said, his voice filled with malice.

Frasier's face colored as he curled his fingers into fists. "God on the bloody cross, how the devil did we allow that bastard onto our island?"

"Most likely he was heralded by Lord Alder," Grace mused. Though the subject was not funny in the least, it seemed enough time had passed since the incident that she might be able to jest a bit...however her little witticism stung.

"I would have skewered the blackguard on the spot," said Frasier, pounding his fist on the table.

"Aye, but as a duke I was duty bound to do the honorable thing and challenge the lout to a duel."

"Who cares what might have been, my husband fled the kingdom without me." Grace clapped her hands together. "Please do not delay, I must know how the Archbishop responded."

Martin drew a hand down his face—his smile nonexistent. "It willna be as easy as we'd hoped. Isidor must seek absolution for his sins. If he does so, His Grace will refuse us. And you ken as well as I that failure to consummate is not grounds enough for an annulment."

Grace's eyes welled and she quickly blinked the tears away. "What if the prince never seeks absolution?"

Martin's gaze dropped to the table as he shook his head while she envisioned herself in a state of limbo until she was withered and grey. "Heaven's no. Can the bishop not be reasoned with?"

"Isidor's ambassador claims he was forced to leave England under duress," said the duke.

"Yet another reason I would have dirked the bastard," Frasier growled.

"But what am I to do? Remain in exile for the rest of my days? A princess with no home?"

"We have naught but to wait to see if Isidor follows through with the Archbishop's edict and seeks absolution for his sins. In the interim, ye canna remain here any longer, if the Canterbury kent you were staying in the laird's cottage, our petition would never be successful." Martin narrowed his gaze at Buchanan. "I trust you upheld the Highland code of hospitality."

"Aye, Your Grace," Frasier replied rather sardonically.

"I will swear on a Bible this very moment," Grace said with every ounce of haughtiness she could muster. "His Lairdship has been more of a gentleman than Isidor ever was."

Martin smirked. "Och, that wouldna be difficult."

AFTER GRACE EXCUSED herself for the night, Frasier poured another round of whisky for the duke and himself.

"We've been friends for a long while," Martin said.

"Aye."

"And we chased our share of skirts when we were lads."

Frasier narrowed his gaze. "We did."

"Ye ken I trust you like a brother."

Their banter had gone on long enough for Frasier to figure out what His Grace was on about. Not that he needed to refer to the duke formally, but he did so whenever he reckoned Martin MacGalloway was behaving like a bloody highborn numpty. "I beg your pardon, sir. I didna chase your sister's skirt."

"No?"

Surely a few stolen kisses didn't count. "Not that it didna cross my mind a time or two. But no. The princess is far too lofty for the likes of a penniless outcast."

Martin's expression softened as he sipped. "That's more like it."

"'Tis a damned shame, though." Frasier shoved the stopper into the flagon with the heel of his hand. "The way Isidor dishonored her."

"It is unforgivable. But dunna fret. The fight isna over by half."

"'Tis good to hear ye say so."

"I'm not as soft as ye think, Buchanan. Just because I'm a duke doesna mean I've forgotten how to march into battle."

"Aye, but ye let the slippery eel slither through your grasp."

Martin scowled. "I challenged him to a bloody duel. His cowardice is reprehensible."

Frasier looked the duke in the eye, for the first time realizing how similar the color of Martin's eyes were to his sister's. "I would have dirked him for certain."

"And what then? Swing from the Newgate gallows for stabbing a prince?"

"Och, I'm already an outlaw. 'Tis just the English havena found me yet."

Martin snorted. "I reckon that's because they stopped looking about thirty years past."

Frasier drank, enjoying the fiery spirit as it rolled over his tongue. His father had abhorred the English and those who had supported the government troops. His father had also instilled in him the distrust of sassenachs.

Perhaps Martin was right, those warrants to shoot on sight were old—though they were still not defunct. But why should he bother trying to clear his name? Frasier couldn't have Grace, and he'd all but failed at trying to find an heiress with a dowry—not that he'd applied himself to the task with diligence. Still, who was he fooling, no well-born lass would ever want to come to the frigid Highlands where she'd be expected to work her fingers to the bone.

"Now that my sister has been found, I have news."

"Oh?" Frasier asked, welcoming the change of subject.

"A cache of treasure seized during the '45 has recently been discovered stowed away in Flint Tower."

Frasier ears piqued. "And just where is that?"

"Built into the curtain walls of the Tower of London. The turret is rather small in comparison to the others, on the north wall bordering The Royal Menagerie."

"God's stones, how the devil am to retrieve the Horn of Bannockburn from London's most guarded fortress?"

"I ken you would relish going in with guns blazing, bayonets attached, but I reckon you might have more success if you ask. Politely, mind you—stay in Town as my guest as well."

"What the devil?" Frasier threw back the remainder of his tot rather than savor it. "Ask the king for the return of my family's treasure?"

"Well, the king has gone quite mad. But perhaps it is time to request an audience with the Prince Regent. Plead your case."

"Right." Frasier had been raised to detest the Hanoverian kings and the fact that George the Prince of Wales had been born in London was little consolation. "And whilst I'm doing that I may as well grow wings and fly to Australia to commence service of thirty years transportation."

"The transportation part might happen, but it is highly unlikely. As I see it, if you ever want to lay claim to the Buchanan treasure again, I suggest you request a pardon for your kin and, whilst you're at it, ask for the horn. The cache from the Jacobites has only just been rediscovered, and the prince is planning to auction it off as soon as it can all be catalogued."

"How long will that take?"

Martin shrugged. "Who kens? Since it is being handled by the Chancellor of the Exchequer, I would assume it will be done in short order."

That soon? These things took planning. On threat of death, a Buchanan hadn't been south of the Scottish border for over seventy years. "Damnation, canna anything be easy?"

"Ye reckon marching into battle is easy?"

Frasier didn't answer. Bloody hell, the last thing he wanted was to ride to London and kiss the Prince Regent's arse.

12

Grace had been gone for over a week, her absence making Frasier's cottage feel like a tomb. He paced endlessly. At first he thought his agitation would fade, but it had only driven him to the brink of madness. Aye, he and Angus were making preparations to travel to godforsaken England, but nothing had been the same since the duke had taken his bonny sister to the lodge. Every time Frasier turned around, he expected to see Grace stitching, or smiling, or proud of herself for making tea.

Finally, when he could tolerate the silence no longer, he saddled his horse, picked his way along Loch Tulla, cut across the path through the wood, and used the enormous blackened-iron knocker on the lodge's medieval door. It wasn't the caretaker who answered, but Tearlach, one of Dunscaby's most trusted footmen.

After exchanging a greeting, Frasier peered beyond the man's shoulder. "Might I have an audience with Lady Grace?"

"Princess Grace," Tearlach corrected.

"Aye. Forgive me. At Druimliart she asked us to refer to her as lady."

"A faux pas which His Grace immediately corrected." Tearlach bowed. "Please come in and I'll let Her
Highness ken you're here."

Frasier was shown to the parlor adjacent to the
hall. At one time it had been an antechamber where
callers were asked to wait for an audience with the
lord. The décor most likely hadn't changed a great
deal over the centuries. The faded tapestries on the
wall were certainly dated, as was the rectangular table,
the wood stained dark, its six matching chairs padded
with red leather. Against one wall was an ornately
carved bench in the same dark tone. Above it were
crossed medieval pikes and a targe mounted on the
wall. Frasier wouldn't have been surprised if those
very pikes were used in the Battle of Bannockburn.

He pulled out a chair but before he sat, Grace
slipped inside, radiant in a frilly day gown.
"Buchanan, how kind of you to pay a call!"

He stepped forward as if to wrap her in an embrace, but when she clasped her hands beneath her
chin, he stopped himself and bowed, albeit awkwardly. This wasn't the reunion he'd anticipated. She
was supposed to fall into his arms and declare she'd
die if she had to live another day without him. But
who was he fooling? "Your Highness," Frasier said
stiffly. Only in his dreams could he ever imagine he
might have a chance to win her love. "It is verra good
to see you."

"Pfft," she teased offering her hand. "I give you
leave to call me by the familiar, if you please. After all,
we are childhood friends."

He kissed it, closing his eyes as his lips touched
her soft skin. The scent of orange blossoms made him
want to trail kisses up her arm all the way to her neck,
though he straightened as he ought. "Verra well, I

shall call you Grace if ye forevermore refer to me as Frasier."

"Done." She stepped aside as Mrs. MacIain brought in a tea service including slices of shortbread. "Will you join me for a cup of tea?"

"What would you think of going riding first?" He gestured toward the hearth. "Keep the tea warm by the fire?"

The caretaker's wife huffed, turning up her nose as she pushed out the doors.

"I take it she doesna approve of riding?" Frasier asked.

"It is not that. Mrs. MacIain hasn't been terribly happy of late." Grace chuckled. "She and her husband are alone up here in the mountains most of the year. But now since I haven't the service of a lady's maid, Marty asked her to step up to the task."

"But MacIain's wife has always done the cooking has she not?"

"Yes, as well as the housekeeping. Mind you, she is quite busy, which is why I am still wearing my hair in a braid. I told her all I require is a few moments of her time whilst dressing."

"That doesna sound all that difficult."

"No, but the MacIains are getting on in years. Perhaps climbing the stairs makes her rheumatism ache. I know not, but I've written to Marty to ask him to send me a proper lady's maid at his earliest convenience."

Frasier looked aside. Of course now that Grace had returned to the MacGalloway household, she would require the multitudes of servants to which she was accustomed. "How much longer will you remain here?"

"Your guess is as good as mine. You might recall

that Isidor must atone to the Archbishop of Canterbury. And, as you are aware, it takes an eternity for news to reach us up here." She stepped toward the door. "I'll send Tearlach out to saddle my horse. Do help yourself to a cup of tea and a slice of shortbread whilst I change into my riding habit."

He again bowed. "Certainly."

Of course, she wouldn't throw a cloak over her shoulders and march out to the stables in her slippers and muslin skirts. Women of her ilk spent half their lives changing clothes. The lassies of his clan were so much more practical. And now that Grace had returned to her privileged life it was a wonder she was even speaking to him.

He mustn't forget that though she might have returned to the lodge, to her this medieval castle was an outpost—a place to hide. When they'd spoken with her brother in Frasier's cottage, the duke had mentioned that his mother had worked to ensure the members of the *ton* believed Grace had sailed to Lithuania with her husband and was still abroad.

By the time Frasier finished his first cup of tea and had eaten three of the delicious biscuits, Grace returned wearing a navy blue winter riding habit, the lapels of her matching pelisse trimmed with gold filigree. Evidently the clothing in her upturned trunks had been recovered from the bottom of the ravine and she no longer had need of an arisaid.

Unfortunate.

"Bonny as always," he said, kissing her gloved hand and noticing the ruby ring adorning the pointer finger. Though it was a reminder of her family's wealth, this was the first time he realized she hadn't been wearing a wedding ring while she was at Druimliart.

As he straightened, she gave him a saucy smile, gazing through the fans of her extraordinarily long eyelashes. "And you, sir, are dashing."

Though Frasier's heart hammered, he tempered her compliment with a chuckle. Grace could charm an adder with her bonny looks and silken tongue. But he was no dandy, no handsome beau to swoon over. He wore a kilt, a leather doublet, and his hair clubbed back. Mayhap it wasn't stylish, but it suited him and he was not about to change. There was nothing he hated more than a fop who put on airs to impress his betters.

After mounting their horses, together they ambled side by side through the forest to where it opened to the loch.

"The lassies all asked after you," Frasier said.

"Did they?" Grace chuckled thoughtfully. "You may find it surprising, but I miss them. Especially Lena."

Frasier stroked his horse's mane, the coarse hair slipping through his fingers. If only the princess had missed him a fraction of how much he'd pined for her.

"I'm glad the snow is melting," she said.

Frasier looked to Black Mount which concealed his home from any passersby. "There's still a foot or two of snow at Druimliart which most likely willna melt until April, May at the latest."

"Truly? How can you bear to endure the frigid temperatures up there so many months out of the year? If you ask me, it is still too cold down here."

As his horse snorted, a cloud of air billowed around his muzzle. "I think one learns at an early age to appreciate one's birthplace."

"Is that why you so rarely come down the mountain?"

He gave her a sidewise glance. "You ken why."

She let out the length of her reins, allowing the mare her head. "Alas, we are two outcasts—I am estranged from my husband with whom I never spent a single night, and you are an outlaw by the circumstances of your birth. What a pair we make."

Frasier wished it were so. But he had nothing to give her. She'd said it herself, he lived in a hovel. Even if everything went his way in London, he'd still be poor by Grace's standards.

But up here in the Highlands, he was a king. He was Laird Frasier Buchanan of the ancient line of Buchanans. He could proudly ride beside a princess and enjoy it when she looked fondly upon him—even if the moment was only a passing fancy.

"Look there," Grace pointed, laughing. "We used to play King of the Hill on that rock."

"I recall."

"You do? Did you play when you were fostering with my father?"

"Aye." He chuckled as well. "And I remember with clarity when Martin and I were dueling it out, you were down below with your nurse wailing because you wanted to climb up and defend your brother. I reckon you could hardly walk at the time."

Grace dismounted and secured her reins around a tree branch while Frasier followed suit. She ambled toward the rock, the ostrich feather atop her velvet riding hat shimmering in the wind. Glancing back, she dazzled him with a brilliant smile—one that made him forget to breathe, one that made him forget the enormous void between their stations. "Marty always protected his sisters from the boys—they're all older, you know."

"I thought Frederick was between you and Modesty."

"Oh, no. Frederick was born in 1794—three years before me. He would have been four years of age when you began your fostering with my father."

Interesting how Frasier recalled Grace so vividly, but he scarcely remembered her closest brother when they were children. Of course, he was now familiar with all the former duke's children not only from his two years of fostering, but because he'd seen them at the odd social engagement over the years. "Forgive my slip. It seems even when you were a wee bairn you commanded all of the attention."

She threw back her head and laughed. "At least I believed I did. 'Tis almost funny how having your entire life crumble about your feet shifts one's perceptions of oneself."

"I wouldna allow a scoundrel like Isidor to coax you into believing you are any less deserving."

"Oh, I suppose Isidor isn't to blame, though he most likely is the catalyst."

Frasier rubbed his palm over the hilt of his dirk. "He's to blame, mark me."

Grace stopped at the edge of the loch, the wind making her skirts billow behind her. "It is ever so peaceful here when I'm not surrounded by several other siblings and a host of servants."

"Aye." Frasier wanted to ease himself behind her and wrap his arms around her slender waist, but instead, he stepped to her side, keeping his hands to himself. "I asked you to go riding with me because I wanted to speak with you in complete privacy."

She faced him. "Oh?"

"I ken I'm not a wealthy man like the swains and

dandies you met in London, but I am loyal—to you and to your family." He cleared his throat, allowing the thought to settle. Frasier could not walk away from this woman, nor could he declare his love. The one thing a man like him could do was protect and defend. "What I'm trying to say is there isna anything I will not do for you, m'lady—*Princess*—*Grace*. I want you to ken you are verra dear to me and if you should ever be in need of anything, anything at all, I hope you will see fit to call upon me."

Though her lips turned up, she did not reply straightaway. It seemed she, too, was in no hurry to move beyond the subject at hand. After drawing in a deep breath she replied, "Thank you. It means ever so much to me to hear you say it. But—"

Her brow furrowed as those eyes shifted up to his, made bluer by the glint of the sun. "Frasier," she said his name with confidence, making him shiver to his toes. "You must know you are more of a man than any of the eleven peers who proposed to me last Season. And most of all, you deserve happiness and a wife who will bear you many healthy children."

There was only one woman he wanted to bear his children, yet she could never be his. "What will you do if Isidor atones for his sins and asks you to join him?"

"Given that the Archbishop doubtlessly will refuse the petition for annulment, there is nothing I will be able do aside from heed the prince's summons."

Frasier's heart bled for her. She would proudly execute her duty and join a man she knew to be a knave and a scoundrel. "You just said *I* deserve happiness," he countered.

She glanced away and nodded.

"So do you, bonny Grace."

"I am afraid it is too late for me."

"I have something for you." He strode to his horse

and retrieved a marionette from his saddle bag—something he'd started years ago but only finished after Martin had taken her away. "I made this Highland lass for you. 'Tis a reminder of your time at Druimliart."

She took the gift and examined it, running her fingers over the doll's painted face. "My heavens, the workmanship has so much detail."

"Lena made the arisaid and linen shift."

Grace smiled at that. "Of course she did."

"And the wee lass has blonde tresses just like yours."

"Blue eyes as well."

"I ken your stay at Druimliart wasna easy, but you persevered and won the hearts of the naysayers. You even won Fiona's favor."

"Well, I'm not sure if I'd go that far, but in the end, I do believe she and I developed mutual respect."

"Aye, ye did. And that is because you are a fighter. You are a Highland lass even with your highborn speech..." He took her hand and straightened the ruby ring which had fallen askew. "...and your finery."

Not replying, she frowned, casting her gaze downward.

"I've said something to upset you?"

The lady shook her head, shifting the marionette over her heart. "I do so love your gift. Thank you."

He nodded. "I must also tell you that Angus and I are leaving for London on the morrow."

Her lips parted with a slight gasp. "To request the abolishment of the warrant for the arrest of any member of your clan?"

"Your brother told you, did he?"

"Yes. I hope you don't mind."

"Not at all."

"Where are you planning to stay? Please tell me my brother offered you accommodations at the Mac-Galloway town house."

"Aye, the duke graciously offered us room and board."

"Good." She reached out as if to touch him but pulled her had away. "When might you return?"

"As soon as practicable. Afterward, I hope I'll be able to see ye afore ye..." He bit his lip not wanting to believe she might actually set sail across the North Sea.

"I doubt I'll be going anywhere for quite some time. If Isidor does atone for his sins, I'm not certain Marty will accept his apology even if the Archbishop does. At least my brother will try to act on my behalf, not that a duke can overrule the head of the Church of England."

Frasier ground his fist into his palm wishing Isidor was nearby so he could thrash the man. "That puts you in an untenable situation. It must be awful not knowing what will happen."

The sadness in her eyes twisted his heart all the more. If only he could do *something*. "I do not know what is worse. Having my entire life hanging in the balance or the loneliness whilst I await my fate."

His tension eased slightly—she was lonely? Lonely for him? "Tell me, why did you come all the way up here rather than go to Newhailes or Stack Castle?" he asked, wondering why he hadn't posed the question before.

"Because nobody ever pays a call at the lodge. Here I am well and truly hidden from all of society."

"Aside from me."

"Well, you are nearly family and I trust you not to

reveal my secret even if you are going to take London by storm."

Frasier didn't respond. Surely she didn't look upon him as a brother?

Grace took a step closer, her expression turning a tad uncertain. "Before coming here, I had never been completely alone as I am in this moment with you."

"Not even Isidor?" he asked, the prince's name bitter to his tongue.

"We were allowed a few moments in the drawing room together when he proposed. Then we did go for a few walks together, though we were followed by servants."

"Did he not kiss you?"

"Twice, though now I wonder if he really kissed me at all."

"I dunna understand."

The lass bit the corner of her mouth, looking ever so tempting and nothing like a family member. "Actually, until you kissed me, I believed kissing to be overvalued."

"Unpleasant?" Frasier asked, his chin dipping as he studied her rosebud-shaped mouth.

"Not exactly, but I failed to see why ladies oft spoke of impassioned kisses when my experiences had been rather tepid." She grasped his hands and squeezed. "Until your lips met mine."

Frasier needed no more encouragement. He lowered his mouth gently to hers and claimed her pliable lips. "Like this?"

"Hmm." The marionette dropped to the grass as she wrapped her arms around his neck and let him mold his body to hers. Then she urged him to lower his lips once again. This time their kiss was what flames were made of. Grace's little purr in the back of her throat was the kindling he needed for his blood to pulse with fire. In each other's arms, a wild fervor consumed them. Their mouths were demanding and searching. Her lips like an all-consuming love potion.

Losing himself, Frasier dove deeper. He moaned, let his hands rove across the supple contours of her hips. As their lips parted, he kissed her jaw, her cheek, her lovely wee ear. Humming with pleasure, Grace turned her head and claimed his mouth again and again.

The sun had begun to set by the time they stepped apart.

Neither said a word. Neither needed to speak in order to understand their love was taboo.

As they rode back to the lodge, Frasier hoped she would still be there when he returned, albeit a voice at the back of his mind, insisted it would be best if she were not.

13

Only a fortnight after Frasier left for London, one of the duke's carriages arrived at the lodge and, rather than bringing her a lady's maid, Grace was summoned to Newhailes on the Firth of Forth east of Edinburgh. Martin had sent a hastily written missive instructing her to meet Mama and Gibb at the estate.

Blast the duke, he mentioned nothing about Isidor or the Archbishop or her present circumstances. In Grace's opinion, his last paragraph was a waste of ink:

My vote is desperately needed in Parliament, and though I would like to meet you at Newhailes myself, Gibb will dutifully ferry our mother northward to join you in Scotland.

It didn't escape her notice that the doors of the carriage had been changed out from the Dunscaby coat of arms to plain black—a certain sign Martin did not desire for her identity to be known or assumed or otherwise conjectured.

Was she being summoned to Newhailes because circumstances were still too precarious for her to show her face in London? Though it was relatively easier to hide at the manor where there would be fewer callers, why had Martin assigned Gibb to the task of ferrying Mama northward?

Well, that one wasn't too difficult to imagine. After all, Gibb was a sea captain and owned a fleet of ships which he operated out of the Firth of Forth.

But why, oh why, had Martin not mentioned a single word about Isidor in his letter?

How dare he leave me in the lurch? Has he no idea how maddening it is to be given no information whatsoever, treated as if I am a child, too fragile to know the truth?

Aside from plotting ways to lambast her eldest brother when she next saw him, Grace had memorized every word of the letter because she perseverated on it throughout the tedious carriage ride down the winding, hairpin turns in the Highlands followed by two days crossing the rutted roads in the Lothians of Scotland. For heaven's sake, the crown had spent ridiculous sums of money improving the roads in England, especially the Great North Road, but little had been done to address the horrible conditions of the abysmal highways in Scotland.

The carriage had not thrown one, but two wheels, on account of the horrendous ruts, one of which was the size of a heifer.

When at last the carriage turned down Newhailes' sycamore-lined drive, Grace did her best to compose herself, using a pin from her reticule to secure an errant lock of hair, then she tied her bonnet with a bow beneath her chin. She tugged on her kid-leather gloves—the same pair she had been wearing since they had left the lodge, upon which she had smudged a drop of raspberry conserve. But she had packed for this journey in such haste, she hadn't included a spare set in her traveling valise.

She ought to have been relieved to finally be returning to civilization. Although Newhailes was a country estate, the manor was close to a large city and was properly staffed with more servants than Grace could count. Obviously, she could count the servants if she so desired, but she had never considered such a task. It had never occurred to her to actually inquire as to how many milkmaids they employed, or laundresses, or scullery maids—positions filled by young women who Grace hardly ever saw or even thought about.

There were upstairs maids and downstairs maids, and at least a dozen footmen, and Lord knew how many chaps worked in the stables—grooms, stable boys, the stable master, of course, and there were two drivers assigned to the Newhailes residence...or were there three?

Well, if she was to be exiled here, she would pay more attention to the running of the household. After all, Grace had done quite well in her house husbandry classes at Northbourne Seminary for Young Ladies, thus qualifying her to run an estate such as this. How had she lived for one and twenty years without truly seeing the people around her? Was everyone in her family entirely shallow?

As soon as she considered the question, she knew the answer. Grace had always behaved as the shallowest, most self-serving of all the MacGalloways—a fact in which she was not proud.

The carriage rolled to a stop, Tearlach hopping down from the rear and opening the door. "We have arrived, Your Highness."

She huffed a sigh. Though at one time she had desperately longed to be referred to as "Your Highness," presently she abhorred the title as much as she hated being called Princess.

After allowing him to hand her down, Grace gave a respectful bow of her head. "Thank you. You have been very dutiful and I have greatly appreciated your assistance over these past weeks. You are also quite adept at changing carriage wheels. I shall ensure His Grace is made aware of your competence."

"Och..." The man blushed profusely, his eyes popping wide as if he didn't recognize her. "Thank you, madam."

Grace started to offer her thanks to the driver, but her younger sister Modesty and her shadow (as Grace had begun to refer to the lass) Kitty dashed down the portico stairs. "The princess has arrived!" Modesty beamed, the red ringlets framing her freckled face bouncing with every step.

Grace welcomed her sister with a warm hug, and a slightly cooler hug for Kitty. "I'm surprised to see you here. Did Charity make the journey as well?"

Charity, the Countess of Brixham, was, of course, their elder sister and married to Kitty's brother, the Earl of Brixham. Kitty and Modesty were the same age and were planning their coming out next Season because Mama had been too overwhelmed with Grace's wedding to give Modesty's wardrobe the proper attention it deserved for the debut of a duke's sister.

Kitty beamed with innocence. "We sailed with Captain Gibb."

Grace patted the young lady's shoulder. "I hope you didn't suffer from seasickness."

"Not I," Kitty said while they climbed the stairs to the front door.

Out of the corner of her eye, Grace watched six footmen struggle with her trunks, taking them through one of the many servant entrances—this one an unobtrusive door hidden behind a large azalea.

Mama met Grace on the portico, her arms out-stretched. "My dear, I have missed you so."

She wanted to fall into her mother's arms and sob, but the woman was the Dowager Duchess of Dunscaby. No one ever fell into any duchess' arms and wept, especially not in a place as public as the front stoop of the Newhailes residence.

"I've been ever so worried about you." Mama's brows pinched together. "My heavens, you must have gone through an awful ordeal up there in those wild mountains. I've never seen you look so haggard."

Grace stopped midstride and glanced down at her attire. She was wearing a green carriage dress with puffed gigot sleeves and broad wristbands, the skirt tipped with two flounces which were hardly creased, considering the amount of time she had been travel-ing. She touched her fingers to yet another strand of hair which had again escaped her bonnet.

"Haggard?" she seethed, keeping her tone to a whisper. "How can you say such a thing?"

Mama's lips thinned as she pointedly escorted Grace directly into the front parlor, dismissing Mod-esty and Kitty with a flick of her fingers. As soon as they were behind closed doors, the dowager whirled around and faced her daughter with a look that could have made Mount Vesuvius explode. "Am I not al-lowed to tell my own daughter she looks drawn, worn, and tired? You are my most poised, most refined child yet you show up with a haphazardly tied bow, your gown looks as if you've been wearing it for days and your hair isn't even curled, and your gloves are filthy. What has come over you?"

"Me?" Grace asked, her temper raging. "The first thing out of your mouth is a comment as to how hag-gard I look and I am the person at fault?"

"Compared to the young woman I saw when you left London, your appearance is quite shocking to say the least."

"Oh, is it now?" Grace asked, not masking the sardonic tone in her voice. "First of all, I'm sure you are aware I lost my lady's maid in an accident that tragically took the lives of everyone except me."

"My dear—"

"Then I spent nearly a month living in a ramshackle cottage as if I had been transported back to the Middle Ages where I had to learn to cook and tend my own toilette—*all* of it. I even mended clothing to earn my keep."

As Mama clapped a hand over her heart, the expression upon her face grew horror-stricken. "Laird Buchanan sat idly by whilst you were treated like a commoner?"

"It was not his idea. The only way I could earn the respect of the clansmen and women was to help in any way I could. And I might say that my skills are quite *lacking* when it comes to living in a community where there are no servants whatsoever."

"Well, I—"

Grace stamped her foot. "Furthermore, after Marty found me, he hauled me off to the musty old lodge where I have been serving my sentence of exile with only Mrs. MacIain to lace my stays. Mind you, if I asked that woman to style my hair, she most likely would have taken a pair of sheep shears to it."

"I cannot—"

"And then—" Grace ferociously cut off her mother once again. "I received a missive from Martin instructing me to depart at once for Newhailes, his letter telling me nothing of my husband or Isidor's response to the Archbishop of Canterbury. I have been tossed around in a carriage for four days, having thrown not one but two wheels. I believe it goes without saying I am tired and angry and *outraged*!"

When her mother deigned to remain silent, Grace threw out her hands. "So, I'm a tad disheveled? Who would not be given all that has transpired since I was forced to flee London in disgrace?"

Mama's expression softened with her long exhale. "I know the past two months have not been easy for you. But you are still a princess, and before that Lady Grace Eloise MacGalloway—"

"Yes, but—"

Mama held up her palm. "I listened whilst you put forth your feelings, now it is my turn to speak."

After Grace clamped her mouth shut and gave a resolute nod, her mother continued, "No one knows what the future holds, but I can tell you without a doubt you will be tested over the next several weeks—months—perhaps years, whatever it comes to. And you have not but to hold your head high and act as the lady of substance I raised you to be. You are still a rare diamond."

"A flawed and ruined diamond is more apt."

"On the contrary. If you behave in a fashion befitting your station, in the end everyone will either see you as the wounded party or you will be happily reunited with your husband."

Grace shuddered. Honestly, after the last two months of reflection, she didn't even like Prince Isidor. Aside from being rather boring, he was about as affectionate as a trout. And now that she had been tainted by Frasier Buchanan's kisses, she never wanted the prince's lips to venture anywhere near her mouth again. "I would prefer the former option."

Taking a moment of respite, Grace turned toward

the window overlooking the manse's front garden. The summerhouse, built to resemble the Palladian Bridge with Roman columns and archways stood as empty as a tomb. The family often entertained guests there, hosting luncheons in summer, but now it looked as abandoned as a mausoleum. In front of the arched bridge spanning the loch swam Ester and Calum, the family's resident swans whose wings were clipped. Alas, she knew all too well what it was like to once be free and now imprisoned with nowhere to go.

"I am going to tell the groundskeeper to stop clipping the swans' wings," Grace suddenly blurted.

"But then they will fly away," Mama replied.

"That is exactly the point." Grace again faced her mother, this time, crossing her arms. "Can you please tell me why I have been summoned?"

"Once Martin told me about your awful ordeal with the carriage, I decided that you were too isolated up there in that draughty old castle. You need a proper lady's maid, which by the way, I took the liberty of promoting Miss Mary Biddle. The housekeeper says Biddle is ever so sensible and never gossips."

"What does she know about the latest hairstyles?" Grace asked.

Mama glanced away. "Modesty and Kitty have been working with her on that."

Oh, how wonderful, Grace was to have a lady's maid whose only experience was cleaning the upper floors of the house. Honestly, she couldn't even place Mary Biddle. "Wasn't there anyone in London you could have hired?"

"Not who I trust enough to keep your secrets, my dear. You are not here, remember? You are in Lithuania with your adoring husband."

"Oh, please, must we keep up with pretenses when behind closed doors?"

As the words left her lips, Gibb strode into the parlor, a missive in hand. "I've news."

It wasn't his usual greeting, but given the circumstances, Grace was too anxious to tolerate hugs, kisses, and the compulsory small talk. "About...ah...my *predicament*?"

"Oh, I do like how you phrased that, my dear," said Mama. "Henceforth we shall refer to Grace's *predicament*." She shifted her gaze to her second son. "Your news?"

"This letter is from Martin." Gibb waved the parchment. "Not only has Isidor atoned to the Archbishop, telling him he was forced to flee England under threat of his life, his ship will soon arrive in London to..." Gibb cleared his throat and read, "...*ferry my wife to Lithuania. However it is incumbent upon me to inform you that if Princess Grace refuses to join me, I shall have no recourse but to immediately commence divorce proceedings in my home country which I woefully regret will ruin the self-serving young lady for all eternity.*"

Mama drew in a sharp gasp. "Why that miserable, white-livered fiend!"

Grace stumbled to the settee and dropped onto her backside, scarcely able to breathe. *Self-serving young lady?* "I knew our marriage was not a love match, but at least I had hoped it would be amicable. Good heavens, if you eliminate his flourish, Isidor's words are nothing short of hostile."

She held out her hand and demanded the letter. When her brother pursed his lips and pulled the missive flush against his chest, she sat forward. "I want to see it now!"

Reluctantly, Gibb gave her the missive.

Grace quickly read. "Look here, I knew it!" She pointed to the sentence with the self-serving bit. Clearly, before he wrote the words *young lady*, he'd written *self-serving wench* but had crossed out the ugly word and written above it the kinder words, which given the preface weren't kind at all. "He called me a wench!"

"Only at first," Gibb replied, retrieving the letter and folding it. "I imagine he changed his prose to a less severe blow once his ire cooled. Surely he was angry at the thought of the possibility of enduring divorce proceedings, the insufferable cad. Regardless, I dunna want you to join him in Lithuania."

"Oh, no? So am I to spend the rest of my days within the walls of the lodge. Or worse, mending hems at Druimliart?" Actually, her second idea did not seem as abhorrent as the first.

Isidor threatened divorce? Things had suddenly gone from untenable to unbelievable.

To Gibb's puzzled expression, Mama frowned. "It seems Buchanan required your sister to earn her keep."

Grace pulled a pillow onto her lap and hugged it. "He did not require me. I volunteered in order to stave off the boredom."

"The thought of my daughter mending—"

"I believe we have more pressing matters at hand," Gibb said. "Isidor's ship is scheduled to welcome Grace aboard at the Pool of London on or near the fifth of May."

"Six weeks hence," Grace whispered, her voice haunted. In six weeks, she would be sailing to her doom. Unless she wanted to be a marked woman for the rest of her days. "Why did he choose the fifth of May?"

"I have no idea unless it was to allow time for Martin to reply." Gibb cleared his throat. "Which the duke has done."

Mama rolled her hand through the air. "Well, do not delay. What was Martin's response?"

Grace sat forward, equally interested to know how her brother had responded on her behalf, especially since he hadn't consulted with her. In fact, she was growing rather irritated by the way the duke was rearranging her life without any input from her.

Gibb looked directly at his sister. "His Grace would like for me to accompany you across the North Sea on the *Prosperity* which will serve a dual purpose. Firstly to give you a chance to reconcile with Isidor, and secondly to allow me to ensure the man is truly remorseful about his behavior before we leave you in his care."

Her jaw dropped. "He called me a self-serving wench. Are those words not clear enough? My husband is a prince. He's not going to change. If you take me to Lithuania, he will most likely lock me in a tower and find a way to murder you."

"This clearly needs careful thought," said Mama lowering herself into a chair.

"Why?" Grace snapped. "No matter what we do, my life is over. I'll never be accepted into the *ton* again, be it in London or Edinburgh or Paris for that matter. If I do not comply with his demands, there is nowhere in Christendom I will ever be able to show my face without being marked as Isidor's debauched bride."

"My dear," Mama huffed. "That is such an ugly word. And you are not sullied in the least."

"Unless Lord Alder comes forward," Grace mumbled, knowing full well he had not because he, too, had committed sodomy. A fact which Martin had made imminently clear to His Lordship.

Gibb stepped toward the door. "I shall write to Martin and tell him we will await his reply."

"No," Grace said, her chin ticking upward. If they left now she might actually... "Inform the duke we will join him in London. We shall sail southward on the *Prosperity* and await Isidor's reply to Martin's request at the town house. That way we will be ready for what may come."

"But you cannot show your face in London," Mama said.

"I disagree. No one knows where I have been. No one knows of my disgrace—Lord Alder wouldn't dare admit to his crimes..." Her mind whirred with possibilities. "Perhaps I've returned from Lithuania to help Charity during her confinement. She is expecting again is she not?"

"Not that I know of," said Mama.

"Well, perhaps it was a lapse of judgement on Charity's part." Grace tapped the tips of her fingers together as she schemed. "But my eldest sister sent for me all the same. I think such an excuse will do quite nicely."

Gibb slid Martin's missive into his waistcoat. "I dunna advise it. Not with so much at stake."

Grace tossed the pillow aside before pushing to her feet. "I am a princess who is fully capable of making her own decisions. I *am* going to London. Either you can sail with me or you can remain here."

14

W hat polite society saw in London, Frasier had no idea. Aye, it might be the kingdom's capital where Parliament met, but it was too bloody crowded. The air was polluted with the pall of chimney smoke, the streets were teeming with carts, wagons, carriages, beasts of burden, and ridiculous sedan cars carried by haggard laborers clad in ragged livery. The mayhem presented the street sweepers with an insurmountable task of cleaning up after horses, not to mention all manner of filth which compounded the stench tenfold.

Perhaps in Mayfair where Dunscaby lived the city was tidy, but his mews was overcrowded with horses and carriages. "I canna return home soon enough," Frasier mumbled under his breath as he used the brass lion's head knocker.

Giles, the butler, opened the door with a gaunt, sour expression, his bloodhound eyes immediately brightening as he recognized Frasier. "Buchanan, what the devil are you doing in London, let alone England?"

He'd been acquainted with the butler since the age of fourteen and it wasn't long after when the two men had dispensed with all formality. Giles had even taught Frasier to play the piano, not that he remembered anything from those lessons so long ago.

"I've come to clear my grandfather's name. My father's as well."

"Och, 'tis about time. His Grace mentioned you might pay a visit, though I had to see it with me own eyes to believe ye would actually come down from your wee dung hill."

Frasier introduced Angus who was standing agape. "I hope it willna be too much trouble to take in a pair of ornery highlanders."

"Nay, nay, not at all." Giles stepped back and opened the door wider. "Come in afore it starts to rain."

"My thanks." Beside him, Angus released a breathy whistle. Indeed, the Duke of Dunscaby's entry was lavishly decorated in finery complete with a gilt sideboard and Grecian marbles, but it wasn't as spectacular as Stack Castle's enormous great hall. Nonetheless, this was the first time Angus had been to one of the duke's residences. The most lavish building the highlander had ever visited inside was most likely the kirk in Crieff where most of their kin had been wed.

Once inside, Frasier removed his woolen bonnet. "Is His Grace home?"

"Unfortunately, no. He's had to take a trip to Brighton on parliamentary business, poor soul."

Frasier scowled. Of course Dunscaby was an important man who was exceedingly busy but having him away posed a conundrum.

Angus looked none too pleased as well. "How long until he returns?"

"It shouldna be more than a few days. Mayhap a week...could be more."

Noticing Frasier had removed his bonnet, Angus followed suit. "Longer than a week?"

"One never kens. The Prince Regent is having one of his banquets at the Royal Pavilion."

Frasier quizzically studied the butler. "I thought you said Dunscaby was on parliamentary business."

"Aye, well he and the duchess didna *want* to go to Brighton." Giles gestured to a grand staircase. "Allow me to show you to your rooms. Of course, ye are to make yourselves at home until he returns."

THOUGH THE DUKE'S town house was not as large as his Newhailes manor, it was still gargantuan. Upon giving a brief tour, Giles had mentioned that most London town houses were built on city lots a quarter of the size of Dunscaby's which afforded the duke a sizeable dining hall, drawing room, two parlors, a ballroom, a library, and enough bedchambers to house the entire family as well as guests. Of course, the nursery was somewhere above stairs, now occupied by the duke's children Lord James and Lady Lily whom Frasier had met at Stack Castle last summer. Giles hadn't taken them up there because the tour had only included the common areas.

Frasier's bedchamber was appointed with a four-poster bed which had blue and gold damask bed curtains and a matching coverlet. In one corner, a pristine washstand appeared as if it had never been used. As did the writing table and chair. The window embrasure, with its blue velvet seat cushions, overlooked the rear courtyard which was bordered with herbaceous plants. Beyond that was the mews housing carriages and horses. The mews itself was at least as large as the stable at Druimliart.

But Frasier was anything other than comfortable. During the tour, he'd discovered everyone aside from the duke's children was away. Martin and his wife Julia had not only gone to Brighton, the Dowager Duchess and Modesty were at Newhailes with Princess Grace. Lady Charity was the only MacGalloway in London but she spent the Season at the Brixham town house with her husband due to his parliamentary duties.

Why was Grace in Newhailes?

Frasier didn't suppose the reason mattered. It would take at least five days of steady riding to reach the manor. She was scarcely closer to him now than she would have been if she'd remained at the lodge.

After a shave and changing his shirt, Frasier stepped into the corridor and looked along the row of opposing closed doors. Angus was bedding down in another wing of the house. This floor was obviously for the duke's family and perhaps Martin's closest friends when not all of his eight siblings were in residence. Did one of these doors lead to Grace's bedchamber? He opened a door—too masculine. Another was too frilly. Another—definitely not.

As Frasier placed his hand on the latch of the next door, tingles skittered up his arm all the way to the back of his neck. He hesitated for a moment, breathing in the faint scent. He didn't need to look to know it was hers, but he stepped inside all the same.

Ah, yes, this was the bedchamber of a woman who left nothing undone, who saw to every detail. The bed itself was a work of art. In the baroque style, the woodwork had been gilded. The canopy was layered with embroidered roses atop a cream silken fabric, edged with a very light shade of rose-corded fringe. The coverlet matched, of course. The princess' writing desk, toilette, and settee were all of the same baroque style —expensive, exquisite, and pristine.

Perhaps it was pristine because she was no longer in residence. If she were there, the lady's maid might have set out a dinner gown or, since the Season was in full swing, mayhap a ball gown?

Frasier moved to the toilette with its large oval mirror. The brushes were gone as were the hat pins, hair pins, and hand mirror. All of her possessions were gone except a rose-colored scent bottle with a brass lid. He twisted off the cap and drew it to his nose.

Lavender.

He should have known Grace wouldn't try to mix together an assortment of fragrances. Hers was pure and soft, definitely not overpowering. Frasier closed his eyes and imagined her in his arms waltzing as they had done in his meager cottage. He had held her closer than was proper, but for his boldness he had no regrets. In that wee moment, he'd almost convinced himself that she was his.

Sighing, he recapped the bottle and replaced it. A slip of paper on the writing table caught his eye. The script was practiced, slim, and feminine.

My dreams have finally come true. By the time the sun sets this day I will be Princess Grace!

Obviously, she must have written the note sometime before she'd left for the cathedral. Frasier could only imagine how excited the lass must have been the morn of her wedding day—the sense of triumph she would have felt. After all, she was the darling who had caught the eye of the most eligible bachelor in Christendom.

He scowled. How dare that bastard dash her

dreams? How could the prince have sailed across the Baltic Sea without raising a finger to fight for her? What kind of man would do such a thing?

Frasier tossed the note aside and rubbed his fingers over his dirk. Och aye, how he would dearly love to grab Isidor by the throat and thrash the smug bastard.

A sound somewhere in the house roused him from his dark thoughts. He shouldn't be in Grace's bedchamber. Moreover, it was futile to imagine himself fighting a man who wasn't even in London, let alone Britain. Frasier had come to London for one purpose—well, in truth there were two objectives— request a pardon for his clan and reclaim the Horn of Bannockburn and or any treasure he might be able to claim.

He made his way down the stairs and slipped into the library where he found Angus staring at an enormous volume opened on a wooden stand. "What have you there?"

The man looked up, his eyebrows arching. "Did ye ken the dictionary is larger than the Bible?" Angus had learned his letters, but he was no scholar.

Frasier chuckled. "By the looks of it, that one most certainly is."

"Och, I didna realize ye lived in audacious luxury every time you paid a visit to the duke. 'Tis a wonder you returned to Druimliart after your fostering."

"Of course, I returned, ye numpty. Druimliart is my home." Frasier gestured from one book-lined wall to the other. "I was merely a guest—a student, really. I wasna ever part of the family."

Angus closed the dictionary. "Ye took your meals with them."

"Aye, but never when His Grace was entertaining,"

Frasier replied, taking a newspaper from the writing desk and sitting in a wingback chair near the hearth.

"So what then? Did they make you starve?"

Frasier glanced at the headlines: *House of Lords to Debate Perilous National Debt*. "I ate in the servants' quarters."

Angus snorted. "Bloody aristocracy and their dependence upon servants."

"Actually, I often felt more comfortable among the working class. No one has to put on airs below stairs. 'Tis more like eating in our hall."

The highlander bent down to examine the globe. "Well, I'm just glad they didna turn you into one of them dandies."

Not interested in the kingdom's debt problems, Frasier turned the page. "Never."

"It makes me realize though…"

"Hmm?" he asked, scanning.

"What a shock it must have been to the princess to awake in your wee cottage. The butler put me in a chamber out toward the mews and I reckon the bed curtains cost more than the contents of my entire home."

Obviously Angus was in the mood to talk. Frasier folded the newspaper. "Dunna compare yourself to the likes of a duke. It will only serve to make ye bitter. We came here to clear our name, and that's what I aim to do."

Angus stroked his beard, lowering himself into the chair opposite. "Except Dunscaby isna here."

"We dunna need him, damn it. I am laird. I can handle my own affairs." At least some things. Others he most definitely could not accomplished without His Grace's backing.

"All right. So, where do we begin?"

"Since we need Dunscaby to gain an audience with His Highness, mayhap we'll pay the Tower a visit on the morrow."

Angus coughed as if he'd just choked on a morsel of dry biscuit. "Have ye lost your mind?"

15

I t took an hour to walk from Dunscaby's Mayfair town house to the Tower of London. Frasier opted to save the fare for a hackney until he truly needed it. Nonetheless, since His Grace was away, they had nothing better to do aside from drink the duke's whisky and it was far too early in the day for spirits.

As they approached, the enormous medieval fortress loomed large on the Thames, hewn of stone, streaked grey-black by centuries of rain, snow, and soot from the multitudes of coal burning fires belching from thousands of chimneys. The White Tower loomed above the parapet of the outer bailey, not white, but its stone walls lighter than those of the fortress. Perhaps the white paint from the time of Henry III now provided a lightening effect. The masonry itself was artful, striped vertically by lighter brickwork at the corners and the four equally spaced decorative columns built into each wall. The same light sandstone was also used in the archways framing the windows.

It was in this place were the Jacobite leaders had been beheaded. Frasier knew the stories well. Though the government troops were not successful in capturing Bonny Prince Charlie who had escaped to the continent, Flora MacDonald, the woman who fearlessly helped him escape had also been captured and imprisoned in this very place.

True, Frasier had been raised in the Jacobite tradition but he was not staunchly loyal to the Stewart line of succession. In this day and age, he saw no reason to be. When Charlie failed, the would-be king had abandoned Scotland, just as his father had done before him. Of course, as a youth Frasier kept his opinion to himself on threat of being skewered by his father. However, when looking at the other side of the equation, Frasier held no great loyalty for the current government because he was technically still an outlaw. Perhaps some things could be changed?

"Are you certain ye want to go in there now?" asked Angus as the steel nails at the bottom of their boots which made it easier to walk in icy conditions, slipped on and tapped the rounded cobblestones.

Frasier took in the enormity of the twin guard towers connected by an archway. In front of each tower, two yeomen stood with medieval pikes, their bright red uniforms topped by Elizabethan neck ruffs and black hats. The guards paid them no mind as they continued under the archway. "I just want to have a wee peek."

It surprised him to see the main gates wide open as they passed over a bridge and into the courtyard. A sign pointed left indicating The Royal Menagerie, the cost of admission, one shilling. To the right was the infamous Tower, the prison where Frasier's grandfather had been held for the crime of high treason before his beheading. Aye, the kings and queens of England had held a great many high-ranking officials in this place before their executions, many English, but Edward I's claim that William Wallace had committed treason had been utterly false. During Wallace's time, Scotland had not yet been annexed into Britain. Who could commit treason against a country to which they did not belong?

Frasier growled under his breath at the burning pulse thrumming beneath his skin. If he had been born in another time, he would have followed Wallace just has his ancestors had done. He would have fought for the Bruce as well.

But now, Scotland did not even have its own parliament. Everything for the Kingdom was decided in London by a vast majority of Englishmen.

Before they walked through the gates, Frasier looked up to the wall-walk, half expecting to see an armed guard glaring down through every crenel. But there was not. This was not only a time of peace, there hadn't been an attack on the Tower of London since the English Civil War in 1642.

It seems I paid more attention to my history lessons than I'd realized.

"What is your plan?" asked Angus as they traversed beneath the thick archway.

Once inside the courtyard, Frasier followed the small crowd to the ticket booth. "We'll purchase a pair of tickets to see the wee beasties. Look there, the sign says they have lions, leopards, baboons, and tigers."

Angus snorted. "Dunna tell me ye came to get your head bit off by a lion."

"Have ye ever seen one?"

"Ye ken I havena."

As they approached the ticket master, Frasier reached into his sporran and pulled out a couple of shillings. "Two please."

"From Scotland, are you?" asked the man, just like

dozens of others had done since they crossed the border.

"Aye," said Frasier contemplating the purchase of a pair of breeches. But then again, why waste his coin?

"What brings you to London?"

"Paying a wee visit to an old friend."

The man slid two paper tickets forward. "Enjoy the exhibit. I reckon the tiger is the most magnificent."

"Not the lions?" asked Angus.

"There's only one lion and he's old and rheumy-eyed. The tiger was a gift to His Majesty just a few years past. He's young and bloodthirsty, that one."

As they proceeded toward the ramp leading down to what once had been the moat, but had been drained to create the menagerie, Frasier glanced at the row of four towers along the north inner bailey wall. He checked over his shoulder, noting the ticket man's attentions were drawn elsewhere as he was serving a steady flow of visitors. Frasier nudged Angus with his elbow. "Stay here."

"And do what?"

"Keep watch."

"Where are ye going?"

Frasier inclined his head toward the inner bailey courtyard. "For a wee stroll."

"But the sign says, '*do no' enter*.'"

"Och, I never should have taught ye to read."

As Frasier stealthily made his way through the inner bailey, the corner tower on the northwest side bore a placard above the first door contained the name *Devereux*. Several paces on, he discovered the second tower was the one he was looking for—*Flint*. He turned full circle to ensure no one was watching—no one aside from Angus, who gaped at him, making a quick gesture with his fingers, urging him to come back. Frasier responded with a whirly circle of his finger, commanding the worrier to turn around. There was no use having Angus stand guard and watch Frasier, the numpty.

He tried the latch. Not surprisingly it was locked.

He removed two iron picks from his sporran and with a couple deft flicks of his fingers, the lock opened. It was several degrees cooler inside, dark and dank as well. Frasier left the door slightly ajar to allow the sunlight to shine in, then waited for his eyes to adjust.

Dozens of trunks in various sizes were stacked haphazardly, some partially opened, looking as if the inventory was well and truly underway. There were weapons of all sorts—Scottish, many of them. Great swords, dirks, a pile of sgian dubhs beside them. In one corner was a cache of muskets, some with bayonets attached, some not. He looked for a journal or papers with a manifest compiled by clerks of the Chancellor of the Exchequer but found none.

Licking his lips, Frasier stooped over one of the crates with the lid askew.

The Horn of Bannockburn is in this room. I can feel it in me bones.

The first item he saw was a broken goblet. He held it to the light, noting it had an etching of two crowns and the initials JR which stood for James VIII. Once the glass had been filled, the etching was invisible and Jacobite loyalists would pay their respects to the glass with a toast of "Long live the King!" Nary a bystander would know they were paying homage to the Stewart line.

The backs of his arms prickled as he bent down for a closer inspection. Frasier only wanted his due, nothing more. Without moving the items within, all he could make out was a tartan kilt and a set of bag-pipes—both of which had been outlawed in 1747 along with Highland weapons. The act had been repealed in 1782, but the thirty-five years of oppression had taken its toll on Scotland's own.

Frasier shifted the lid to see more, dropping to his knees. He ached to rummage through every last trunk until he found his precious horn, but now was not the time. He'd first gain a pardon and then—

"Thief!"

The accusation was followed by a whistle and the clap of dozens of footsteps.

Where the bloody hell is Angus?

Gnashing his back molars, Frasier stood, holding up his hands. "I havena touched a thing. I was only having a wee peek."

His accuser sauntered inside, pointing a flintlock pistol at Frasier's heart. "You're a bloody Jacobite thief. How did you know this treasure was here? Certainly not from the lips of one of my clerks. Only a handful of peers know of it."

On closer inspection, the man addressing Frasier was quite well dressed. He used the tongue of the English nobility which sounded a bit as if the orator was suffering from a bout of indigestion. "I'm surprised to see the chancellor here himself," he hedged.

"Why?"

"Because men such as you employ others for such busy work."

"Who are you?"

"No' a Jacobite, but a highlander. And in this pile of old relics is most likely something dear to my family. But ye have my word I would not take so much as that broken goblet without asking first."

"Your word? I find that difficult to believe, considering I myself assured the lock on this door was sound." The chancellor turned to the guards who had gathered behind him. "Arrest this man!"

Frasier ran for the sliver of daylight. Snarling, he shoved one guard aside while jabbing the heel of his hand into another's chin. With two more steps, he broke through the human barricade, until a blunt object hit him from behind. Stumbling, Frasier set his sights on the gates as stars darted through his vision. One more step and his knee buckled, sending him crashing to the cobblestones. Four guards jumped on his back, wrenching his wrists up his spine. "You just earned a dozen lashes for that trick," growled the chancellor, giving him a sharp kick in the ribs.

As they dragged Frasier to his feet and led him away, Angus was nowhere to be seen, thank God.

AFTER THE GUARDS removed his dirk and sgian dubh, Frasier struggled against his manacles while the bastards used the blunt end of their pikes to prod him into moving forward. "I didna take anything, ye bleeding maggots!" he shouted, his head throbbing with pain, the spinning inside his skull making him stumble.

"Who are you thief?" the chancellor demanded.

Frasier pursed his lips shut. The more he said, the more likely he'd be damned for eternity.

"How did you know what was locked away in Flint Tower? Did you come down from Scotland to rob the king?"

He scowled while they led him to a post—one with an iron ring attached three quarters of the way up.

Damn them to hell!

It took six men to wrench Frasier's arms upward while another locked the chain between his manacles in place. "I am no' a criminal!" he shouted while a guard used a knife to slice through Frasier's doublet, waist coat, and shirt. He turned and glared at the bastard through strands of his hair. Somewhere in the scuffle, his leather thong had disappeared.

The chancellor reached in and yanked away Frasier's pocket watch. "Look what we have here. You're a Buchanan—you're the spawn of the first man to be beheaded in this very square." The bastard held up the watch and strutted in a circle. "Do you see this men? This ruddy Highland scourge has come to thieve His Majesty's purse!"

"I did no such thing!" Frasier jerked downward in a futile attempt to free himself. "I came to clear my name and that of me kin."

The chancellor threw the watch to the cobblestones, smashing the glass. Then he ground it into the stone with his heel. "I do not believe you." The bastard gestured to someone behind Frasier. "Twelve. And make them sting."

The high-pitched whistle of the whip sent a shock of dread up his spine right before the first strike slashed through his flesh. Unable to help his initial grunt, he closed his mouth, his legs shuddering with the shock of pain.

The chancellor bellowed with an ugly laugh. "You are guilty of treason, admit your crimes!"

Blood oozed down Frasier's back while the breeze off the Thames cooled the sting. "I am innocent. I did no' steal anything from the tower and I have never in my life entertained a treasonous thought!" Well, given his father's influence, Frasier could boast because he had never actually acted out against the crown.

"I found you among that pile of rusted Jacobite relics. Admit to it!"

Frasier sneered over his shoulder. "I only wanted a wee peek—as I already said."

"Lie! Who told you about the treasure?"

The whip's tines hissed through the air, ripping through his skin like the blade of a dull knife. Frasier clenched his teeth and hissed.

"You are a Jacobite traitor just like your kin!" bellowed the bastard.

Another strike ripped through his flesh on his back, and another, coming so fast, his knees buckled.

"Admit to your plot to undermine the kingdom!"

"Never!" Frasier growled. Sweat streamed into his eyes while his fingers grew numb from straining against the iron manacles chained above his head. "I only want to clear my name. That is all."

Frasier gritted his teeth harder and harder as he withstood the remaining lashes, each more savage than the last. But he did not cry out, and he did not faint.

As the twelfth and final strike cut through his skin, he closed his eyes and conjured an image of Grace's face. On the shore of Loch Tulla she had gazed into his eyes with love. She had kissed him with such fevered passion, there was no denying her feelings for him. If only she weren't already wed, he would speak to her brother. He would take a hundred lashings to win her for his own.

But that could never be.

16

"My heavens, sister, what a surprise to see your bonny face gracing my parlor!" said Charity, sliding onto a settee. "But are you not supposed to be hidden away at the lodge?"

Grace snapped open her fan and cooled her face. As soon as the *Prosperity* had arrived in London, she first discretely enquired as to whether the duke had guests. After one of the footmen confirmed Laird Buchanan was visiting with his "henchman" but had stepped out for the day, she'd gone directly to the Earl of Brixham's town house to see her sister. "I felt it was of utmost import to see you forthwith to explain certain circumstances."

"Oh? Has something happened? Is Mama well?"

"The question is are you well, oh, sister mine?" Grace slowly wielded her fan. "Are you once again in the family way, perchance?"

Charity placed her palms atop her slender stomach. "Not that I am aware of."

Grace closed her fan with a resounding clap. "Drat!"

The butler brought in a tray of lemonade and Charity gestured to the low table. "What is this about?

I canna believe Mama allowed you to come to London whilst you are...ah..."

Grace picked up one of the leaded-crystal glasses. "Enduring my predicament?"

"Precisely."

"Mama decided my estrangement from Isidor ought to be referred to as my predicament."

"Very astute of her."

"Yes," Grace said, taking a sip, the tartness making her lips pucker. "But my excuse for being here is of my own design. I have come under the pretense that you summoned me."

Charity's mouth opened as if suddenly rendered speechless. "I did?" she asked doubtfully.

"Yes. Because you believed yourself to be in the family way, but it seems your summons must have been premature."

"I see." Charity smiled—her lips curling as if she were unconvinced. "My dear sister, I've known you far too long. You havena come to London to attend the theater or balls or Vauxhall, have you?"

"No. I've come to see you."

Charity rolled her eyes to the ornate plasterwork on the ceiling above. "Grace, of all our mother's children, you are the least...shall I say *attached*?"

"Are you inferring I am not dedicated to the Mac-Galloway clan?"

Charity smoothed her fingers along the satin ribbon on her day gown. "I suppose I am."

"Well, then you are wrong. I may have previously, in my youth, been a tad overly motivated by my desire to marry well, but I assure you I have seen the error of my ways."

A pinch formed between Charity's auburn eyebrows. "Is all well? Has someone taken ill, perchance?"

"Good heavens, can I not turn over a new leaf without someone being mortally ill?" Grace looked at the lemonade and decided she wasn't thirsty. "I doubt Marty has had a chance to tell you, but Isidor atoned to the Archbishop and has requested that I join him in Lithuania."

"I kent about the Archbishop's refusal to approve the annulment, but I had no idea Isidor had apologized or had summoned you." Charity sat forward, her auburn eyebrows pinched. "You simply canna go to Lithuania, I forbid it. Not after the way that scoundrel behaved!"

"I do not intend to sit idly by and wait for my doom." Grace most definitely did not wish to re-assemble the shards of her broken marriage vows but if the family knew the extent of her feelings, so would the servants, and at some stage, so would all of polite society. "I simply need an excuse if I am seen in Town, and I would be dearly indebted to you if you would corroborate my itty-bitty ruse that I have returned to provide support for a most beloved sister."

A rather indelicate snigger burst from Charity's nose. "Beloved? I certainly should like to see such a declaration in writing."

"Excuse me, but I do love each and every member of my family." Grace threw back her shoulders. "Dearly."

Charity sipped her lemonade, smiling over the glass. "You're scheming, are you not? What is it you canna bear to miss? A royal ball?"

"I beg your pardon, but my entire life has been ruined for the rest of my days, and you accuse me of scheming?" Of course, Grace did have an ulterior motive, but it was innocent, and most likely would amount to nothing. Moreover, regardless if she wanted to sail to Lithuania, the odds of avoiding the crossing of the North Sea did grow slimmer by the day. Indeed, her future appeared to hold anything but happiness. She only desired an opportunity to see Frasier once again—spend a little time in his company before she actually had to face her fate. "I do not intend to show my face at a ball or anywhere else for that matter. However, because I am here, I could be recognized and if I am, I'd be most grateful if you played along with my reason for not being in Lithuania."

"Goodness, mayhap this whole debacle has helped you to find your heart." Charity had never uttered more truthful words.

"Exactly," Grace replied, looking down and helping herself to a slice of shortbread so her sister could not accuse her of smiling triumphantly.

"Verra well, you have come to comfort me, but my summons was premature and I am not with child. Will that do?"

"Perfectly."

"Are you planning to stay?"

"Here, with you and Brixham?" Grace almost laughed. She was already well aware His Lairdship was staying at their brother's town house two streets away. "Of course not."

~

GRACE CLIMBED the steps of the Dunscaby town house, somewhat surprised to see Tearlach open the door. "Where is Giles?" she asked.

"Angus has returned."

"Angus?" She cocked her head toward the whisper of muffled voices coming from below stairs. "What of Buchanan?"

Tearlach ushered her inside. "I believe that might be what Angus is discussing with the butler."

Grace pushed through the hidden servant door behind a panel in the entry and dashed down the winding staircase. The light in the corridor was dim, but that didn't prevent her from seeing fear reflected in the Buchanan clansman's wild eyes.

Both men ceased talking and looked as guilty as two deerhounds who had pinched the cook's leg of lamb. Grace moved nearer, the heels of her shoes tapping the floor tiles. "Where is Buchanan?"

Angus released a gasp. "Och, thank the kelpies, ye're here, m'lady."

Giles cleared his throat. "It appears Buchanan was arrested at the Tower of London."

Forced to place her hand on the wall due to the wobbling of her knees, Grace also gasped. "Are you certain? What was he doing at the Tower?"

"Since the duke isna here, Frasier wanted to have wee peek at the Jacobite treasure, seized during the '45. Sealed in Flint Tower, it was."

"Treasure?" She knit her eyebrows—Buchanan was visiting London to clear his name. He hadn't mentioned anything about Jacobite treasure. "What treasure? And where is Martin?"

Angus quickly explained that the riches stolen from the Jacobite clans had been recently rediscovered and Giles added that the duke was presently in Brighton and ought to be back within a week—a fortnight at most.

"A fortnight? They could sentence Buchanan to ten years transportation by then!" Grace paced, wringing her hands as her mind raced. Drat, drat, drat! Why must everything in her life go calamitously awry? What had she done to anger the powers that be?

One thing was for certain, she was not about to sit with Mama and embroider. Not now, possibly not ever again. She was sick to death of everyone and everything shoving obstacles in her way and snuffing out her plans. "Angus, go to the stables and have my horse saddled at once. Yours as well."

As the highlander gave a nod, she looked at Giles. "Who else knows about this?"

"No one. Angus just arrived.

She thrust her finger at the stairs. "Inform Captain Gibb at once. Tell him I insist he send for Martin—"

"Och, insist, Your Highness?"

She stamped her foot. "I am a princess, am I not?"

"Aye, but I am a servant. I dunna reckon an order of such magnitude would be taken well coming from me."

"For the love of Moses," she cursed, turning on her heel. "I shall speak to Gibb myself!"

17

F razier sat at the edge of the rough-hewn bed, made from knotty pieces of beechwood. He crouched forward, leaning his elbows on his knees. Every time he moved, his back screamed with pain. Worse, the bedframe was so wobbly, even the slightest movement jarred. The crude straw mattress was covered with canvas and beneath ropes crisscrossed for support—sagging support.

The bastards had thrown him into this cell along with his ruined clothing. They didn't bother to allow him to remove his clothes before they cut them off and took the whip to him. Dammit all, his shirt, waistcoat, and doublet were entirely useless.

No matter, I'll not be able to tolerate anything touching my skin for a sennight or more.

No one had given him bedlinens nor had anyone offered a blanket, though the cell was larger than he might have imagined. There was a wooden table under the barred, paneless window. Perhaps there had been a chair at one time, though no longer. The sandstone hearth was stained inside and above with black soot. And since there was neither wood nor coal for a fire, it seemed the staining most likely had happened through the centuries. Aye, the grey stone walls and masonry were the same as the floor—drab, dirty, and dusty.

It wasn't difficult to imagine William Wallace awaiting his fate in this place. Or Queen Elizabeth when her sister Bloody Mary had imprisoned her for a short time. For centuries, the Tower had been synonymous with wrongful imprisonment as well as wrongful death.

Had Frasier's grandfather been detained in this cell? Some of the stones in the walls were etched with crosses, initials, dates. One was of a fleur-de-lis, denoting a French captive. He strode across the floor and examined the etchings—the oldest date was from 1218 —six hundred years ago. He read dozens of names he did not recognize. But it was the Gaelic motto: *"Clarior Hinc Honos"* that caught his eye. Tingles spread across his flesh. Gaelic was still outlawed by the crown, but he knew some. Most of all, he recognized the words as the Buchanan motto, translated as *"Henceforth forward the honor shall grow ever brighter."*

The guards could not have known Frasier's grandfather had awaited his fate in this very cell.

Will I suffer the same? As the wounds on his back tortured him with agony, he feared he had already been judged. Why had he been so reckless? Damnation, when he'd walked along the courtyard there were no guards to be seen.

Absently, Frasier reached down to his flashes for his *sgian dubh*, but it had been taken when the soldiers confiscated the knife along with his dirk. He may have hated London when he'd first arrived. Now he loathed it doubly so.

He'd been accused of theft.

Except he hadn't taken anything.

He hadn't even planned to.

Yet.

"You cannot hold an innocent man without bail!" seethed a woman.

Grace?

The voice sounded similar, but certainly could not be. The lass was still in Scotland. Besides, never once had Frasier heard Grace sound shrill. Obviously, he was imagining things.

He could not make out the guard's reply, but the woman grew even more enraged as well as more assertive. "He had best be in conditions befitting his station. Buchanan is a laird—a man of high esteem, close allies with the Duke of Dunscaby!"

Damnation, it is Grace!

The soldier on guard mumbled something about treason, which earned him a flabbergasted reply, "You are utterly wrong! His Lairdship's grandfather might have been at fault but that was three and seventy years ago. I may not be an expert, but I am quite certain it is against the edicts of the Magna Carta to punish consecutive generations for any crime whatsoever. Furthermore, doing so is positively *barbaric!*"

Frasier snorted as he held in a laugh, his back punishing him for his sudden jolt. Good God, had the princess been born a man, she would have made a formidable barrister.

"I am not taking my leave until I am satisfied that Buchanan is unharmed and assuredly is not locked away in some rat-infested pigsty."

Keys jangled as Frasier moved to face the door. "Only one of you is permitted inside," muttered the guard.

He didn't need to hear the soft tap of feminine shoes in the corridor to know Grace was the person allowed to proceed. The woman most likely would have caused a riot if they had not allowed her.

The key screeched in the iron lock and she slipped inside, the glow from the torch on the wall illuminating her hair as if she were an angel...until the door slammed closed behind her.

Though she was wearing his mother's arisaid with her tresses pulled back in a simple braid, she still looked like a princess, albeit worry etched those lovely features. A wee cry squeaked from her throat. He'd only been incarcerated for a matter of hours, but by God it was good to see her. "Grace!" he said, pulling her into his arms and kissing her. Their bodies fitting together like two halves of a broken heart. In that moment pain did not exist. Worries faded. Happiness swelled through him.

Until her fingers brushed his back.

Gasping, she recoiled, staring in horror at the blood on her fingertips. She peered around him. "My God, Angus did not tell me you had been whipped!"

Frasier grabbed his ruined shirt and set to cleaning her hands. "He didna ken. 'Twas after he went for help."

"You knew?"

"Aye, the man isna daft. If he'd stayed behind and tried to fight, both of us would have been behind bars and nary a soul would have been the wiser."

"The guards surely know who you are."

"Perhaps, but ye wouldna have kent would you?"

She shook her head, then gently tapped his shoulder. "Please allow me to have a better look."

He considered arguing but was well aware doing so would be futile. As he turned, she hissed. "Only twelve lashes—most likely 'cause I am innocent."

"Clothing can be replaced. You need a salve forth-with lest your wounds mortify."

"I'll be all right. Just having ye here makes me forget the pain."

"Hogwash." She pounded on the door. "Guard! This man needs a doctor immediately!"

The panel on the window of the door slid open. "He looks well enough to me."

"That is because you are an imbecile. I demand you send for a doctor at once!"

"It'll cost ye."

Grace thrust her finger in the direction of the exit. "The bill will be paid by the Duke of Dunscaby. Now go, before I file a complaint against you and arrange for *you* to receive a dozen lashes for your impertinence!"

Though Frasier's legs were on the verge of giving out, he admired the woman's spirit. If anyone ever questioned her station as a princess, they would be sorely mistaken.

Her eyes blazed as she faced him. "You will be tended. And I will see to it they give you proper linens. This cell is a disgrace."

Unable to stop himself, he reached for her. "You are the most astonishing, vivacious, commanding woman I have ever met."

Her reaction was to skitter away, her expression worried. "Should you not be lying down?"

"Nay." He tried again, and this time she fell against his chest, her sweet mouth turned up to him. He cupped her cheeks with his big hands. "I need to kiss you."

As her eyelids fluttered closed, he lost himself in the softness of her mouth, in the soothing way her breasts pressed against his bare chest. Kissing her was akin to coming home, like being far away from London and those who wanted him dead.

When finally their kisses ebbed, Frasier whispered into her ear, "Why are ye in London, lass?"

She met his gaze, her forehead furrowing. "Because you are here."

"But I thought—"

"A great deal has transpired since we last spoke at the lodge, but none of it matters at the moment. Because you told me you were coming to London, I made up a tiny ruse that Charity needed me. Mama eventually agreed and Gibb sailed us down from Newhailes, taking only two days, mind you." She bit her lip as if she had more to say but decided against it.

As Frasier recalled, she had been planning to remain at the lodge for quite some time. It seemed a great deal must have changed very quickly. "Why were you at Newhailes?" he asked.

With a sigh, she tsked her tongue and led him to the bed where they both sat. "I have never been good at harboring secrets."

"Oh?" Frasier asked, closing his eyes and trying to block the pain. "Come, we have shared a great many secrets between us. What is it now?"

She leaned back, wincing as she took a wee peek at his wounds. "I do not wish to add to your woes."

He took her hand and kissed it. "Grace, something has happened and you will only be adding to my misery by keeping it to yourself. I implore you, please tell me."

Again she sighed, this time with more of a huff. "Isidor atoned to the Archbishop for his sins."

Frasier's shoulders fell. He should have known her news wasn't good.

Grace released him and covered her face with her

hands. "Worse, I have been summoned to Lithuania on threat of *divorce*."

Damnation, that man was truly a bastard. Why could the prince not leave well enough alone and agree to a bloody annulment? Why must he drag this dear woman through the mire? She had done nothing to deserve such malice. His mouth dry, Frasier placed a hand on her shoulder, well aware he must choose his next words carefully. "Is a divorce something you would deign to consider?"

"How can I? Divorcing the prince would put a stain on my family forever and would ruin Modesty's chances to marry well." She gently rested her fingers atop his. "But my fate is not the issue at hand, is it?"

Frazier glanced at the barred medieval door and shook his head. Why had he tempted fate? Locked inside, he was powerless to help her. "I suppose it isna."

"I thought you were coming to London to clear your name, not to recover your clan's lost treasure."

"Mayhap it was a little of both. I wanted to see the spoils of the Jacobite raids led by the Duke of Cumberland. And since His Grace is presently in Brighton, I thought there was no harm in having a peek."

A pinch creased her brow. "Why did you not give them a false name?"

"I gave them no name whatsoever, but they found out who I am easily enough. My pocket watch has Buchanan engraved on the back—or it did. The chancellor ground it into the cobbles with the heel of his Hessian boot."

"Oh, dear." Grace pressed praying hands to her lips. "You are aware they're already calling you a traitor?"

Frasier's fingers curled, tightening into fists. The chancellor had taken but one look at his list of Jacobite rebels and the man had pronounced him an outlaw on the spot. "Aye. They said I was hewn of the same cloth as my grandfather."

"You must know Angus came to the town house straightaway."

"At least he was smart enough not to try to intercede when the chancellor hailed the guards."

"Thank heavens."

"I want to show ye something." He stood and offered his hand, then led her to the clan motto. "My grandfather must have etched this."

Grace ran her finger over the letters. "'Tis Gaelic."

"Can you read it?"

"I'm not fluent. I think it says something about honor growing brighter."

"Aye. Henceforth forward the honor shall grow ever brighter."

"He was here," she whispered, turning full circle and rubbing her arms as if cold. "Knowing that your grandfather suffered incarceration in this cell fills me with trepidation."

Honestly, Frasier had yet to come to grips with it, but he sure as hell was not planning to succumb to the same fate. "Has there been any word as to when Dunscaby is expected to return from Brighton?"

"Not as of yet, but Gibb himself is riding southward to intercept him. You should not have left the town house until Martin returned."

"I should never have come to London."

"Perhaps not, but you're here now, and I will not rest until your name is cleared."

"You?" he asked, stopping himself from reminding the woman that she had been summoned by her scoundrel of a husband.

Grace eyed him with fire in those blues. "Do you believe I cannot help because I am a mere woman?"

In truth, if he knew Grace, she would stop at nothing to pursue whatever her bonny heart desired —aside from an annulment it appeared. But he could not allow her to further cast a dubious light upon her circumstances. He grasped her arms and held her firmly. "I believe you have a crisis of your own to attend."

She dropped her head to his chest. "I do not want to attend my crisis."

"But you must."

"Not immediately."

He kissed her forehead. "Dear *Princess* Grace, merely your presence here will draw speculation."

"I do not care."

"Ye should. A man as powerful as Prince Isidor surely has eyes and ears in all corners of Christendom. Ye mustn't come here again even disguised as a Highland lass. It is too dangerous."

Heaving a sigh, she gave a single nod. "Nonetheless, I will not rest until you have been released."

She rose onto her toes and gave him a gentle kiss on the lips. Not satisfied by half, he wrapped her in his arms and kissed her deeply, her wee sigh making him grin, making him remember how much he had enjoyed her deep-seeded passion and how she applied it to everything she pursued.

"I was verra impressed with your argument when you arrived," he said, touching his forehead to hers.

"Hmm." She chuckled softly. "I was not going to take no for an answer."

A pounding rattled the door. "You've had long enough," shouted the guard.

"Has a doctor been summoned?" she demanded.

"I sent a messenger boy to fetch him."

"Thank you. I shall require a moment longer. You are dismissed," Grace said over her shoulder as if she were in command of the world. God save any man who chose to stand in her way.

Unable to stop grinning at her ability to disparage the guard with a few sharply spoken words, Frasier, crooked his finger beneath her lovely chin. "I have one wee question."

"Oh?" she asked, her expression adoring with no hint of the fire she'd just unleashed on the guard.

"Where did you come up with the Magna Carta?"

Grace buried her face in his shoulder, shaking her head. "It was the only thing I could think of. We brushed on it at Northbourne when we were studying the English kings. I was referring to Clause Nine and Thirty: *'No free man shall be seized, imprisoned, dispossessed, outlawed, exiled or ruined in any way, nor in any way proceeded against, except by the lawful judgement of his peers and the law of the land.'*"

Though inordinately impressed with her recall, Frasier had one thing she might have overlooked. "Except there has been a lawful judgement exiling my clan."

"Ages ago." She looked up, those blue eyes filled with defiance. "And if you ask me, because of the wording of that clause it is *unlawful* to exile a clan for the duration of eternity!"

If only she had had been present when his clan was banished Frasier mightn't be in this predicament. "You are so dear to me." He kissed her. "Go home. Wait for Martin to return."

"But I hate to see you suffering in this awful dungeon."

"It is no dungeon and I will survive." He kissed her

again. "Besides, I'll wager the physician you sent for will be here within the hour."

The door burst open, a scowling guard baring his teeth. "'Tis time, milady, else I'll have to arrest you."

Grace pulled the tartan over her head and blew him a kiss. Frasier watched her follow the guard, his heart squeezing as if clamped by a vise. This might very well be the last time he ever set eyes upon her bonny face.

The thought completely sapped the remaining vestiges of Frasier's strength and he all but collapsed onto the bed.

Since Prince Isidor actually had atoned for his sins, she doubtlessly would have no choice but to go to him. After learning of his character, Frasier imagined Isidor would not bow to anyone, even the Archbishop of Canterbury. Nonetheless, the penance paid had clearly been nothing but an empty promise. The lout hadn't even bothered to come after his bride. He'd summoned her from the safety of his homeland, threatening divorce if she did not obey—and though Martin and the dukedom might not be ruined, Grace was right when she said her unmarried sister would be.

If the bastard proceeded to divorce her, Grace would be ostracized for the rest of her days. She'd never be able to show her face anywhere. Being exiled for a few months was one matter, but the lady was too bright of a star to be cosseted away and hidden for long. Grace was intelligent and vivacious. She was bred to be an exceptional hostess, a vibrant mother, and the lady of a vast estate, if not several vast estates.

The damned prince had the rights of a husband. She could not fight him. Neither could Dunscaby stand in Isidor's way. At least not legally.

Frasier buried his face in the dank canvas mattress. Who was he to desire such a woman? His family had been hiding for three and seventy years. They may have once been powerful and fierce supporters of the Scottish crown, but they had taken up arms for the wrong side of the Jacobite rising.

All he could hope for was to have his name cleared. He was a fool to think he might one day recover the Horn of Bannockburn, or any of the riches his kin once possessed. He never should have left Druimliart. He never should have given Flint Tower a second glance. It was full of worthless, rusted weapons and broken keepsakes from a forgotten realm.

The only realm Frasier cared to be a part of was that of his clan. So what if they suffered long winters in the Highlands? Up there they were left alone. Up there they were free.

18

"You cannot possibly concern yourself with Buchanan's affairs at a time such as this. I say, you are exceedingly lucky the reporters didn't sniff out your visit to the Tower. What if you'd been spotted? Your name would have been smeared across the headlines of the front pages!" said Mama, pulling her needle through her embroidery with a fair bit more force than necessary.

Grace stole a glance out the window, which she had done countless times since she'd sat five minutes ago. "I wore an arisaid and made certain I looked as if I'd just climbed down from the Scottish Highlands."

"That may will be, dearest, but you do not want people thinking something untoward is going on between you and His Lairdship. Not when there will already be speculation as to why you have returned from Lithuania so soon regardless of if Charity agreed to play along with your ruse."

"I am well aware. That is why I wore the arisaid and asked Angus to accompany me. We also hailed a hack so no one would be the wiser."

"But you told the guard who you were."

"I told him I was the sister of the Duke of Dun-

scaby and demanded to see Larid Buchanan at once."
Grace examined the torn set of stays she'd taken from
Biddle this morning. Her new lady's maid's skill with
needle and thread was somewhat lacking, though
rather than chastise the lass, Grace had given the
woman a few helpful pointers. "You above all people
are aware that Marty has more than one sister."

Mama glanced up from her work. "Good heavens
what is that in your hands?"

It might be against all manner of etiquette rules to
mend undergarments in the family's parlor, but Grace
did not give a whit. "The boning in these stays had
frayed the cloth. I'm merely making a few repairs."

"Why are *you* mending stays?"

"Because I'm quite good at it," Grace replied,
smiling before she anxiously cast her gaze out the
window. "I am using a basket stitch which is quite effective. It ought to make this set last another two
years."

Huffing, Mama pushed her needle through the
back of her hoop. "I say, your time at Druimliart
tainted you for life."

Grace was too absorbed in the traffic on the street
to take exception to her mother's comment. There was
a reason Grace had chosen to sit by the window in the
front parlor, and it wasn't to make better use of the
light. It had been two days since she'd visited Frasier
in that awful cell and as Mama had put it, it was very
risky for her to make one appearance at the Tower, let
alone two. Surely Gibb would soon return with Martin. Of course, since Julia had been with her husband
in Brighton they most likely were traveling by coach
rather than on horseback.

*They would have been here by now if they were riding
their horses.*

Though she had listened to her mother's advice, Grace did not turn her gaze away from the window. Polite society mightn't be aware of it yet, but she was already ruined one way or another.

With her distraction, the set of stays dropped from her lap, the needle and thread slipping from her fingertips as well. As Grace stooped to retrieve her sewing, her ever-plotting mind touched on the predicament from a different angle. Of course it was of utmost importance to keep her debacle under wraps until Modesty married—perhaps three years at most. The dukedom wouldn't suffer too terribly if Grace's reputation was besmirched, but her younger sister's prospects would be dashed. Could Grace draw things out for such a long time or would Isidor insist upon immediately proceeding with his threat to pursue a divorce?

After finishing the repair, she selected green embroidery silk to give the contraption some character by adding a green stem with a red rose. Would Frasier wait for her for three years? After all, he had come to Stack Castle last summer in search of a bride.

For the love of Moses, why did this disaster have to happen to me?

It was nearly impossible to think clearly about her own affairs while Frasier was locked in the Tower of London as if he himself had committed treason.

He ought to be compensated by the crown for wrongful imprisonment!

What if His Lairdship had actually found the treasure stolen from his family? Would the clan stop hiding in the Highlands? Would Frasier have enough coin with which to build a home more fitting to his station?

What if...

"Mama, do you know if Martin has paid my dower funds to the prince?"

"I beg your pardon? The duke does not discuss financial affairs with me, nor should he. Such transactions are to be conducted in utmost secrecy. It is very unbecoming of you to even ask such a thing."

Grace jammed her needle into her work simply to keep her hands occupied. Mama was too old fashioned at times. "Hogwash. I believe I have a right to know if that charlatan fled from London with my dowry, yet *without* me!"

Ever since word came that Isidor had atoned for his sins, she had spent countless hours imagining ways in which she could avoid his uncouth demand that she join him. She had even considered sailing to Australia or America, though that would mean leaving everyone she loved including Buchanan because he would never abandon his clan. The idea had been completely ruled out with Frasier's warning that Isidor had ears and eyes in all corners of Christendom. The prince most likely would find her wherever she opted to flee.

And who was she fooling? She couldn't hide from the cur for three years, not even at the lodge or Druimliart. Doubtless, if Isidor did proceed to divorce her, he would devise ways to tarnish her reputation even if she adopted an alias.

Modesty's chances would be dashed and Grace's reputation would be stained forever. Grace stared at the partially completed stem, her eyes welling. Would Frasier want a fallen woman if Martin had already paid her dower funds to Isidor?

Mama reached across the empty space between their facing chairs and grasped Grace's hand. "I told you on the eve of your wedding that no marriage was perfect."

"I didn't doubt you." Grace shook herself from the frenzied wandering of her mind. "However, I did not expect the groom to take a lover so soon after we recited our vows."

"Many husbands take mistresses. It is just that Isidor's tastes evidently do not comply with British..." The dowager sighed as she glanced toward the floor.

"Law?" Grace finished.

"I suppose," Mama said, resuming her embroidery. "It might be inevitable for you to be reunited with the prince, but keep in mind his wealth is at least equal to ours. You will be the mistress of five vast estates. You will live in the comfort to which you have always been accustomed."

Honestly, Frasier's cottage wasn't entirely unbearable.

At the sound of an approaching carriage, Grace craned her neck to better see down the residential street, lined with the opulent town homes of London's wealthiest. "Splendid," she said, her tone anything but cheerful.

"Heed me—all you must do is provide an heir. Then you will be free to enjoy whatever you please. Pick one of the estates and make it your own—you might only see your husband at Yuletide, perhaps Easter."

The dratted carriage rolled past at a fast trot. "But I am his wife—his *property*. What if he doesn't allow me to retire to one of his country estates? What if he is merciless with me? What if he locks me in a dungeon and feeds me only bread and water?"

"Goodness, you do have a vivid imagination." After tying a knot, Mama snipped her silk with a small pair of shears. "When Isidor visited Stack Castle, his manners were impeccable. I do not believe him to be a tyrant."

The Dowager Duchess of Dunscaby was not naïve, but she presently had either forgotten all that had transpired since Grace's wedding day, or she was choosing to ignore the signs that Isidor might indeed be a tyrant of the worst sort. He had already started calling her names even if he did cross out *wench* substituting it with *young lady*. What would he threaten next? Violence? Malevolence? She'd seen him with his falls lowered in the Prince Regent's home as he made love to a man. What other perversion might he subject her to?

Frasier's cottage was most definitely cozy.

Though another carriage rattled on the cobblestones, the shod horse hooves clomping, Grace was too incensed to look this time. "Anyone can be on their best behavior for a sennight. And have you forgotten my husband referred to me as a self-serving wench? How will he refer to me behind closed doors? A hostile shrew? An ill-bred bitch."

"My dear child, you must curb your vulgar tongue!" Mama fanned herself with her embroidery. "You ought to look to the positive things you observed that made you believe he would make a good husband. Obviously, he is angry at the moment, but the prince feared his life was in jeopardy and he was forced to flee England without his bride."

Grace smirked. "His life *was* in danger."

"Think of it this way: Had Martin shot the prince, your brother could have incited a war. Though Isidor's actions may have appeared cowardly, he did save our country a great deal of posturing to say the least."

Grace was rescued from the need to reply to her mother's blather by the appearance of the butler.

"There is a Lord Alder here to see you, Your Highness," Giles said, presenting her with a silver tray with the man's calling card.

"How dare that man come to call," said Mama, her face coloring.

Grace's shoulders tensed. "He is aware of my presence?"

"Oh, my word, I'm going to have one of my spells!" The Dowager Duchess drew a hand to her forehead. "Lord Alder of all people knows Grace went to the Tower of London!"

"I wouldna go that far, Your Grace," said Giles, stoically still holding out the tray. "I asked him how he kent the princess was in London, and he indicated that it was his understanding she had never left."

Somewhat relieved, Grace withdrew the card from the tray and set it on the table. "I shall see him." She shifted her gaze to her mother. "Alone."

Of course, Mama tried to argue, but after Giles confirmed Alder had requested an audience with the princess, not mentioning Her Grace, Mother acquiesced, suddenly remembering she had promised to visit the shops on Oxford Street with Modesty and Kitty and decided she must go above stairs to change.

Grace hid the stays beneath a seat cushion and opted to stand as Giles showed Alder in, sliding the slot doors closed behind the man. His Lordship bowed deeply, his expression unflappable. "Princess Grace, thank you for seeing me."

Unable to help herself, she glanced downward to his neatly buttoned falls, then swiftly snapped her gaze to his face. "I daresay you are looking far more composed than you were the last time I saw you."

Alder had a handsome visage—perhaps pretty, framed by stylishly cut blond locks, though he possessed not a whit of Buchanan's ruggedness or size. His shoulders were slight, his coat fitted to a narrow waist. A bead of sweat trickled from the man's forehead and he withdrew a handkerchief from his coat, drawing Grace's attention to graceful fingers that appeared to be soft and uncalloused.

She was reminded of Isidor's touch—she'd thought it velvety. Now the memory of his caresses made her realize they were merely limp and affectionless. How had she not seen through his deceit? How had she thought him virile—the best catch in Christendom?

Alder tipped up his chin, it being somewhat masculine, shadowed with slight whiskers. "Isidor bade me to come."

"Oh?" she asked, wondering why her husband seemingly had written to everyone except his wife.

"You are aware he is sending a ship to take you home?"

"I am."

"And he has appointed me as your escort."

"You?" She turned away, her hand covering her mouth to prevent an unbidden scream. Alder of all people, the man her husband chose above her. "Can you tell me why?"

"Why?" he asked, his voice cracking. Surely he knew the reason, he just didn't have the fortitude to utter it.

I'll wager Isidor cannot wait to hold this dastard in his arms again.

Dropping her hands, Grace whipped back around, shoulders square, head held high. "Are you in love with my husband?"

His Lordship's expression was horrorstruck—either that or he was quite adept at playacting. "W-why would you ask such a thing?"

Good Lord, he had deigned to call upon her and now Grace was not going to allow the cad to play dumb. "Because you were making love with Isidor. I saw the pair of you with my own eyes." She leaned in allowing a modicum of her ire to boil to the surface. "Are. You. In. love with him?" she demanded, glaring unblinkingly at his eyes.

Alder recoiled. "I-I-I do care for him deeply."

"And you are attracted to him," she said, her tone not quite as stern.

"Yes, yes I suppose I am," he agreed while two more beads of sweat drained from his temple. "After all, the prince is quite a handsome man."

At one time Grace would have agreed. Though Isidor was polished and well-mannered, he, too, was prettier than many of the ladies of the *ton* who worked for countless hours to make themselves beautiful. His stature was more akin to Napoleon than it was to the Duke of Wellington—*or to Laird Frasier Buchanan.*

"I want to understand more about your love affair. How long have you known Isidor?" she asked.

"Years, actually." Alder carefully dabbed the perspiration from his forehead like a doddering old woman. "We attended Oxford together."

Grace wanted to rip the handkerchief from the man's fingertips and wipe his face with one hearty swipe as Frasier would do. "You roomed with Isidor, did you not?"

A slight nod confirmed her suspicions. So, her husband had been having a love affair with Alder since they were boys. She should have known. When she was about the age of twelve, Grace had found a book in her father's library about Marcus Aurelius who as a lad, it claimed, had fallen in love with his male tutor. On top of that, since her coming out, she had heard rumors of ill-reputed dens hidden in London's East End where men who happened to be attracted to other men enjoyed mingling, even though such intimacies were strictly against the law.

"Are you acquainted with many fellows who have your same...predilection regarding the gender of their affection?"

He smirked, neatly folding his handkerchief. "I do like your phrasing, Princess." Returning it to his inner pocket, he cleared his throat. "To answer your question, yes. Though I cannot and will not admit to anything further."

Grace finally took a seat and gestured to a chair, opposite. "Did Isidor ever speak to you about me?"

Alder sat and crossed his legs—a fribbling fop. "Indeed."

"But he loves you and not me?"

The lordling remained quiet for a moment, studying her as if deciding whether or not to answer. "Surely you did not expect your marriage to be a love match?"

No, she hadn't. But she had rather foolishly expected a modicum of faithfulness, if not hoped for her husband to eventually fall in love with her. "Why did he marry me?"

"Isn't it plain enough?" He smirked, the lout. "Isidor desperately needs an heir or else upon his death his title will be forfeit to the Russian crown. You are the vessel he chose to be the mother of his children."

Good heavens, Grace had just been reduced to a vessel—not a woman with feelings, a woman who deserved respect, and care, if not love. "Are you aware that the prince referred to me as a self-serving wench?"

Alder had the audacity to laugh. "Did he?"

"You find his insult humorous?"

"I have known Isidor for a very long time. Though he is generous, he is the most self-serving man I know. There is a great deal of irony in his accusation for certain."

Alder's words hung heavily in the air as if tightening Grace's stays.

"So, you have been appointed to ferry me to the Baltic Sea?" she asked, changing the subject.

"Yes."

"Have you been to Lithuania before?"

"I have."

"What if Dunscaby prefers for me to make the voyage aboard one of my brother's ships?"

"Isidor has made it clear that he does not want assistance from His Grace or Captain MacGalloway."

Her gaze narrowed. Perhaps Martin had paid her dowry, else Isidor mightn't be so bent on keeping her brothers away?

Pity that.

"Imagine yourself in my predicament for a moment. If you were me, the sister of a duke who had no fewer than eleven proposals of marriage in her first Season, how would you opt to proceed?"

Alder examined his fingernails. "I believe you have no choice in the matter, especially since the entire kingdom was made aware of your esteemed wedding. Though somewhat of an egoist, Isidor isn't exactly tyrannical. Once you are with child and produce a male heir, I would wager he'll leave you to your own devices as long as you remain discreet."

Mama had said the same, aside from the discreet

part. With Grace's next blink, she imagined inviting Frasier to visit her at a country estate. But as soon as the thought entered her mind, she knew it would never be. Frasier was an honorable man. He would not sail to the continent to engage in an illicit affair even if he did love her. And she ought to not wish him to compromise his values.

His Lordship stood. "I shall send word as soon as the prince's ship arrives in the Pool of London." He took her hand and gently kissed it. "I do hope you and I can become amicable. You might find I am a good ally to have."

Grace drew her hand away and gave a humorless nod. She waited until Alder took his leave before she wiped the remnants of his kiss away. Becoming friends with that man was akin to charming a snake. Anything she might tell him in confidence would doubtless make its way to Isidor within the blink of an eye.

But there was no time to think about Lord Alder now. As the lordling's barouche rolled away, the Duke of Dunscaby's carriage approached from the opposite direction.

19

F rasier's heart sank when the approaching two pairs of footsteps clapped the stone floor too heavily to be feminine. His back stung from the burn of the lashings, making it difficult to do anything including breathe. Every time he took a deep breath, he swore bleeding fissures opened.

Since he'd been arrested, he had been visited by a doctor who'd bled him, which served to make him feel weak as well as worsen the pain. The man hadn't given him anything to help ease Frasier's discomfort, or even bothered to use a salve on his welts.

Aside from the doctor, he'd seen no one except the guards who brought his meager meals. He wasn't a man who needed to constantly be around people, but there was one very bonny lass he craved to see again regardless if she was married to another. God save him, every time he closed his eyes he saw Grace. He breathed in her scent. He sensed her nearby.

Even though she was not physically present, Frasier imagined her there beside him, whispering that everything would be all right, whispering such lovely things he dare not believe them. Damn her marriage. Damn him for loving her. Damn London and damn this bloody cell.

The key screeched in the lock and then the door opened, revealing the imposing form of the Duke of Dunscaby, his expression grave. He stepped inside, eyeing Frasier with his vivid blue eyes as the door slammed closed behind him. "Ye look like shite."

Still sitting on the bed, Frasier glanced down his bare torso to his beltless kilt. "Feel it as well."

Martin sidestepped, craning his neck to look at Frasier's back. "My sister told me you were given a dozen lashes."

He turned so the duke wouldn't be able to see the damages. "Aye."

"If I were in the Chancellor of the Exchequer's shoes, I would have given you more."

Frasier stood, his legs weak, but he gritted his teeth and looked eye-to-eye with the man who had been his boyhood friend, and now posed his only hope for freedom. "Dammit, Your Grace, I didna take anything!"

Martin stared, his lips pursed. "Exactly why could you not wait for me before you barged into Flint Tower and started rummaging about?"

"I didna ken ye would be away to Brighton when I arrived in London."

"Only for a matter of days. You could have done anything—seen the sights, enjoyed a pint at the Fox and Hounds, taken a stroll along the Thames, done a spot of shopping along Piccadilly or Bond Street."

Frasier shrugged, the movement stinging like a thousand angry hornets. "I did go to The Royal Menagerie."

"Housed in the Tower of London. How convenient. The guards didna even have to transport you to prison."

"I dunna why they arrested me. As I said afore, I had no intention of removing anything from Flint Tower."

"I suppose you also had no intention of picking the lock either?"

Frasier groaned and rubbed the back of his neck, which had been spared from the whip's tongue. "The Horn of Bannockburn is among that pile of rubble, I can feel it in me bones."

"Dammit man, if you had used the brains God gave you, it would have been clear your chances of seeing your bloody horn were far greater had you not picked the lock of a royal tower." Dunscaby threw out his arms. "Everything in Flint Tower was seized by the crown—it was forfeit to the king years ago. Those relics are the property of His Majesty until they are auctioned."

Frasier did not care for the duke's change of mind. "But you told me some of my kin's relics might be returned if I asked politely."

"Aye, that was before you were caught snooping around inside a chamber holding a portion of the king's treasure."

"So now what?" Frasier looked at the clan's motto carved into the stone by his grandfather and rubbed his fingers across his throat. "Am I to suffer the same fate as my grandfather just because I was born a Buchanan? Because I foolishly thought I might gain a pardon for my clan so that we may freely move about the kingdom without fear of retribution or arrest?"

"I told you I would help, did I not?"

"Aye, but ye marched in here as if I'd broken into the His Majesty's Treasury."

"Dunna ye understand? You *did* break into His Majesty's Treasury—at least a wee part of it. And now it will be all the more difficult to secure a pardon for you and your clan."

Frasier raked his fingers through his hair. "Bleeding, bloody hell. The only thing I want is the Horn of Bannockburn given to the Seventh Chieftain of Buchanan by Robert the Bruce. It canna be worth much to the crown, but it is a priceless treasure to me kin."

"Verra well. Mayhap you ought to use that as your excuse for your wee lockpicking adventure—at least the part about it having little value."

"What if I'm wrong? What if it isna in that pile of rubbish?"

"If it is, the Chancellor's clerks will have added it to the manifest."

"And then what?"

"I told you everything is to be auctioned."

Frasier shook his head, recalling the assortment of rusty weapons. Who would want them? And why must his name carry with it unmitigated bad luck? "How long am I to be held in this cell?"

"Actually, that is where I have a smattering of good news. I was able to have a word with the Regent before I spoke to the Chancellor—mind you had it been the other way around, the outcome would have been far different."

Frasier nodded, his spirits lifting a tad. "So-o-o?"

"Because you indeed did not attempt to remove anything from Flint Tower and were discovered empty handed, you are to be released into my care. Because I have vouched for your honesty and sincerity, two days hence the Prince of Wales has agreed to allow me to present you—with armed guards, mind you."

Frasier grasped Dunscaby's forearm while the

weight of an anvil lifted from his shoulders. "Ye did it?"

Martin nearly grinned. "I promised I would."

"Thank you. I am indebted to you."

"You are not out of trouble yet, my friend. I am now responsible for your whereabouts and you'd best heed me: You are not allowed to set foot outside my town house. And I expect you to apologize for your antics."

"But all I did was look."

"Tell that to Prinny. You are to have his attention for no more than five minutes and whatever you say must manifest great impact and effect."

What the hell can a man like me say to move the Prince Regent?

Dunscaby looked at the rickety bed, now stained with Frasier's blood. "Now tell me true, you're as pale as bed linens, are you well enough to walk out of here?"

"Give me a dirk and a targe and I'll fight my way out if need be."

"I dunna advise it." The duke clapped Frasier's shoulder—his fingers brushing a tender spot. "Gather your things, I'd like to arrive home before the evening meal."

Frasier winced. "All I own is on my person. They cut off my shirt and coat to issue my punishment. And the guards took my weapons. I'd like to have them back."

"I tasked Angus with the retrieval of your dirk and *sgian dubh*. He will meet us at the carriage where we also have a clean shirt at the ready." Dunscaby opened the door. "Shall we?"

As Frasier walked past, the duke grunted. "My God, Buchanan, your back looks like minced meat."

"Feels like it as well." He smirked over his shoulder. "Not to worry. I'll survive."

WHEN GRACE DISCOVERED Martin was bringing Frasier back to the town house, she surreptitiously suggested to the duchess that Buchanan might feel more welcome if he were seated beside her during the evening meal. Julia had thought it an excellent idea especially since (as Grace had pointed out) Frasier had saved her from certain death after her carriage had careened off the cliff and then he had been so kind as to take her in during the height of winter in the Highlands.

Except at seven o'clock when everyone had assembled in the drawing room for the evening meal, Frasier had not yet come downstairs.

When the clock struck half seven, Martin offered one elbow to Mama and the other to Julia. "Let us go in. Buchanan can join us in the dining hall."

"M'lady," said Angus, presenting his arm to Grace.

She took it with a smile. The man had yet to refer to her as Your Highness for which she was grateful. "Are you certain Buchanan is well enough to come to dinner?"

"He's hurting for certain but if I ken Frasier, he'll no' be passing up a good meal."

Eleven places had been set at the dining table. Gibb was there, of course. Charity had come with her husband the Earl of Brixham and his sister Kitty. Regardless, everyone in attendance was part of the Mac-Galloway family aside from Angus and Frasier (once he joined them).

"How was Brighton?" asked Brixham as he held the chair for his wife.

Martin gave his duchess a knowing grin. Grace had heard of Prinny's outlandish affairs at the Royal Pavilion, though she had never been. Word was the palace had been decorated with extravagant chinoiserie and though it was undergoing an expansion, the prince hosted outrageously lavish dinners in his banquet room.

"If Grace hadn't summoned us back to London," said the duke, "I'm afraid my tailor would have been forced to let out all my waistcoats."

"I understand the prince served forty entrees when the King of Spain visited from the continent," said Grace. Yes, she had been duly impressed at the news—a bit jealous as well. How foolish she had been, always so impressed by wealth and status.

"Well, I lost count whilst sitting with those dragons staring down at me from the chandelier, but I do not think we were presented with quite forty entrees. Though I did have to pace myself," said Julia. "We started with eight soups, then several removes of fish, followed fowl, roasts, entrees..." She looked at Martin at the other end of the table. "I recall fifteen desserts?"

"Sixteen, and then we had the great rounds with Madeira."

Modesty coughed and patted her chest. "My heavens, it would have taken an entire day to eat all that food."

"Believe me, it was well past midnight when the men withdrew for their cigars and brandy." Julia sat back while a footman filled her wineglass. "I've always been more of an early bird. I daresay it was all I could do to stay awake long enough to find my bedchamber."

The slot door slid open and Frasier stepped inside, moving rather stiffly. He was wearing an oversized coat atop his shirt and neckcloth, his hair damp and neatly clubbed back as usual. A mahogany lock hung down beside his cheek as if it had been hastily tied. "Please forgive my tardiness."

The men began to stand, but he held up his hands, urging them to remain as they were. "No need for formalities." His gaze shifted to Grace. It was but a brief shift of the eyes, but the emotion in his, one glimpse was enough to set her heart afire.

She smiled with a slight lift of her chin. "Buchanan, you are in fine form after your ordeal. I was afraid you'd be unable to join us."

"Aye, m'laird," Modesty agreed. "How is your back? Does it hurt awfully?"

Of course, when the men had arrived, Grace had watched from the upstairs parlor window. Frasier had gingerly stepped down from the carriage and followed Martin and Angus into the house, his shoulders hunched as if the shirt touching his wounds caused him great pain. From within her bedchamber, she had listened to the footmen as they'd toted heavy pails of water for his bath. Desperately, she had yearned to tiptoe through the corridor and tap on his door—inquire as to how his wounds were healing, offer to apply a soothing salve—ask for a kiss.

However, even within the confines of her family's home, she was not free to do so.

"I shall be soon set to rights," he said, settling into his chair, though not sitting back. "I hope I have not made you wait overlong."

"Not at all, the first course has yet to be served," said Julia as the footmen placed bowls of curried chicken soup in front of each person.

Angus did not wait for Her Grace to take the first

bite but dug in and smacked his lips. "Och, a man could grow accustomed to this fare. 'Tis delicious."

Smiling and seeming unconcerned with the fellow's manners, Julia took a dainty spoonful. "I shall pass your felicitations on to the cook."

"Has there been any news regarding Prince Isidor?" asked Martin looking between Grace and Gibb.

As the sea captain shook his head, Grace cringed. "Actually, Lord Alder paid me a visit yesterday morning right before you arrived from Brighton."

"Why was I not informed?" Gibb demanded as if he were the all-powerful captain on one of his ships.

"How could you have been? You had gone to bring your brother home," said Mama. "And Grace would not allow me to sit in. A fact which I cannot understand."

"Exactly," Martin agreed. "Why the devil did you meet with Alder alone?"

"I am no longer a debutante who must be chaperoned at all times." Grace daintily spooned a bit of soup. "Besides, I wanted to ask him a few questions in confidence."

Mama signaled to a footman to top up her wineglass. "I can hardly imagine what you would want to say to that fiend."

Well, with half of her family present along with Angus and Frasier, Grace wasn't going to admit to being curious about men who behaved like Marcus Aurelius. First of all, the book she had found had been in Papa's locked cabinet. She had never been intended to read it. "Alder told me little, except that he and Isidor roomed together at Oxford and had been acquainted for years."

"Why did he come to call?" asked Julia, her tone far more curious than accusatory.

Grace regarded Frasier out of the corner of her eye. If only His Lairdship weren't here at the moment, it would be easier to discuss the topic at hand. "He came to inform me that Isidor had requested Alder act as my escort during the voyage to Lithuania."

"I'll be damned if I'll allow that!" Martin said, earning a sharp clearing of the throat from his wife. "Well," he rephrased, "if Isidor has appointed Alder, then you shall require a battalion of armed guards."

"I'll take her with a ship full of fighting men," Gibb growled.

"Enough posturing," said Mama as she spooned her last bite of soup. "Perhaps my daughter needs one armed guard and I would think a lady's maid as well as a female companion who will share the same berth."

Grace continued to observe Frasier out of the corner of her eye while the soup bowls were removed and the entrées of rabbit pie on a bed of laurel and sauteed pheasant in foie gras sauce were served. The only sign that the present conversation caused him consternation was the twitching of his jaw.

Across the table, Modesty's blue eyes sparked with a flicker of candlelight—or else a flicker of mischief. "I will go! I'd love to see the continent and I'm quite a good markswoman. I've been practicing I'll have you know."

Grace didn't bother to reply to her sister. If the imp shared a berth with her there would be no peace from the incessant chatter.

"Regardless, I will sail out the Thames right behind the prince's ship," said Gibb.

"But Isidor was clear that you are not to accompany me," Grace replied.

"'Tis just posturing. Since the prince is too milk-livered to fetch you himself, he'll be too milk-livered to take on an eighteen-gun barque," said Frasier, earning a dark scowl from Martin.

Brixham sliced his pheasant. "I say, Gibb, is Isidor afraid you'll incite a war? Surely, he's not about to be the first to fire his cannons."

Forever the rugged sea captain, Gibb smirked. "Aye, he'd best be afraid."

Mama, sitting across from Grace at the table's center clapped her hands. "I daresay before this conversation degrades further and the lot of you start scheming about wars and blasting Gibb's canons, let us speak of more amiable subjects."

Silence fell over the dining hall, cut only by the sounds of silverware tapping china plates, which continued until the dessert was served.

"Since Kitty and I will be coming out next Season, we would like to propose we spend the remainder of the evening dancing," Modesty suggested as Kitty grasped her arm and giggled.

Though Martin frowned, Mama beamed. "I think that is an excellent idea." She turned to the butler. "Giles, you will play the pianoforte for us if you please."

"I would be delighted, madam." He looked to Julia and cleared his throat. "That is unless you'd prefer to play, Your Grace."

Shaking her head, Julia dabbed her lips with a serviette. "If I were to play, I wouldn't be able to dance with my husband now would I? I do so prefer private gatherings at home where I can have the duke all to myself."

Frasier turned his lips toward Grace's ear. "Will you dance with me?"

His Lairdship's whisper was barely audible, but the warmth of his breath made tingles skitter up the sensitive part of her neck right beneath her earlobe. The corners of her mouth turned up slightly as she gave him a subtle nod. If only they were alone, she would wrap her arms around his neck and beg to dance only with him every night until she had to sail away to pay her penance.

"Mama," Charity said with a bite of apple and rum pudding balanced on her fork. "You must dance as well."

The dowager frowned. "I'm afraid my dancing days are over."

"Hogwash," said Gibb. "I shall dance with you."

"But there are five men and six women present," said Mama. "Not to worry, I enjoy watching my children more than anything."

"I agree with Gibb," said Grace. "Tearlach can partner with Kitty as he does during rehearsals, and Mama can dance with our illustrious sea captain. After all, his wife is still in Edinburgh."

"Do you miss Isabella awfully?" asked Modesty, forever the dramatic one.

"I do," Gibb replied. "And I am looking forward to sailing home and staying there for a fortnight or two. I'm actually leaving on the morrow, but I shall return to accompany Isidor's ship, not to worry."

The footmen must have made quick work of lighting the chandeliers in the ballroom because the hall glowed as resplendently as it did when the duke hosted dances. Though there hadn't been time for décor. The rather middling hall appeared quite large with only chairs lining the walls and a mere eleven people in attendance.

Over the years, Grace had spent many hours in this very room with Charity and Modesty as they learned to dance. And once Charity had married Brixham, Kitty often joined them. The music played by the butler was more familiar than anything she ever danced to at the dozens of balls she'd attended during her Season.

Oddly, Frasier had never asked her to dance while she was out, not that he had many opportunities to do so. But now she had not only danced with him at Druimliart, she stood across from him as everyone clapped and laughed, dancing one country dance after another. Since this was a family affair, laughing out loud was permissible. Even the Dowager Duchess threw her head back and howled as Gibb swung her in a circle.

After the reel, Giles played a fanfare, then loudly cleared his throat. "A waltz."

Grace glanced at her mother who only a handful of years ago had condemned waltzing as vulgar and uncivilized. Though now that Mama had ushered two daughters through two Seasons and was preparing to introduce Modesty, she said not a word as she curtseyed to her son and stepped into position.

When Frasier took Grace's hand, his eyes shone with his smile. "I canna recall ever seeing your mother enjoy herself so."

Grace stepped nearer, reminding herself not to touch his back. "Honestly, I cannot either. In fact, I've rarely seen her dance since Papa passed."

"Has she…"

"Hmm?"

"Had gentleman callers?" he whispered.

Grace resisted the urge to scoff. "My mother? Oh, no. She is far too busy ordering her children about to entertain callers, especially those of the male persuasion."

"She has been a widow for how long now, seven years?"

"Aye," Grace said, forgetting herself and allowing the Scottish affirmative to slip.

"Do you not worry that she might be lonely?"

In truth, she'd never considered that her mother might want to remarry—or have a rendezvous with a gentleman. However, once Modesty married, Mama would have little with which to occupy her time.

"You are right," Grace replied, feeling quite remiss for her lack of concern. She didn't like that she had been so self-absorbed before her life had spun out of control. "Upon reflection I think my mother ought to put some thought into attending soirees for her own benefit."

Giles played the introduction to a slow waltz and together they danced, Frasier leading her through the intricate steps as if with ease, but as soon as she shifted her gaze to his face, she stopped dancing. "My word, you are quite pale. Are you feeling poorly?"

"I'm a wee bit weary, lass. The exhaustion set in when prison's doctor bled me." Frasier pressed his hand against her back, urging her to resume the waltz, though he curled forward, his head nearly bending all the way to her shoulder. "This shall be my last dance of the evening."

"No, this is but a family gathering if you need to rest then—"

Frasier fell forward, straight into Grace's arms. "Buchanan? Are you well?" she asked again, staining to hold his bulk upright.

The music stopped.

"Good God!" shouted Martin as he and all of the other men in the ballroom rushed to their aid.

Angus arrived first and slid beneath Frasier's arm, looping it across his shoulders while Brixham took to other side. "I told him to take a tray in his room, but he wouldna listen to the likes of me."

Grace hardly heard the man as she pressed her hand against Frasier's forehead. "He's burning with fever. We must take him to his bedchamber straightaway."

"Giles," said Martin as he and Gibb each took one of Frasier's legs. "Send for my physician at once!"

20

The duke's physician was away in the country and Grace had never met the fellow who came in his stead. In her opinion, the new doctor was too young and appeared to be far too inexperienced to treat Frasier. Nonetheless, after Martin and Angus went into Frasier's bedchamber with the doctor, she stood outside the slightly cracked door, wringing her hands and turning her ear toward the gap to better hear what the doctor was saying.

"His wounds are beginning to fester," said the man.

"Can you heal him? Have you a salve?" asked Martin.

"I shall leave a preparation of blackberry vinegar and grapeseed oil. 'Tis the best thing I know of to treat the infection."

Grace nudged the door slightly to allow her to see inside as well as listen. Frasier sprawled awkwardly atop the mattress, laying on his stomach.

The physician reached into his black leather bag and withdrew a tin bowl along with a tied leather parcel—she'd seen such a parcel before, the type doctors used in which to stow their lancets. "I'll need to bleed him to help ward off the fever."

"Absolutely not!" Grace said, giving up on her efforts to remain discrete and marching inside. Though she herself had been bled when she was fevered, it had done nothing to help whatsoever. And clear in her memory was not too long ago she had helped Fiona reduce Aggie's fever with the use of snow and a cold bath—not bleeding, even though Fiona had applied leeches. Perhaps there was no snow to be found in London on the first of April, though they could send for a block of ice. But first she needed to stop this man from killing His Lairdship. "Only moments before Buchanan collapsed he informed me that the bleeding he'd suffered whilst incarcerated in the Tower had done nothing but make him feel weaker."

Martin slipped the leather parcel from the physician's grasp. "Och, she has a point, sir. I also had a wee peek at his bed linens at the Tower and he did lose a fair bit of blood."

"I should have been told all of this straightaway, Your Grace," said the physician, his nostrils flaring as he tugged down his coat. "And I might add that if this man is a criminal, what, pray tell, is he doing in your home?"

"He was wrongfully imprisoned," Grace said, tipping up her chin.

Martin returned the doctor's lancets and bowl, depositing them into the man's black bag. "His arrest was a misunderstanding."

"Aye," said Angus, though when both Grace and Martin gaped at him sternly, the highlander closed his mouth.

"So..." Grace began counting on her fingers. "I believe Lard Buchanan requires icy cold cloths applied to his forehead to help bring down the fever; secondly, he needs a saline draught made from willow bark boiled in white wine; and thirdly, I agree with your suggestion of regular applications of blackberry vinegar in a grapeseed oil tincture."

"You agree?" asked the doctor, the color of his face turning scarlet. "I'll tell you here and now, young lady—"

"She is a princess," said Martin with a ducal air. "And I suggest you treat my sister with her due respect."

This was a most inappropriate occasion for pride, but at the moment, Grace appreciated her title for the first time since her wedding day. She assumed the most commanding stance she could muster given she was quite a bit shorter than everyone in the chamber.

"I beg your pardon, Your Highness," said the doctor, with an irreverent bow. "Are you not the sister who married the Lithuanian prince?"

Oh, dear, perhaps her feelings of pridefulness were premature. "I am," she said with her most radiant smile. It was time to employ her ruse. "I recently returned from the continent to comfort my sister who we believed was with child, but once I arrived, she learned that she had been merely suffering from a bout of biliousness."

"Very well. Since the patient has been recently bled, I shall leave you with the salve." He turned to Martin. "I take it your household is equipped with a saline draught?"

"We are," Grace answered. Though they most likely had the willow bark tonic in the kitchen, she also had a full bottle in her medicine chest which had been replaced after being ruined in the carriage accident.

"Well, then I believe there is no more to be done here as long as you have someone to tend him. A competent soul must sit up with him and notify me if his condition worsens."

"Of course, we shall take excellent care of His Lairdship." Grace gave her brother a pointed stare, silently requesting he not argue. "We have a house full of servants," she added, though she had no intention of allowing anyone near Frasier's bedside.

The physician collected his bag and walked with Martin toward the door. Though Angus followed, Grace opted to remain where she stood.

"Buchanan must meet with the Prince Regent the day after tomorrow," said Martin as they moved into the corridor.

"Oh, no," the doctor replied. "I doubt this chap will be out of bed for at least a week, perhaps a fortnight."

Grace gasped when one of Frasier's fingers brushed the back of her hand. Though still quite pale, he turned his head far enough to wink at her. "I'll up by the morrow, mark me."

As the men continued away, Grace turned her attention to Frasier. "How long have you been awake?" she whispered but he did not reply, his eyes again closed.

Though when he'd come to dinner his hair was clubbed back, it had come loose and she smoothed it away from his face, his skin still much too warm to the touch. "'Tis best if you sleep now, my love."

AFTER GRACE SENT Tearlach to collect everything Frasier needed, Martin returned and sauntered inside the bedchamber. "You should not still be here."

She had little doubt her brother, her mother, and three quarters of the household would object to her plan but they'd have to first put her in shackles and drag her away screaming. She was going to tend Frasier and she would entertain no arguments. "How quickly you forget this man pulled me from a devastating carriage wreck in the midst of a blizzard and saved my life."

Martin crossed his arms. "I have forgotten nothing."

"Well, if you think for one minute that I will leave Buchanan's care in the hands of someone else, you are gravely mistaken."

"Is that why you so quickly dismissed the physician? Because you believe yourself far more capable than a man who has studied medicine at Oxford?"

"You misstep!" Grace dunked a cloth in the bowl and wrung it out. "The esteemed doctor was preparing to bleed Frasier. Had I not intervened when I did, your dear friend would be the worse for wear."

"So now you are referring to him by the familiar?"

She shook the damp cloth beneath her brother's nose. "Bless it, Marty, why are you fighting me on this? Who gives a fig if I referred to Buchanan by his given name?"

"If you dunna care, you certainly ought to."

"Why? Because my husband has sent for me and I must provide him an heir? My life is in a shambles and no one can fix it. I *shall* sit by Buchanan's side and apply cool cloths until he wakes—which I pray is in time for his meeting with the regent."

"You heard the doctor. Buchanan will not be able to meet with Prinny as planned."

"Though he opened his eyes long enough to refute him."

"Regardless of what the laird might have done, on the morrow I shall ask the regent's secretary to reschedule."

Pursing her lips, Grace turned toward the hearth. "I do not need to tell you that gaining a pardon for the Buchanan name has been his life's dream."

"I ken. Most likely better than you."

Yes, Marty was Frasier's friend long before Grace had ended up in the laird's cottage but her brother had no idea she had fallen in love. That she would protect Frasier Buchanan with her life. Rather than turning around and confessing all, she closed her eyes and drew in a deep breath.

Martin placed a firm hand on her shoulder. "You have feelings for him."

Her shoulders shook as she fought the urge to sob. If she denied his statement, the duke would see straight through her. "So what if I do? It is not as if Isidor cares one way or another." With another deep breath, she faced him. "Yes, I have developed a fondness for His Lairdship and he for me."

Martin's heated gaze darted to the bed. "Did he take advantage of you?"

"No!" She thwacked her brother's arm with the wet cloth. "No, no, no' you assuming numpty! Frasier Buchanan would never importune me. Never! And if you do not realize it, then you truly do not know the man as well as you think you do!"

Rubbing his arm, Martin's expression softened. "Och, sister. Ye're no' so bad with a wet facecloth."

"Stop." Had circumstances been less dire, she might have laughed, but instead she asked, "Tell me something, if you please..."

He nodded.

"When Isidor atoned to the Archbishop, you told

Frasier," she lowered her voice to imitate him, "'*The fight isna over by half.*' What did you mean? Please tell me you have a plan to thwart the fiend."

Martin began pacing. "I wish I did. One of the reasons I went to Brighton was because The Archbishop of Canterbury was there, which gave me an opportunity to speak to him away from the cathedral, man-to-man."

"Oh?" she asked while a stone sank to the pit of her stomach.

"I'm afraid to say he refused to budge on the matter."

She placed the cloth onto Frasier's head as best she could considering he was on his stomach. "Even though you are a duke?"

"Aye, well, Isidor is a prince. But His Grace behaved as though our request for an annulment was a personal affront because he presided over the ceremony."

"Unbelievable. Did you explain we caught my newly married husband in the act of..." She couldn't say it.

"I did. That was when he suggested Isidor atone for his sins."

"Yes, of course. Why would he need to do so otherwise?" As tears dribbled from her eyes, Grace withdrew a handkerchief from her sleeve. "So that is it. In five weeks' time I have no choice but to board Isidor's ship and sail to my doom."

As she realized she had been counting down the days, this being number thirty-five, Grace was cut to the quick by the reality of how little time she had left until she must walk the proverbial plank. A cry pealed from her throat.

"Och, Grace." Martin pulled her into his arms and

kissed the top of her head. "Of all my sisters you are the most stalwart, industrious, and—"

"Self-serving?" she sobbed.

"I didna say that. But you do always find a way to be utterly remarkable at everything to which you apply yourself. And I shall tell you right now, if Isidor does not perform his marital duties or if he in any way mistreats you, I shall personally send a fleet of ships to escort you home."

"But why do I have to go in the first place?"

"Ye ken why." He took a step back and held her shoulders at arms' length. "You promised to love and obey the prince. And he promised to love and protect you and he upheld that promise through his apology to the Archbishop of Canterbury."

"But he called me a self-serving wench."

"Though he changed it to young lady. However the fact that he even wrote the slight wasna nice, which is another reason for Gibb to be sailing behind Isidor's ship and seeing to it that you are well settled before he returns home." Martin grimaced. "Besides, God save us all, Modesty will be introduced at court next Season. She deserves the same chances you had to find her match."

"I am aware, and you have my word I will do nothing to damage our sister's reputation."

BY THE TIME Tearlach returned with all Grace had requested, it was after midnight. Most everyone in the family had stopped by Frasier's bedchamber to check on him and to express how deeply sorry they were that he had been treated so poorly by the chancellor and the king's guards. Of course, Mama had tried to talk Grace into permitting one of the housemaids to sit at Buchanan's bedside.

That he saved her life was a convenient excuse to insist on holding vigil. But Grace would have stood up to anyone who tried to persuade her otherwise, even the dratted Archbishop of Canterbury.

For hours, she chatted softly while continually changing the cool cloths. Early on, Tearlach had brought up a bucket with a block of ice in a bit of water. Thank the stars it was still cold, and it hadn't melted. Since she could only reach half of his forehead, she opted to cover his entire head with the cloths. She also cooled his legs and his shoulders while applying the blackberry vinegar tincture to his wounds.

Every time she applied it, Frasier's welts turned angry red.

What she found most difficult was feeding him the saline draft of willow bark boiled in white wine. When two teaspoons slid over his tongue and out the corner of his mouth onto the pillow, Grace sipped it herself and, holding it in her mouth, she took his head between her hands and turned his lips upward just enough for her to feed him.

When his Adam's apple moved, she nearly danced for joy. If only she could shower him with kisses. But her elation was short lived. As the hours passed, it was clear his fever was still raging.

The ice had melted down to a chunk the size of her fist, but the water was still cold. She gathered a pile of clean cloths and doused each one, carefully placing them as before, but this time, she draped two over his back.

Frasier moaned and shifted.

She moved to his legs and removed his stockings,

placing cold cloths over his calves. Her gaze meandered to his thighs, peppered with dark hair, his kilt hitched halfway up.

No, she mustn't go any farther. His fever would come down. It had to.

"When you arrived at Stack Castle for Mama's house party, I had to force myself not to look at you or I would have fallen in love with the wrong man...or the right man, as it turns out. I endeavored to ignore you in my haughty way, showering Isidor with all the attention I could manage." Grace sat in the chair beside the bed, her eyelids heavy. "During the party I overheard Marty telling Mama that you had come to find a bride and..."

Grace didn't finish her sentence. It hurt too much. Besides, she should not be overjoyed that no woman caught his fancy at the house party. How terribly selfish of her to even think it.

"At the ball, I was secretly relieved that you didn't ask to sign my dance card." She moved the cloth so she could gaze upon his ruggedly dark features. "I suppose I should say I was secretly relieved as well as incensed. You may think I didn't notice, but every time you were present at a gathering where there was dancing, you did go out of your way to avoid me. Was that because you are Martin's good friend, or because you were...?"

She didn't utter the words, "afraid of me," because she couldn't imagine Frasier being afraid of anything, especially her. Besides, she had always reasoned he didn't dance with her because he was beneath her station.

How utterly thoughtless of me to believe myself superior.

"I am not superior." She stroked his cheek, loving

the coarseness of his dark stubble. "My past behavior shames me."

"It shouldna," he whispered, his voice barely audible. "To me ye have always been a princess...a queen... a goddess." He drew out every compliment as if uttering them sapped him of his strength.

Shocked, Grace leaned in and placed her hand on Frasier's forehead. It was still warm, but if she wasn't wrong, he may have cooled a bit. "Are you awake?"

When he did not answer, she doubled her efforts, draping cold cloths over him, applying the tincture, and feeding him the saline draught from her own mouth. She rang for more ice and by the time the sun rose, Frasier's color was not quite so pale, and though the fever hadn't entirely broken, he was definitely cooler to the touch.

21

Not long after dawn, Angus slipped into the bedchamber and insisted she rest. She slept until noon after which she went straight back to Frasier's bedside where she read to him, talked to him, and tended his wounds with utmost care.

She had hoped Frasier's fever would be short lived, but the laird did not speak lucidly again for three days. His sleep was fitful and he oft tried to roll to his back which brought on agonizing shrieks of pain.

On the third day, as Grace applied the tincture to His Lairdship's welts, she was heartened to see the wounds were not as swollen, nor were they as warm to the touch. "Frasier?" she asked, holding her breath while listening to the rain ping against the windowpane. When he didn't answer, she continued, carefully applying the tincture. "It would be ever so reassuring if you would open your eyes today."

After a knock on the door, Modesty popped her head inside. "May I come in?"

Grace nodded, assessing the lass as she tiptoed across the floor. Though her sister's freckles were endearing, neither her red hair nor her freckly face was fashionable. She also had opted to stay at home with her governess rather than attend Northbourne Seminary for Young Ladies. Unfortunately, all three strikes against her would make it difficult for the lass to find a match even if she had a sizeable dowry.

If only I looked like Modesty as well, I never would have ended up married to Isidor.

"Tell me something that will make me smile," she said, desperate for a moment of respite from her worries.

The lass leaned against a bedpost. "I believe Marigold is pregnant."

"Modesty, how gauche!" Grace scolded, though she did chuckle.

"Leave it to Marty to give me a mare who has been covered. We've only just started to develop a mutual understanding for each other and soon I willna be able to ride her."

"Are you certain she's going to have a foal?"

"Either that or she's eating too much hay."

"How old is she?"

Modesty leaned over the bed while she examined Frasier's wounds. "Ten years of age."

"And she's well-broke?"

"Aye. Our brother would never allow me to ride through Hyde Park on a spirited mare."

"My dearest, all mares are spirited."

"Wheesht," Modesty cupped a hand beside her mouth. "Let it be our wee secret."

Grace put the stopper back into the bottle and set it on the bedside table. "So, to what do I owe the honor of your visit? Do you not have fittings today? Planning a jaunt to the haberdashery?"

"That's later." Modesty gripped her hands behind her back and swayed in place. "I have a couple of things to ask if you dunna mind."

"Oh?" Grace led her sister to the window embrasure where they sat facing each other. "Is something troubling you?"

"Aye...a great many things." Modesty's red eyebrows slanted over her bright blue eyes. "But first. I want to say I've been watching you of late, and I reckon you've changed."

"Me?"

"Mmm-hmm, you Grace Eloise, and dunna deny it. Afore you went to the lodge, you would have told me mind my own affairs had I stopped to ask you a few questions."

"I would not."

"I beg to differ. Come now, sister. You've always enjoyed snubbing me at every turn. At least you used to, but now I'm not so certain." Modesty picked a bit of lint from Grace's shoulder. "And what I dunna understand is why."

Sighing, Grace regarded the injured highlander sleeping atop the bed. "Perhaps my predicament has made me see myself in a different light."

Modesty snapped both fingers as her expression brightened. "I kent it. I kent there had to be a silver lining in all this mess."

Grace didn't agree. Her affairs were dangling precariously. "Would it make you feel better if I apologized for tormenting you all those years?"

"Are you truly regretful?"

Grace narrowed her gaze. Knowing Modesty, if she admitted her remorse, in recompense there would be some unbearable task attached, which she neither had the time nor inclination to do. "Perhaps now that we're grown, we ought to start anew."

Rather than show exuberance, the lass cringed as if she wasn't convinced she wanted all that came with becoming an adult. Perhaps that was another reason Mama had postponed her come out for a year. "Grown. I can hardly believe it."

"So, tell me," Grace said, nabbing the opportunity to shift to a different topic. "What has you worried?"

Modesty glanced out the rain-splattered window, a deep furrow in her brow. "I feel awful. 'Tis my fault His Lairdship collapsed."

Grace not only smiled, it was all she could do to hold in a snicker. "Why would you say such a thing?"

"Well, it was my idea for us all to dance after the evening meal."

"I assure you, dancing had nothing to do with his illness. Though the vigorous activity may have precipitated his collapse, Buchanan's wounds were already beginning to fester. He was—*is*—very ill as oft happens when a man is savagely whipped."

Modesty twirled a ringlet around her finger—a habit she'd developed in the nursery. "Do you think he'll recover?"

Frasier moaned as if on cue.

"Absolutely. I have never met a man more robust than Laird Buchanan."

"You care for him deeply, do you not?"

"Yes, I suppose I do. After all, he rescued me and I will be forever grateful to him for it."

As the clock chimed the hour indicating time to reapply the tincture, Grace moved to stand but Modesty stopped her. "There's just one more thing I'm a wee bit anxious about."

"What is it?"

"I ken you have never been one to mollify the truth."

Grace gave a nod. Honestly, she had been rather horrid to her younger sister over the years.

Modesty pressed her hands together and pointed her fingertips forward. "Promise me you'll not try to do so now."

Reminding herself how dear family truly was, Grace resolved to take whatever time necessary to address Modesty's concerns—after all, she had reformed from her previous self and must no longer be impatient or impertinent. "Very well, if it is not His Lairdship's health, what is weighing upon you so heavily?"

"I do not want to have my coming out."

All young ladies looked forward to experiencing their first Seasons. And the MacGalloway daughters were no different. Throughout their entire lives everyone from Mama to their nanny to their governess had drilled into them the importance of becoming a lady and entering the marriage mart—the importance of finding a good match. Moreover, Modesty wasn't one to suffer from flighty nerves. "No? Why?"

"Do I have to say it? You of all people ought to ken why." She hid her face in her hands. "I am hideous."

Grace reflected back to a time when she'd accused her sister of that very thing, though never in a hundred years did she expect Modesty to believe her. *Good heavens, my behavior was reprehensible.* She had treated her younger sister as the girls at Northbourne had first treated her.

"First of all," she said, carefully, "you are not hideous."

Not looking up, the lass shook her head. "I'm certainly not beautiful."

"I wouldn't say that. Your beauty is, however, different than mine—*unique*. As such, it shall not be easy to shine in a ballroom filled with vying debutantes all sparkling like diamonds. But remember that you are an opal, layered with many facets, sparkling at the most interesting times. You have iridescent beauty that must be studied before it can be appreciated."

"Studied? That's a verra long-winded way of saying I look as though I stood behind a cow with flatulence!"

"It is not! Goodness, don't go putting words into my mouth." Grace moved across to Modesty's bench and draped an arm across her shoulders. "You are as darling as a pixie—mayhap as mischievous as well."

As her sister shook her head, Grace held up her palm. "You have the most beautiful eyes I've ever seen —blue like the sky on a midwinter's day. They're perfectly set, not too wide and not too close. And your freckles are incredibly endearing."

"Nay, they are awful and unseemly."

"Hear me now, sister, you must embrace them. They define you. Any man who turns away from you just because of a few freckles is an idiot."

Modesty peeked out between her fingers. "How do they define me?"

"They give you character—and you must already be aware you have character in droves. Your freckles make a statement announcing to all that you are not perfect and you were never intended to be—just like the rest of us. Furthermore, your lovely countenance proves without a doubt beautiful women come in an assortment of packages."

"I wish you would have been born with freckles. Then you'd ken exactly how *imperfect* they are."

"Little did you know, but I wished the same thing as you walked through the door."

"But you are ethereally beautiful—and dunna deny it. The papers reported those exact words."

Grace tightened her grasp on her sister's shoulder. "Very well, I might be ethereally beautiful, but you are *quintessentially darling.*" She kissed Modesty's cheek. "And you'd best never forget it."

FRASIER LAY VERY STILL on the bed. Regardless of whether he was utterly sapped of strength, the conversation Grace was having with her sister was too good to allow himself to drift off to sleep again. Over the years he had heard an unkind turn of phrase from the older to the younger sister as was not uncommon among siblings. He himself had teased Fiona mercilessly on occasion. That Grace was speaking to Modesty as an elder sister really ought, was touching. Many regarded the lass as ostentatious, but Frasier believed it was just a ruse the princess had adopted at a young age to prevent others from getting too close—or from hurting her.

After Grace ushered Modesty out the door, he opened his eyes and smiled at her. "I do so adore your dubbing her 'quintessentially darling.'"

Her eyes brightened in tandem with her jaw dropping. "You're awake!" She dashed to the bedside, but rather than grasp his hand as he'd hoped, she plastered her fingers against his forehead. "Oh, my heavens, I do believe your fever has broken!"

Frasier tried to sit up but he was weaker than a bag of boneless limbs. "How long have I been abed?"

"Three days."

"What?" With renewed effort he forced himself up enough to sit, the movement causing not only his head to spin but agonizing pain to his back. "I've missed my meeting with the Prince Regent," he said, unable to keep the strain out of his voice.

"Not to worry." Grace urged him to lay down on his side. "Martin was able to postpone."

"For how long?"

"Until you are well enough to do so...at least that's what he said."

"Ballocks!" Frasier ran his palm over his hair which was in a riot of wavy curls. "I had planned to be heading home by now."

"But you are not." She touched his shoulder with cool fingers, softer than rose petals. "And, might I say, now that you are healing, I for one am glad you are still here."

He grasped her fingers and kissed them. "Please tell me the Archbishop has had a change of heart."

With his words, her smile dropped along with her shoulders. "I'm afraid he has not."

Frasier released her hand and turned away, his chest suddenly aflame with rage.

I am a damned fool.

If Grace was to soon join her husband, then he needed to clear his name and head for Scotland at the first opportunity. He also needed to stop lusting after her, kissing her, wanting her. As he shifted the bed-clothes, he was appalled by his stench. "Bloody oath, how can you stand to be near me?"

"I beg your pardon?"

"I need a bath."

"But—"

"Order the bath and fetch Angus. I'll not have you hovering nearby whilst I'm as weak as an invalid!"

He hated the stricken look on her face as Grace hastened out the door, but what was he to do? Pull her onto the bed and make passionate love to the woman? God knew he had been on the brink of doing so ever since...hell, ever since the woman had awakened in his cottage.

Angus burst in, slamming the door behind him. "What the bloody hell did you say to Her Ladyship?"

"Wheesht, and help me get out of this damned bed."

"Och, I'll no' have ye waking up after hovering on the brink of death and barking at everyone who tended ye. I'll tell ye here and now that woman held vigil at your bedside for hour upon hour, only sleeping a wee bit when I made her do so. You are alive at the moment because of her!"

Frasier hung his head. Damnation, he knew it. The time had passed in a fog, but there were many moments when he was aware of her presence. Grace had talked to him endlessly. She had soothed him. Her lips had lovingly brushed his as she'd given him the bitter saline draught.

That much he knew. He had saved her life, and whilst he had been abed, she repaid in kind. She was an angel and he was but a lowly outcast.

He couldn't continue their romance, pretending she would one day be his.

She will never be mine!

Kissing her caused him grievous pain. No more could he continue to kiss her without taking it further, without making love to her.

"I need to go home," he said.

"We will go home just as soon as you finish the task ye came down here to accomplish," Angus replied, as several footmen came in with a copper tub and buckets of water.

Once they finished, Angus faced him with his fists jammed onto his hips. "What has got into ye? Ye remind me of an agitated bull."

Agitated bull was spot on for describing Frasier's frustration. But he couldn't tell the highlander that he was madly in love with Grace. He could never admit that being unable to make love to her was driving him to the brink of insanity. Angus already had guessed Frasier's infatuation with the lass—he just did not know how deeply the laird had fallen in love.

"I dunna ken. I suppose anyone would be out of sorts after three days battling a fever." He reached out a hand. "It pains me to admit, but I'm weaker than a bleeding sparrow. Help me into the bath. I reckon a good dousing will do me good."

22

F or the first time since her father had died, Grace was well and truly melancholy. She'd spent the past five days avoiding Frasier, not because he had barked at her, but because she knew he was right to do so. She had been daft to hope they might have some sort of flirtatious liaison where they kissed and cuddled and stared into each other's eyes, all the while hiding their affection from everyone in the household.

She was not free to love Frasier the way he wanted to be loved. She was being entirely selfish to think she actually might enjoy a few moments of happiness before leaving for the continent. Perhaps she was still a heartless shrew. Perhaps she had not changed as much as she'd thought.

Today it was raining yet again as it tended to do in mid-April, so rather than go for a ride in Hyde Park with Modesty and Kitty as she had planned, Grace found a copy of *Pride and Prejudice* and sat in the over-stuffed chair by the library's window. The rain tapped the glass, running down in streaks as if to mirror the bleeding of Grace's heart—as if to weep with her.

She read for a time, turning the pages but not

comprehending. Too many things vied for her attention—things she did not want to think about.

Her conversation with Modesty had served to reinforce the fact that Grace absolutely mustn't cause a scandal. Grace had meant it when she'd told her sister she was quintessentially darling, but she had also been utterly truthful when she'd more-or-less said it would take a special man to see beyond the red hair and freckles. Indeed, Modesty had her own special type of beauty both within and without, but she was not a rose. She was a dandelion. People try to weed their gardens of dandelions, but they always come back. They are resilient. They are brilliant and bright and have ever so many uses from tea, to delicious greens, to ingredients in jams and soup, to a host of healing tinctures and tonics.

Many people believed dandelions were a nuisance, but those ignorant fops had never really studied the gems. Each flower had one hundred and fifty to two hundred ray florets. And when they went to seed, children delighted in blowing on the pappus and scattering the seeds on the wind.

Grace turned the page and stared at it, quite at a loss for what she had just read even though she'd somehow ended up on page fifteen.

She looked up when Frasier entered, her heart suddenly hammering like hummingbird wings. He didn't see her at first, but not wanting him to suddenly realize she was present, she closed her book and stood. "Your Lairdship, I hope you are well."

He spun from the wall of bookcases and bowed. "Princess, I didna realize you were in here. Angus told me you were to be out with Modesty and Kitty today."

Evidently Frasier was using his brother-in-law to

track her whereabouts. Moreover, it appeared they had reverted to formalities.

No matter. We should never have permitted familiarity.

She gestured toward the rain-splattered window. "Unfortunately the weather decided not to cooperate. I believe the girls are enjoying a game of chess in the front parlor."

"I see."

They stood for a time awkwardly staring at each other, Grace trying to think of something witty to say, while he appeared to be in pain.

Pain!

"Goodness, how thoughtless of me not to immediately enquire as to your health. How is your back faring? Your color is looking quite good."

Frasier smiled. Heaven help her, did he have any idea how he was able to twist her heart into a thousand knots just by the slight upturn of those wonderfully full lips? "I am verra much improved, thanks to you."

"I—"

"I—"

They both spoke at once. She nodded, unable to help smiling at him like a lovesick nymph. "You first."

"Thank you." He took a step nearer. "I have been meaning to..."

She closed her eyes and prayed he had been meaning to spirit her away to a place where they could walk barefoot on beaches of warm sand. Where they could lie in each other's arms every night and no one would give a care...

"...to thank you for tending me so much watchfulness and vigilance. I am in your debt."

Grace's heart sank. Alas, there would be no fairy

tale romance. "I believe I owe you a great deal more than you do me. After all, you did rescue me from certain death."

"I wouldna say that. Shall we call it even?" he asked, taking another step closer.

I will never consider it so. "If you wish," she replied, trying to sound indifferent. Blast the highlander, he was standing so close, the light scent of bergamot nearly caused her to swoon.

"Why is it...?" Oh, no, she could never again utter her feelings aloud.

"Hmm?" he asked.

"Hmm?" she countered.

"You were about to say something."

Grace started to bat her hand through the air, but he caught her wrist with those rough, calloused, strong hands. Her breath stopped. "I-It was nothing."

He bowed and kissed her hand, his lips soft and warm and tender. "I owe you an apology."

Her knees trembled. "No."

"Aye." He straightened, meeting her gaze with those fathomless cobalt-blue eyes. "I shouldna have been cross with you, especially not after all ye did for me."

She had done too much, none of which he was aware. She had fallen in love and stolen his heart as if it could possibly be hers. "I need no apology but to beg for forgiveness."

"Och, lass, what are you saying?"

"I had no right to kiss you. I should have let someone else tend your sickbed, but I couldn't bear to stand aside when you were so gravely ill."

As an unbidden tear dribbled onto her cheek, he pulled her into an embrace, his arms feeling so wonderfully good, exceedingly protective and caring. This was where she wanted to be, bless it.

"Ye are and will always be verra dear to me, *mo leannan*. Whatever may come, if ever ye should need me, I shall answer your call."

"Even in Lithuania?"

"Aye, if you find you canna bear it." He kissed her forehead. "I ken ye must go to preserve your family's honor. And I respect your steadfast loyalty. Soon Angus and I will be heading back to Scotland and I shall no longer pose a thorn in your side."

"Please do not say that." She hugged him tightly. Frasier might pose a distraction, but he served as an elixir—a welcome diversion which was keeping her sane. "I don't want you to go."

"I ken," he whispered, kissing her cheek.

Her breath ragged, Grace turned her head, their lips meeting in a slow, languid joining, imparting enough fire to turn her blood molten. They clung to each other, both fully aware this may be the last time they kissed, the last time their bodies molded together like malleable clay. Their tongues entwined in an intimate dance as if time did not exist, as if nothing existed outside that very room.

"What is the meaning of this!" Martin boomed, marching inside.

Nearly jumping out of her skin, Grace skittered away, but as her brother focused a deadly glare at Frasier, she changed directions and stepped in front of the big highlander. "It is not what you think!"

Martin snorted sardonically. "I dunna need to think, I saw you kissing with my own eyes."

"But we were merely—"

"Enough!" The all-powerful duke glared at his

sister and thrust his finger toward the door. "Go to your chamber. I shall speak to you anon."

~

FRASIER STOOD in the middle of the library feeling like a wee laddie who had been caught stealing the crown jewels by the Lord High Executioner.

"I trusted you!" Martin seethed.

"I ken. I want—"

"But you betrayed my trust. My sister is not only married, her predicament is dangling on the precipice of a vast abyss. If this affair were to become known, she would be utterly ruined." Martin smacked the globe and jammed his finger onto what must have been Lithuania. "Grace deserves a chance to make something of the tatters of her marriage even if that bastard across the Baltic Sea has threatened divorce. Do you have any idea what a divorce would do to a woman like *Princess* Grace?"

"I do." Frasier nodded, spreading his palms apologetically.

"Grace may fancy herself in love with you," Martin continued as if Frasier had said nothing. "But she is a princess. Of my three sisters, she has embraced the edicts of polite society more than any of them. She loves to attend balls and the theater. She loves London. As a divorced woman, she will enjoy none of it."

"I ken!" This time when Martin tried to speak over him, Frasier raised his voice. "Which is why I was saying goodbye."

"I beg your pardon?" Martin stepped in with a menacing snarl. "That looked like no goodbye I've ever seen. I'm going to ask you one more time, have you importuned her?"

"I. Have. Not!" Nose-to-nose with the duke, Frasier clenched his fists, ready for Martin to take the first swing. "I have kissed her and that is all."

"Kissed her?" Martin narrowed his gaze. "Just this once?"

"On more than one occasion."

"How many times?"

"A few."

"Do you swear on your father's grave that you have not ravished my sister?"

"I do." Sensing the tension ratcheting down a notch, Frasier uncurled his fingers and let his hands hang at his sides. "Bless it, God kens I wanted to. But out of respect for you—"

"What about respect for her?"

"Aye, *and* Princess Grace, I tried my damnedest to keep my feelings at bay."

"But you failed did you not?"

"I bloody kissed her. Do you wish to invite me for a duel so you may shoot me dead?"

Martin turned on his heel, grabbed a book from the table, and slammed it down. "At this moment I canna tell you the thought hasna crossed my mind."

"I love her," Frasier whispered. "More than anything."

The damned book sailed past Frasier's head. "But you canna have her. Bless it, do ye not understand my sister deserves a chance to reassemble the fragments of her marriage?"

"I ken." The one thing that had been shredding his insides was the very reason he could never love Grace as deeply as he desired.

With a huff, Martin marched to the sideboard and poured a tot of whisky, threw it back, then poured two more. "Here," he said, handing Frasier a glass.

"Thank you."

"Do not thank me. It is only because of our long-standing friendship I havena booted you out of my house." Martin sipped, his brow creased in thought. "In fact, that is a verra good idea. You canna remain under the same roof as Grace."

Frasier bit his bottom lip. Dammit all, he was so close to meeting with the Prince Regent. First he was unconscious, now he'd been caught with Martin's sister in his arms. Why did he have to go and ruin his chances at every turn? "I understand. Angus and I will leave at dawn."

"Nay. You will leave now."

Frasier gaped. "If that is what you wish."

"Good God, ye numpty. I'm sending you to Brixham's town house." Martin indicated southward with his glass. "I came in here to tell you Prinny has agreed to meet with us whilst he attends the boxing match at Covent Garden."

"The Prince Regent attends boxing matches?"

"Aye. 'Tis good sport." Martin dropped into a wing-back chair and crossed his hairy knees. "Furthermore, the Chancellor of the Exchequer has announced the auction of the Jacobite treasure. There was a notice in the papers—a list of some of the finer items as well."

Frasier sipped. "May I see it?"

"Top left drawer of the writing table. I stowed it there after breakfast."

After retrieving the newspaper folded open to the article, Frasier opted to stand as he read. "The auction is on the seventeenth of April—a week away."

Martin nodded as Frasier continued to read, quickly scanning the list of seized Jacobite treasure. "The Horn of Bannockburn isna listed."

"Do ye reckon they'd refer to it by name? How

many Englishmen would ken the relic was given to the seventh laird by Robert the Bruce?"

"None." Frasier leaned against the desk and took another sip of whisky, scanning slowly this time. "I'll be damned."

One item on the list simply read: *Medieval horn.*

He slapped the newspaper on his thigh. "This mentions nothing of precious stones on the medieval horn. Makes me think the Chancellor might have kept it for himself."

"Aye, it may not be what ye are looking for." Martin dismissed him with a flick of his wrist. "Go on fetch Angus and collect your things. I'll take you over to the earl's town house myself. 'Tis a rather delicate situation best explained by my lips."

FROM THE DRAWER of her writing table, Grace retrieved the note she'd written the morn of her wedding. When she'd returned to London, she'd found it, crumpled it into a ball, and tossed it into the drawer. Though nearly three months had passed since that fateful day, it seemed like an eternity.

She smoothed out the paper until it was nearly flat, the words glaring at her:

My dreams have finally come true. By the time the sun sets this day I will be Princess Grace.

She dipped her quill in the ink and drew two thick black lines through the silly musings of a child. Grace might now be a princess, but she had realized there would be no happily ever after for her. She jammed her pen into the holder and tore the paper into shreds, watching as the pieces fluttered into the white wicker rubbish bin.

What is wrong with me? I wouldn't last long in the Highlands, living in a cottage that is no larger than my bedchamber. Up until now, I thought only of dress fittings, balls, attending the opera, flower arrangements, what I would embroider next and for whom.

She answered a knock by asking Martin to enter, for she knew it was he. "Have you challenged Buchanan to a duel?" she asked, standing with her chin held high.

"I have sent him to stay with Charity and Brixham."

"Oh..." She said, a bit of her sanctimoniousness deflating. "Good of you," she added, turning away and facing the hearth.

"Och, Grace, I ken the past few months havena been easy for you."

She tensed as he placed his hand on her shoulder.

"Hell, had I been you I reckon I might have fallen into the arms of a good man myself—looked to him for comfort when all seemed lost."

Her head dropped forward as she fought to keep her tears at bay. Had she turned to Frasier because he was kind and caring and generous? Had she turned to him because she desperately needed to be loved?

Over and over again she'd told herself Frasier deserved a woman who was free to love him, free to bear his children.

She sobbed into her hands. "Life is not fair!"

Martin grasped her shoulders and pulled her into his arms, patting her back as if she were his daughter. "There, there. A man like Buchanan was never meant for the likes of you. You were born to languish in luxury, to manage vast estates, to host grand balls and soirees. You would be miserable freezing up there in Druimliart."

Grace's shoulders shook as she nodded, her tears dripping onto Marty's coat. "I-I keep trying to convince myself of tha-a-a-t!"

"It is never easy when everything seems to be mounting against you, but I said it before and I stand by my words, you are the most resilient person I ken." He patted her hair. "Look at how quickly you convinced Mama and Gibb to bring you back to London. You love it here."

Sobs wracked her body. The only reason she wanted to return to London was because Frasier was here.

Martin held her at arm's length. "Look, give it a go with Isidor—mayhap after a year things will be different. You may find that life as a princess is everything you dreamed it would be. However, if that bast—ah—your husband dares to mistreat you as you fear, send for me."

"What if he reads my outgoing letters before they're posted?"

"Hmm. Let us agree upon a secret code."

She nodded, though unable to manage a smile. "Oh, I do like that—something simple."

"How about a question...say...'Are the puffins nesting?'"

"Yes, yes. I so love those little birds, the way the flit about."

"I ken. You have always adored them." Martin stepped toward the door. "Are you feeling better now?"

She wasn't, though the mention of puffins had lifted her spirits somewhat. "Yes."

"Buchanan will be meeting with Prinny soon."

"Good, I hope he fares well."

Martin turned, placing his hand on the latch.

"What about the Jacobite treasure?" she asked.

"There will be an auction. One week hence." The duke eyed her over his shoulder. "I suppose it goes without saying I dunna think it a good idea for you to see Buchanan again. You'd best leave him to his own affairs. He will be gone soon enough."

"As you wish, brother," said Grace, looking to the hidden drawer of her writing desk—the one she kept locked. The one where she'd stowed the pin money she'd been saving over the years.

23

Three days after Frasier and Angus moved to the Earl of Brixham's town house, Martin arrived with his shiny black town coach dressed like an English duke, complete with breeches, pink waistcoat, top boots, and a neckcloth tied high enough to strangle him above his well-cut coat. When Frasier balked, His Grace introduced his valet after which the Buchanan laird was marshalled upstairs to don the same attire.

"Are you certain this is necessary?" asked Frasier, the smalls he'd donned beneath his nankeen breeches hugging his loins more than a bit too tightly. "I reckon I've heard tell of the Regent wearing a kilt when he posed for a portrait in Edinburgh."

The damned duke paced the floor, wearing a path through the Persian carpet. "We'll be attending the boxing match with His Highness's retinue. If you want to meet with him, you'll finish dressing and stop complaining."

"Shall I cut his hair, sir?" asked the valet, tying the starched neckcloth like a noose.

"Ye're not touching my bloody hair," Frasier snarled.

"Leave it," said Martin, smirking. "Some things cannot be tamed."

After the valet handed Frasier a top hat and gloves, he stood in front of the mirror, barely recognizing himself. Everything itched—especially since his welts had scabbed over. He tugged the crotch of the breeches downward and shook out his leg. "This seems awfully lavish for a trip to a wee fight."

His Grace stopped pacing and crossed his arms, eyeing Frasier from head to toe. "When meeting the Prince Regent, appearances are important."

The pox to appearances.

He was trussed like a hog and moved like one of the wooden soldiers he and Martin had played with as lads. All he needed was an apple in his mouth and the fops would feast upon his naivety.

The ride to Covent Garden took but a quarter of an hour, even though the arcade was on the edge of the more squalid part of Town. After disembarking on Bow Street, the two men walked a short distance to a sprawling marketplace. All the colors first caught Frasier's eye, brilliant silks and brocades, dyed in every hue imaginable. Vendors with wagons sold vegetables and fruits, and by the pall, some on the verge of turning. The odors were overpowering and changed as they walked, from baked goods to the musky, iron pall of freshly butchered meat. It seemed everything was for sale from flowers to tobacco and pipes to porcelain snuff boxes painted with pastoral scenes. An enormous tent had been erected in the center of the pandemonium and as they neared, the noise grew louder, the excitement in the air palpable.

"Here we are," Martin said, walking with a silver-tipped cane and leading the way through the tightly packed crowd. They hailed from all walks of life, shouting over one another, while tickets and coins exchanged hands.

Dunscaby strode right through the gate and straight to the King's box, erected higher than the ring to ensure a good view and to keep the crowd from mobbing His Highness. Quite a gathering of aristocrats had already assembled and it wasn't difficult to pick out the rotund form of Prince George, not only was he the center of attention, he was quite large as the newspapers had described him. As they climbed the steps, for the first time today Frasier was glad to be dressed like a peacock. He fit right in with the prince and all the gentlemen in his company. Fortunately the Chancellor of the Exchequer was not present. Nonetheless, this was a rather unconventional place for a meeting especially when a man was asking for his clan to be reinstated into the realm.

He'd dreamed of standing before a man seated on a throne surrounded by knights in armor. Perhaps his imagination had lapsed a few centuries since armor was a thing of the past. Still, Frasier envisioned a private audience, perhaps with a headsman standing at the ready.

Down below, a ringmaster was shouting above the crowd, or he was attempting to do so. Frasier couldn't make out a word. The dozen or so dandies in the box were all sipping champagne. He found it odd, but Dunscaby fit right in with the highborn fops. Though Frasier shouldn't have been surprised. Martin was a duke and sat in the House of Lords. He interacted with these men a great deal even though he was Scottish through to the bone.

His Grace made the introductions and Frasier found himself standing by the Prince Regent as the fight began. Two shirtless men faced off in a bare-knuckle brawl—they were both large and beefy, one a few inches taller than the other. If Frasier thought the crowd was loud when they arrived it was doubly so now. At least the crazed men down below were yelling. Though it seemed shouting at a boxing match was beneath the aristocracy. Dunscaby and the others watched on, the corners of their lips tight with an occasional squint or tensing of the jaw the only outward sign of excitement.

The shorter boxer was the first to attack, throwing a left jab followed with a right hook. The taller ducked and eluded both strikes, landing a punch in his opponent's solar plexus, hard enough to lift the lad off the ground.

"Are you a fighter?" asked the regent loudly, his gaze glued on the ring.

Frasier tugged on his starchy collar and stretched his neck. "Only if someone else throws the first punch."

The regent smirked. "Dunscaby mentioned you were a man of honor."

The shorter boxer's next jab it home, striking the other's jaw.

"So, my secretary tells me all the Buchanans were thought to have fled the country after the rising—those who did not were executed or transported."

The boxers were both already bleeding, sweat and blood dripping to the dirt floor. But after the crown's hospitality at the whipping post, Frasier had little stomach for blood sport and turned away from the fight. "Aye, many were, aside from a handful of my ken who fled into the Highlands."

"And you've been living up there all this time?" the

regent asked as the first round came to an end with the clang of a bell.

Frasier nodded as the noise from the crowd lowered to a hum.

His Highness looked him up and down. "It is astonishing the troops have not yet weeded you out."

With a wave of panic, Frasier wondered if the soldiers were in Druimliart now opening fire on his kin.

"You look as if you're ready to race home and build a fortress." The prince's belly shook with deep, rumbling laughter. "Not to worry, Laird. I'm told any Jacobite sentiments that may exist are quashed before they grow out of hand. So, you are prepared to pledge your fealty to the crown?"

"Aye." Frasier bowed his head. "If my name is cleared."

"And what if I don't grant your pardon?"

A moment of tension swelled between them as Frazier carefully considered his reply. He ought to kiss the man's arse. But doing so would betray his very character. His shoulder ticked up. "Then nothing will change, I reckon."

"Oh, that's where you're wrong. By coming to London you have precipitated a great deal of change." The prince flagged a footman who presented him with an open snuff box. He inhaled a bit of tobacco with a miniature spoon, then sneezed. "Now tell me about breaking into—" He glanced over his shoulder. "What tower was it?"

"Flint Tower, Your Highness," replied the hovering secretary.

"That's it. Why the devil did you break into the tower when you came to London seeking a pardon?"

"If I may interject," said Dunscaby, speaking over Frasier's shoulder. "It is my fault. I told Buchanan the

Jacobite treasure had been unearthed and mentioned there was to be an auction. He did not intend to steal anything but wished to view the pieces. Furthermore, His Lairdship received twelve lashes for merely picking an old lock that most likely would have come open with a good tug."

"Oh, that's right, did you not say he suffered a fever as a result of the Chancellor's action?"

"I did," Frasier said, preferring to answer his own bloody questions.

The bell for the second round rang and the men were at it again, looking the worse for wear.

"Tell me," said the Regent. "Was there something in particular were you looking for among those rusted relics? It seems rather odd that you would bother entering a locked room if there wasn't an item of import."

"As you may be aware, my grandfather's assets were taken as were his lands." The crowd roared as the taller boxer stumbled and fell, the referee shouting the count. When the man used the ropes to pull himself to his feet, Frasier continued, "Among them was the Horn of Bannockburn given to the Seventh Chieftain of Buchanan by Robert the Bruce."

The prince eyed him, his lips pursed as if he'd swallowed a bitter tonic. "After the battle, I assume?"

Frasier nodded. "It is one keepsake I'd like to have returned."

"I'm told you didn't find it."

"No, but I was only in the tower for a matter of moments."

The tall boxer fell again, this time he appeared to out cold and motionless. With a huff, the Regent tore his betting ticket and threw the pieces off the dais. "Well, if the horn is there, it will be auctioned along with the other items seized by The Duke of Cumberland. Though I say, the Battle of Bannockburn is nothing in which to be proud. After all, it was a loss which kept Scotland and England from uniting for another three hundred years."

Frasier gulped at the mention of Butcher Cumberland. All his life he'd been taught to believe that man was a heartless murderer.

Dunscaby pushed in, making Frasier sidestep. "It is also worth mentioning the Buchanan lands are but a wee isle on Loch Lomond, presently uninhabited."

"Owned by the crown, I'd venture?" the prince asked over his shoulder.

"Yes, sir," said the secretary. "Though it is among the properties we have listed for sale."

"Sale?" Frasier asked, the word bitter, but if it meant he could reclaim the lands of his forefathers, he'd spend his last farthing to do so.

The secretary used a pencil to make a note in his journal. He tore out the page and handed it to Frasier: £500. Martin leaned in to have a peek, but Frasier folded the document before the duke had a chance to see it. After all, he had pride, and though he couldn't afford five hundred pounds, he would take the information back to Druimliart and discuss options with the clan.

"I shall expunge the order commanding the troops to shoot you and those associated with your clan on sight," the Regent said as casually as if he were commenting about the weather. His gaze shifted from the ring where they were introducing two more fighters. He met Frasier's gaze for a brief interchange akin to staring into the eyes of an eel. "Evidently after three and seventy years, the order has not been terribly effective, considering you are standing here on the dais beside me."

IT WAS the seventeenth of April when the countess donned a black mourning gown, with matching gloves, veil, and shawl. Her husband had already left for Parliament. Today was a significant day in the House of Lords where they were hearing arguments for and against the National Debt Commissioner's Act. The Prime Minister was doing everything in his power to reduce the national debt and if he didn't succeed, the country would be thrown into bankruptcy yet again.

The countess hadn't dressed in mourning since her father passed away when she was nineteen years of age. After birthing a daughter, she was afraid it wouldn't fit, but there wasn't time to have the modiste make a new ensemble. Thanks to her lady's maid's deft needlework, ten years later, the gown fit—barely.

She quietly slipped away from her home via the mews, careful to ensure she wasn't seen by anyone who might be inclined to follow. Once she was several streets away from her town house, she hailed a hackney, giving the address of an auction house in Pall Mall.

The driver gave a gap-toothed smile. "There'll be quite a crowd, madam. Everyone wants a piece of the Jacobite treasure. Word is there are bargains to be had."

Her Ladyship nodded, allowing him to hand her into the carriage. She didn't give a whit that he didn't know her title. After all, her veil was so dark, she

hadn't been able to make out her own visage in the
looking glass.

Nonetheless, she had but one objective in attending the auction—actually two. She would do her
part to raise money for the crown and reduce the kingdom's debt. The other objective was of a deeply personal nature.

24

A gain, Frasier found himself in the midst of an avaricious crowd, but this time he was accompanied by Angus. Dunscaby had left early this morning for Parliament—had given his apologies. Evidently there was to be an important vote about righting the national debt.

The mayhem was similar to the boxing match with people from all classes mingled amongst each other. At the boxing match, the excitement in the air had been that of blood lust—of the crowd watching modern-day gladiators fight while they placed wagers and cheered on their man. This crowd was no less lustful, though their hunger was for the spoils of war.

The auctioneer was dressed like a dandy with nary a hair out of place, his loquacious banter filled with florid descriptions, his manners impeccable, his charm too syrupy for Frasier's taste, but the man seemed to have won the crowd. The excitement was infectious as the auctioneer persuaded, goaded, and cajoled the mob into a frenzy of raving excitement.

With each hammer of his gavel, he sold mostly rubbish, from the rusted weaponry to the broken glass Frasier had seen in Flint Tower—because "a glass of sweet sherry had been served in this vessel to Bonny Prince Charlie himself!"

It didn't sell for much, but the woman who'd won the bid wore a mobcap and an apron over her dress and, by her rapt expression, she had just won a treasure to be cherished for all eternity.

Frasier's gut roiled while item after item was sold, portraits, silver tea services, silverware, crystal glasses, lockets and jewelry, pieces of furniture. Some things were Jacobian and others were just relics of another era—once treasures of forgotten families like the Buchanans, the crowd vying for them like dogs fighting over a bone.

Hours had passed and Frasier grew all the more unsettled. The prices were climbing as the buzzards fed. The crowd must have sensed the end was nearing. Aye, the excitement ratcheted up while the auctioneer's words sped, spewing half-truths and tall tales.

The winner of a decent basket-hilted broadsword stood and thumped his chest, giving Frasier a sardonic grin as if to say, "take that you Highland bastard."

Angus elbowed him in the ribs. "Have a look at that."

Following his friend's pointed finger, a clerk handed the auctioneer a large horn—a ram's horn, greyed with age. Frasier's heart raced.

"Will you bid on it?" asked his friend.

"Perhaps," he said, though it was difficult to make out the detail from the back of the room. The relic might have belonged to someone other than his grandfather.

"Ladies and gentlemen," the auctioneer drawled, flashing a row of gleaming teeth. "This horn is very old, *very old*. Merely the stones inset are worth a fortune! Our assessors have verified as genuine, two garnets, three rubies, and no fewer than nine peridots! I tell you true, this artifact will shine above your mantel!" The man held it up for all to see. "Look here, the mouthpiece is hewn of solid gold."

"That's ours," growled Angus. "I'd stake my entire fortune on it."

Frasier smirked. "You have no fortune." The admission made his gut twist. The problem was he had but fifty pounds in his sporran, and the feeding frenzy most likely had risen to its peak.

The bidding started at five pounds and quickly shot to twenty. Several people dropped out as the price soared to thirty-five. Frasier's heart hammered faster as he raised his hand every time he was outbid.

His gaze shot across the eager faces. Damnation, the competition had to be among the best dressed—a man wearing a well-tailored coat and John bull, a woman dressed in mourning complete with a veil shrouding her face, a man wearing a raffia top hat, another with no hat at all, but his hair fashionably styled with black whiskers extending down his cheeks, nearly touching his high collar starched and held in place by a pristine neckcloth.

Frasier's heart sank as the bidding soared to a hundred pounds, two hundred, three hundred, and higher until the gavel pounded, naming the woman in mourning as the buyer at the outrageous sum of four hundred and seventy-five pounds.

The auction continued, the pieces ever more valuable, but Frasier moved around the edge of the crowd, keeping his gaze on the woman. Something about her was familiar. But from where? Aside from Dunscaby's family, he knew no one in London. Most likely, his senses were fooling him. The lass was a good four inches taller than Grace. She moved swiftly, stopped at the clerk's table, bent forward as if to tell him a secret. Then without collecting her prize, she headed for the door.

The woman was lithely fast for a person bereft, and Frasier nearly trampled people as he sped to keep pace with her. "I beg your pardon, madam!" he called as a hackney stopped at the curb alongside her while carriages and wagons rattled past on the busy street.

The woman didn't turn as she spoke to the driver.

Frasier arrived at the coach in time to offer the lady a hand. "Good afternoon, madam, it is of utmost urgency that we speak. I believe the horn you purchased belonged to my grandfather."

Though he was unable to see her face, he could have sworn she gasped—right before she ignored his outstretched palm, gathered her skirts, and climbed inside unassisted.

Damnation, she couldn't just leave without a word. "You have paid dearly, madam. All I ask is to view the wee piece. Please!"

She leaned forward, but rather than reply, she grabbed the latch and slammed the door.

As Angus lumbered out to the footpath, Frasier inclined his head toward the hall. "Go ask the clerk for the name of the woman who purchased the horn. I'll meet you at Brixham's town house."

"Ye dunna aim to follow that hack?"

"That's exactly what I'm doing," Frasier shouted over his shoulder, running for the carriage before it disappeared in the mayhem of London's traffic.

He was able to keep up at a jog, his gaze set on the lantern swinging behind the driver. Running on the uneven cobblestones made the going difficult, his shoes sliding awkwardly, threatening to turn his ankles. Frasier dodged a cart with a stubborn mule, which nearly got him run over by a racing phaeton. "Move out of the road, you damned fool!" shouted the driver as he wielded his whip, hissing over Frasier's head.

The woman's hackney turned into Green Park and picked up speed. Keeping it in his sights, Frasier sprinted faster, when all too late, the warning of impending disaster came from his right. Not even knowing what was about to collide with him, he gnashed his teeth and ducked.

With a sickening thud, a barrow full of manure caught Frasier's heel, sending him careening face-first to the grass only saving his chin by the buckling of his knees.

"Watch where ye're goin' ye daft Scot!" shouted a man who smelled as foul as the contents of his cart.

Not bothering to respond, Frasier pushed to his feet, limping as he tried to run off the pain in his knee. He crossed through the park and stopped at the curb, looking all directions, but the hackney was nowhere to be seen. Bracing himself with his hands on his knees, he inhaled deep gulps of air. Damnation, this godforsaken city was going to end up sending him to the grave.

Downtrodden, he limped for Brixham's town house, hoping Angus had at least found the woman's name and address. He headed down the close to the mews, finding the highlander waiting for him at the back gate, his arms crossed, his expression cantankerous.

"Who is she?" Frasier asked.

"Dunna ken." Angus pushed open the gate and led the way along the path skirting the horse stalls. "The damned clerk was gone by the time I went back inside."

"Gone? How can that be? The auction wasna over!"

"Well, he'd been replaced. I asked the new fella where the other went, and he said an urgent errand. And dunna bother asking me if I got her name. The blighter didna ken that either."

"That damned woman must have asked him to deliver the horn straightaway. Did ye follow him?"

"I would have if I kent where he'd gone."

Frasier pounded his fist on the wall beside the rear door. "Ballocks!"

Angus scoffed. "She can take the bloody horn and go straight to hell."

The man wasn't wrong. "'Tis just a relic," Frasier growled. "We've lived without the miserable thing for three and seventy years. I reckon we dunna need it."

"Agreed. Ye accomplished what we set out to do. Let's go home."

Home. That single word never sounded so comforting. "Aye, we've been here too long for certain."

"Thank God ye still have some sense left in that miserable head of yours."

"Some sense? What the hell are you talking about?"

"Och, ye're a grown man, but ye let Dunscaby boot ye out of his house—and after Her Ladyship nursed ye back to health."

Shoving his brother-in-law in the shoulder, Frasier growled, "What the blazes are you on about?"

"Ye're a bloody eejit."

Frasier's fists curled. The man didn't know what the hell he was saying. Didn't he know Frasier lay awake every night trying to figure a way to win her? Didn't Angus realize that if Frasier did indeed win the lady's heart, he would be asking her to live a life so far beneath her station she would eventually fall into an abyss of despair? "Excuse me, but Princess Grace is married," he snarled.

"Aye, but I reckon ye gave up too easily."

Frasier grumbled under his breath. Gave up? The Archbishop of Canterbury made the everlasting decision for him...and for *her*. "You ken I canna ask her to divorce the prince as he so threatened."

"Nay?"

"Of course no'. Her younger sister is to be introduced to society next Season. If Grace divorced now, it would ruin Modesty's future."

The black-bearded highlander batted his hand through the air. "So she's ruining her own instead."

Frasier watched as Angus opened the door and disappeared into the kitchen. The bloody muttonhead didn't understand a damned thing. He was honoring her wishes. The entire week he'd been at Brixham's town house, Grace hadn't come to call on her sister, or at least she hadn't come to call upon him. She hadn't sent a note. It was as if he'd already left London. As if she was already reunited with her prince.

Whatever Martin had said to her, it must have been dire. Worse, the duke was right to chastise them both and stop their romance before it grew further out of hand.

Frasier ought to be relived to be going home. He had achieved the most important goal—he now could walk into Fort William or any military outpost without fear of being shot. Frasier had finally achieved his father's dream. Moreover, his back had healed enough to ride—aye, it would take months for the welts to completely stop stinging, but Frasier could manage his horse well enough. The problem was he felt as though he was leaving a piece of himself behind.

Frasier dropped onto a bench, propped his elbows on his knees, and hung his head. Aye, Angus was right, Frasier was a bloody eejit. Except his friend was wrong as well. Frasier had never been in love before. How in God's name did he manage to give his heart away to a woman who was already married? And why the hell did said woman have to be in such an untenable situation? Her brother had insisted that Grace needed a chance to find out if her marriage was capable of being saved.

She deserved happiness. She deserved to be put on a pedestal and treated like a queen.

Except Frasier hadn't the means to care for a woman like Grace. How daft was he to allow himself to fall in love with a princess? He couldn't even buy his family's heirloom because he hadn't enough coin. He doubted he'd ever see five hundred pounds all at once.

His mind flickered back to the woman in mourning. Who was she and why did she not give him the courtesy of answering him? If she was wealthy, why had she hailed a hackney? And she was alone. Didn't she have a companion? A carriage? Footmen?

The Horn of Bannockburn had well and truly slipped through his grasp. He'd received twelve lashings and suffered a fever, he damned well deserved the chance to hold his family's most treasured heirloom for his troubles. But he was leaving on the morrow and he'd never see that woman again.

Good riddance.

What value would the horn grant him even if he'd won the bid? He needed nothing to prove his heritage. He needed nothing to prove to his future children that their forefathers were good men—highlanders who fought for king and country, who loved and were loved. What mattered was a man's character, his integrity, his kin.

It was nearly dark by the time Willaby, Brixham's butler opened the back door and ushered him in. "What the blazes are you doing out here, sir?"

As Frasier stood and sauntered in through the kitchen, he removed his bonnet—damned right, he wore a tartan bonnet just as all proper highlanders did. "I merely needed a moment of respite is all."

The butler nodded, his expression perplexed, but Frasier didn't stop to explain. He used the back stairs to head to his room.

Brixham's town house wasn't as grand as Dunscaby's, but it was still luxurious by Frasier's standards. Hell, most likely a modest room in a boarding house by the east end would be luxurious by Frasier's standards. But at least his cottage was his own. He'd never once gone hungry or without clothing. A few times as a lad he'd gone without shoes but doing so only made him tougher. In the Highlands he had everything he needed.

Everything except a wife.

Aye, he'd flirted with his share of lassies—enjoyed the arms of the odd alehouse wench as well. But love had eluded him...was eluding him still.

Weary, he opened the door of his bedchamber and loosened his neckcloth. He strode directly to the bowl, poured in some water, and splashed his face. It wasn't until he looked in the mirror that he noticed a wooden box atop the bed. Made of polished dark wood, it appeared to be very old, the knicks and grooves shadowed by the vestiges of the setting sun streaming in through the glass.

Frasier dried his face and hands before reaching

for the letter resting atop—addressed formally to *The Buchanan*. He broke the seal and read.

Dear Frasier,

I have missed you terribly these past several days, even though I have no right to miss you at all. I will never forget my time at Druimliart. I shall also never forget you. Please allow me this small kindness. Not only did you save my life, but I believe the forces of nature or God or whatever it may have been, sent me to you because I needed to open my eyes and see all that existed around me, not just what I wanted to see. You and your clan showed me a different side of life that I may have known existed, but I chose to ignore. I realize now I chose to ignore so many important things. I have also gained a much keener appreciation of the importance of every living soul. Yes, I in one way or another appreciated servants, but I never gave much thought to them—to their lives outside of service. I had always believed in the class system and assumed people were generally content regardless of if they were born into a dukedom or born into the serving class.

I will always remember you, no matter what may come. You are honorable and good and fair. Felicitations on earning your pardon. There is no man more deserving.

Yours lovingly,

Princess Grace

He stared at the salutation. *Lovingly.* She did not use sincerely or faithfully. Such a salutation had to be deliberate. His heart nearly burst out of his chest.

With trembling hands, Frasier opened the box and removed the Horn of Bannockburn from where it rested atop a blue velvet pillow. It had been taken from a great-sized beast, but even so, it was much heavier than it looked. Though old, the luster of the stones faded with age, the relic was stunningly beautiful—a piece that announced this gift had been given by a great king, not just as a thank you, but in recognition for extraordinary valor on the battlefield.

When a knock came at the door, Frasier gently replaced the horn and answered. "Lady Brixham," he said, noticing Charity stood about four inches taller than Grace. Good God, *she* was the woman in mourning! "I see you've already changed for dinner."

Her Ladyship offered a sheepish smile. "I'm sorry I didna speak to you when I climbed into the hackney. If I had you might have realized it was me and that would have spoiled the surprise."

"Grace had you bid on the Horn of Bannockburn? Why did she not do it herself?"

"Och, can you imagine the gossip mongers? Tomorrow's papers would be raving about how the Princess of Samogitia attended a Jacobite auction without her husband. Especially with Isidor on the continent, they would twist the story into a riotous scandal."

Frasier understood Grace's situation, though not Charity's. "But you were there and you're a countess. I would think you took a great risk as well."

"Not as great a risk. Had my identity been revealed, I would not have created as much cause for gossip. After all, my husband is in London. My sister's is not."

Frasier closed the box, fastened the brass hasp, and picked it up. Goodness by its weight, he reckoned the box was lined with lead. He had initially planned to hand it to Her Ladyship, but he didn't expect a lady to carry anything this heavy. "This was a verra generous and thoughtful gift. But I couldna possibly accept it."

"Hogwash," she said, gently nudging it toward him. "Grace told me the auctioneers appraised the piece and were hoping to fetch close to a thousand pounds for it."

"A thousand?" he asked, his voice cracking.

Charity smiled as if she were a conspirator in a great heist. "Aye. You see, we practically stole it."

"Shall I take it to your library perchance? It would be a lovely addition atop the mantel." He hated to part with such a cherished heirloom from Buchanan history, but knowing it was kept in the care of a dear friend lightened the burden somewhat. "Truly, I canna allow such a gift."

"You would deny Grace this one opportunity to express her gratitude to you and to Clan Buchannan?" The countess thwacked the top of the box, nearly making him drop it. "I beg your pardon, but not only will my sister find your rebuff hurtful, I do as well. Do you have any idea the lengths to which we went in order to acquire that horn? Grace had to convince the chancellor's clerk to admit it was indeed included among the items they were putting up for auction. You have no choice but to accept the horn and return it to its rightful place!"

"Ahem." A footman appeared in the doorway. "I beg your pardon, Laird Buchanan, but whilst you were out we received word that Prince Isidor's ship has arrived."

"So soon?" Her Ladyship asked.

Frasier replaced the box on the bed. "The boat wasna due until the fifth of May—not for at least another fortnight."

The man shrugged while Charity stepped forward. "Why wasn't I notified straightaway? I have been home for over an hour."

"When did Grace write the note?" Frasier asked as the footman turned scarlet.

"She sent it to me via messenger yesterday," replied the countess.

He leveled his gaze at the footman. "How long has the ship been in port?"

"I've really no idea." The lad spread his palms apologetically. "Forgive me, madam, but I was away with the carriage to fetch Brixham from Parliament. I came up here as soon as I returned."

"I understand, Randall, but it is verra important for us to know if my sister has already departed from Dunscaby's residence."

"Would ye like for me to run over and ask? It won't take but a moment or two."

"Please do," Frasier said—looking at the footman. "Meanwhile, I'll fetch my horse. I owe the princess my sincere gratitude."

He could make all the excuses in the world, but Frasier was not about to let her go without a fight.

25

G race fumed throughout the entire coach ride from Mayfair. She, a princess and the sister of a duke, had been given a mere hour to pack her trunks and make haste to the wharf. An hour! Anyone else in all of Christendom would realize it takes at least a week to pack, regardless if her new lady's maid had already begun to organize her effects. An hour was hardly time enough to don a proper traveling gown.

She wasn't surprised when, after a Lithuanian dragoon dressed in a navy-blue coat and white breeches handed her down from the carriage, she was met by Lord Alder. "My Lord, I should have known you would conspire against me."

He offered his elbow which she ignored with a sniff and toss of her chin. "Good evening, Princess. I trust your ride was comfortable."

"I beg your pardon? Do not try to tell me that you give a rotten fig about my comfort. I was allowed but an hour to collect my things. Furthermore, I am convinced that you colluded with someone to assure I was summoned the very night that today's session of Parliament was to run late as it often did when there was an important vote which fiercely split the Tories and the Whigs. Not to mention my brother Gibb is presently in Edinburgh. You, sir, have been spying on me!"

He merely shrugged, his face impassive as a retinue of Isidor's dragoons marched them toward the gangway of the *Royal Lithuania* with its sails already unfurled while a growing crowd watched in awe.

Grace glanced to a man wearing a tricorn hat who looked at her as if she were being forced to board a prisoners' schooner on her way to serve a life sentence of transportation. "The ship is over a fortnight early," she seethed out of the corner of her mouth. "And you cannot tell me you had nothing to do with it."

Alder stepped onto the plank and offered his hand this time. "Very well, I shall deny nothing."

She used the rope rails rather than allow this slippery eel to touch her gloved hand. "Exactly why am I being treated as if I am not trustworthy? I had resolved to set aside the..." She glanced over her shoulder to ensure no one was close enough to overhear—which several onlookers were. "I was so looking forward to reuniting with my husband," she rephrased. Alder knew what she meant, the fiend.

"He is waiting for you inside his stateroom."

She stopped mid-stride, gripping the ropes. "Isidor is here?"

"Yes. Which is why—"

"Princess Grace!" a rider called from the wharf.

Gooseflesh rose across her skin as she recognized Frasier's voice.

"Princess Grace!" he hollered again, dismounting. "Might I have a wee word afore you set sail?"

Alder grabbed her arm. "Who the hell is that brash Highland yokel?"

She wrenched away and backed a step. "He happens to be the man who saved my life after my carriage overturned in the midst of a blizzard. I owe him a moment."

"But—"

She dashed down the ramp while thrusting a defiant finger at Alder. "I *will* have a moment, sir!"

As His Lordship stood gape-mouthed, she hastened along the busy wharf, wanting nothing more than to run into the welcoming warmth of Frasier's arms. Instead, with a retinue of dragoons flanking her, she reached out and grasped his hands.

His brow furrowed with worry, his eyes pleading. "I couldna allow you to leave without saying goodbye."

"I'm so glad you came."

His gaze shifted to the soldier on her right and his jaw twitched. "Though this isna quite the send off I had in mind."

Dear Lord, how she hated being accompanied by armed guards as if she were a criminal! "I assure you it isn't anywhere near what I expected either."

"You are certain you want to go through with this?"

"It is my duty and I cannot turn my back on the vows I took... Before the eyes of God." Grace gestured to the domed roof of St. Peter's Cathedral, dominating the London skyline. No matter how deeply it hurt, she had to end things between them once and for all. "You must go on and live your life as if I'd never existed."

"What I said afore still holds true. If ye should need me, send word and I shall take on Isidor's entire army if need be."

"Thank you, but I must do everything in my power to see to it that I make my husband happy."

"But what of your happiness?"

She gulped. This was no time to cry. To enable him to move on, Frasier needed to believe Grace had made her decision. "My mother reminded me that I always see to it that I make my own happiness. She was quite right. Besides, you ought to know me well enough by now. I shall be fine—as will you."

His eyes seemed to go out of focus as he gave her a sharp nod. "I ken you will." He bowed and kissed her hand. "M'lady, I wish you every happiness."

Grace pursed her lips. "And I wish you every success."

A dragoon touched her elbow. "We must go, Princess."

She gave the guard a thin-lipped glare. "We will go when I say we are ready to do so."

"Thank you for your assistance in returning the Horn of Bannockburn to Clan Buchannan," Frasier said his voice almost in monotone.

If only she could tell him why she had done it—not for the clan, but for the man. She loved him with every fiber of her body. And now she was doing the most selfless thing she'd ever done in all her days. "Go. Find a spirited woman to marry—someone who can cook and clean and bear you a multitude of healthy children. I swear to you it will be best if you never think of me again."

With her words, Frasier seemed to have lost his tongue. Looking utterly forlorn, he released her hands and backed away, his powerful form being swallowed by the mass of humanity.

When she could no longer make out the tartan of his cap, she finally turned and gestured to the presumptuous soldier. "Lead on."

After she stepped aboard, Grace grasped the rail of the ship and looked out along the river's edge. The streetlamps had been lit, their yellow halos shining in regular intervals among the dark blue shadows of humanity. Across the street, Frasier sat his horse, partially illuminated by a lamp, his head held high. Never in her life had she been so ashamed of her lofty birth.

Lord Alder tapped her elbow. "This way, Princess. The captain gave the order to weigh anchor as soon as you stepped aboard."

Her heart as hollow as a gourd, Grace followed aft along the deck. "I thought Isidor had planned to remain on the continent."

"No," said Alder, not explaining further. He opened a door and walked through a narrow corridor, it's wooden paneling polished to a pristine sheen. They passed by three doors until they arrived at the fourth. He knocked before opening the latch.

Grace stepped inside, meeting the gaze of her husband for the first time since her wedding day. Isidor did not approach but remained in place with his back to the ship's stern-facing windows. He appeared thinner, perhaps a tad gaunt. Isidor gave her a nod, then shifted his gaze to Alder. "I trust everything went as planned?"

"It did," said His Lordship, confirming Grace's suspicions. He had been spying on her and her family and Isidor had come at a time when he wouldn't be challenged to a duel. *The coward.*

She curtsied, bowing her head as she ought. "Your Highness, I wasn't expecting you for another fortnight."

"Are you not happy to see me, wife?" he asked, coughing.

"I didn't say that." She glanced around the stateroom, where she should have spent her wedding night. It was everything she'd imagined and more complete with a mahogany four-poster bed, but none of it impressed her. Grace felt nothing but emptiness and heartbreak. "Surprised is more apt. However, I must express my dismay at not being given enough time to pack."

"Anything you may have left behind you can buy once we arrive in Klapedia." Isidor drew a handkerchief to his lips and coughed again, this time more robustly.

"Are you unwell?" she asked, stepping toward him, but he held up a palm demanding she stop, then moved to Alder's side and showed him his handkerchief.

The alarm on His Lordship's expression spoke volumes about Isidor's condition. "How long have you had the cough?"

"A few weeks. I do believe I contracted a touch of influenza in Brussels."

Grace moved forward. "We mustn't set sail. If you've been ill that long, you should be seen by a doctor straightaway."

"She's right," said Alder as the ship groaned and creaked, listing into the Thames current.

Isidor shook his head of wheaten hair. "Not in London."

"Then where?" she asked. "If we sail into the North Sea and hit bad weather, you could grow worse."

"There's sure to be a doctor in Southend," said Alder while the foam from a wake roiled behind the ship. "With a favorable wind we ought to be there within the hour."

26

Throughout the long journey home, Frasier had more time to think than he would have liked. The Buchanan name was clear. The Horn of Bannockburn had been returned to its rightful place. There was a great deal to be thankful for and he tried to force himself to look on the bright side. But his heart could not be convinced. Aye, he'd never pursued Grace MacGalloway because she was too far above his station. Hell, he never would have met the lass if it weren't for his father sending him to foster with the duke. But how could he do as she asked and live his life as if she'd never existed?

Though he had no answers, it was time to stop living his father's dreams and start following his own. Life at Druimliart was comfortable.

After stabling his horse and ensuring the gelding had an extra ration of oats, he wearily trudged to his cottage. As soon as he stepped inside, an enormous weight lifted from his shoulders. He set the box with the horn on the table and after lighting a few tallow candles and starting a fire in the hearth, he poured himself a dram of whisky.

Damnation, it was good to be home. Even if the

cottage was as quiet as death. He glanced back to the bedchamber and half expected Grace to emerge. But she had sharply told him never to think of her again. By now the princess ought to be settling into one of the duchy's vast estates. She was where she was meant to be—living in luxury, wanting for nothing, with countless servants to cater to her every need. No, her marriage mightn't be a love match, but she had never expected it to be. She was a woman of many talents and she would prosper come what may.

Would she not?

As he sipped his whisky, he examined the box, running his hand over the aged surface. The thing was so heavy, he'd had to buy a mule to pack it into the Highlands.

He opened the lid and carefully removed the horn, first examining the gold mouthpiece. He blew on the opening, his air going nowhere. He swapped ends. Upon his first inspection, nothing seemed amiss, but when he held it to the light, the damned thing wasn't even hollow.

What the devil?

Frasier explored inside with his pointer finger, his nail scratching a bit of sealing wax. After taking his sgian dubh from his flashes, he blindly ran the tip of the blade around the edge of the seal. It took a bit of effort, but the wax eventually popped out and flew across the table, landing on the floor, the jingle of metal tinkling behind it.

He upended the horn and out slid a cache of gold coins embossed with the image of a crowned unicorn —one of the heraldic symbols of Scotland. The reverse presented Scotland's royal coat of arms. The writing encircling each side was inscribed in Latin.

Frasier gathered a handful in his fist. "These are nearly as old as the horn itself."

They were also worth more than his cottage, worth more than Druimliart, worth far more than the five hundred pounds the crown wanted for the Buchanan's ancestral seat on the Isle of Clairinsh. In fact, this coin would most likely be enough to purchase the entirety of Loch Lomond.

His gaze shifted to the box and his heart raced. It took but a minute to find and remove the false bottom.

"Whoaaaaa!" he shouted, a high pitch screeching from his throat. If Frasier thought there was a fortune hidden in the horn, it was only a quarter of the gold in the box.

Angus burst through the door. "Holy Christmas, I thought ye were dying!"

In two steps, Frasier wrapped his arms around his friend and spun the heavy, black-bearded bag of bones in a circle. "Dunna unpack your satchel, we're heading to Edinburgh come morn!"

"Och, ye earn a pardon from the Prince Regent and all of the sudden ye're paying calls to the nobles?"

"Nay." He gestured to the gold coins. "We're off to purchase the Isle of Clairinsh and whatever we need to rebuild our castle."

Angus gaped at the cache. "Where the bloody hell did all that come from?"

While Frasier explained about the sealed horn and false bottom, he poured two more drams of whisky. "I thought that damned box was hewn of petrified wood."

"'Tis a good thing the Chancellor of the Exchequer didna look too closely."

Frasier tapped his glass against Angus'. "Bloody oath."

"So ye reckon we ought to leave Druimliart?"

"The heart of our homeland is the isle—has been the time of King Alexander II—afore Robert the Bruce and the Wars of Independence when Scotland was a sovereign nation."

"There may be some folk who want to stay put," said Angus as if he might be one of them.

"I see no reason those who wish to stay canna. The summer grazing here is far better than in the Lowlands. Besides, we'll not be running herds of cattle on the island." Frasier's mind raced as he spoke. "We'll need caretakers here to mind our livestock."

Angus' smile fell. "But you'll no' be here?"

"I've a castle to rebuild."

"She's no' coming back."

Frasier's excitement deflated as if he were sailing at a fast tack and the wind suddenly died. "I ken," he mumbled. He mightn't be able to marry Grace, but he now had the means to find a wife and keep her in style.

"Lady Modesty is coming of age," Angus mused.

"Wheesht."

Frasier might love the MacGalloway family as much as his own, but if he couldn't have Grace, he didn't want to marry into the family and hear tell of Grace on a daily basis. It would drive him mad. Besides, since he was making a new start, it was time he stopped using the duke's family as a crutch. He'd find his own damned wife and love her as much as he loved Grace.

If such a thing were possible.

~

TWO WEEKS after they dropped anchor in Southend and brought the local physician aboard, Isidor passed away. As soon as the doctor examined the prince, he diagnosed consumption which came as no surprise considering the blood in his handkerchief when she and Lord Alder had boarded the ship. To her chagrin, Grace was not allowed to approach her husband's bedside. Instead, she was assigned a small berth adjoining his stateroom from where she could observe but was instructed not to enter.

From the doorway she learned how deeply Isidor and Alder loved each other. During the entire fortnight, Lord Alder sat beside the prince. He fluffed his pillows, he held the cloth when he coughed, he cleansed the perspiration from his body and spooned a willow tincture into his mouth. Grace felt as though she were on a cloud looking down upon a heart-rending scene of a man at the end of his life saying goodbye to the one soul he cherished most in this world.

Lord Alder also refused to allow Isidor's valet to help with anything. Alder himself shaved the prince, his every caring and fluid motion filled with adoration, respect, and love. Yes, Grace had heard horrible things about men who engaged in "shameful" acts with other men, but from her observation, Isidor had found his love match in Lord Alder. If only society could understand as she now did, these two men should have never been kept apart. She should not have walked down the aisle—had she known, of course she would not have done so. Isidor also should not have promised to love and cherish her. True, the prince needed an heir, but such a requirement had cost him dearly. He would die along with an enormous list of men who left no male legacy. The sun would still rise every morn just as it had always set every evening.

When it was clear that her husband would not survive the crossing of the North Sea, Grace sent for Charity to join her. Together they spent quiet hours tending to their embroidery aboard ship where they remained in the comfort of the royal suites. Charity had always been the most caring of the MacGalloway sisters, and she proved so now. She seemed to know when to speak, when to ask questions, and when to remain silent as with each passing day, Isidor's spirit faded.

From the door of her berth, Grace watched as the man she married drew his last breath while clasping the hands of his one true love. She gently closed the door and left Lord Alder to his grief, then gave the order to set sail for Klapedia where he would be buried.

The crossing was turbulent, but swift. The funeral was attended by hundreds of mourners all of whom wept for the passing of who they saw as a good man. Grace also wept behind her black veil, wishing she'd been able to come to know him better, wishing the rift between them had never happened, yet realizing she had been meant to find him with Lord Alder because that moment was a catalyst that had opened her eyes to so many things.

The day after the funeral, Grace and her sister meandered through the palace's long gallery which displayed portraits of one prince after another who had filled the eldership in the Duchy of Samogitia.

"The servants have been very accommodating," said Charity, stopping at the portrait of Isidor's father, gazing up at the near life-sized image.

"Exceedingly so," Grace agreed, though she felt

akin to a kitten placed among a household filled with dogs. Words were not necessary to know they somehow held her responsible for Isidor's demise. The servants went about their duties, tight-lipped with eyes downcast, seeming to have an aura of negative bias oozing from their pores. She could only imagine the gossip below stairs after their lord had gone to England to marry the sister of a duke and returned without her, then he'd sailed for England again (by way of Brussels) and returned home in a coffin, his widow making an ill-timed appearance.

Charity moved along, strolling forward, and looping her arm through Grace's elbow. "I know you said you wish to return home, but you could stay here. After all, you are inheriting a quarter. And this palace is as splendid as Carlton House."

Grace chuckled, fluffing out her black bombazine skirts. "I suppose I could sit here and play the grieving widow alone in a strange country. Some gallant Russian ought to take pity on me."

"You deserve no one's pity."

"No. But I do not belong here," she said, the words reminding her that she had been told the same by Fiona not so long ago. Would she ever find where she belonged? "I don't even feel as if I deserve a quarter of Isidor's estate."

"After all he put you through? After you were certain your life was ruined forever?"

"Even after all of it. Isidor loved Alder but needed me only as a vessel for his heir."

"Vessel?"

"Yes, well I had the same reaction at first, but after spending two weeks watching His Lordship dote over my husband, I feel differently. After Martin told me to give my marriage a try I feared Isidor might be a tyrant. Alder even came to the town house and told me Isidor would allow me my freedom once I bore an heir, but I didn't believe him at the time."

"I dunna think I would have believed that man either."

"But now my husband is gone, and I am left feeling as empty as a soap bubble." Grace stopped and grasped her sister's hands. "I do want to go home—but to Scotland. I'm finished with London and the snobbish airs of polite society."

"My heavens, sister, I never thought I'd see the day when you snubbed the *ton*." Charity opened her fan and cooled her face. "Or chose Scotland over England —you are the only one of Mama's children who endeavored to affect an English accent. Are you certain you dunna have a fever?"

"I am quite sure and am feeling well, thank you."

They strolled along the long hall until Charity led the way into the front parlor with an ornate Rococo ceiling and lavish furniture of the same French style. "What about Laird Buchanan? The two of you seemed to get on awfully well when we were dancing at Marty's town house. At least until he collapsed on top of you."

Grace chuckled into her fingertips. Evidently Charity had not been apprised of the fact that the princess had spent three entire days at the highlander's bedside. Furthermore Grace had cajoled her sister into bidding for the horn because "she merely wanted to recognize the laird for rescuing her from certain death."

"And he did save you from perishing in that horrendous carriage accident," Charity continued. "I assume things were rather bleak at Druimliart?"

"Yes, bleak is a good name for it. How did you know?"

"I paid a visit once with Martin and was a wee bit shocked to see the laird's cottage was so—"

"Primitive?"

"Exactly." Charity sat on a settee and patted the seat beside her. "It was very thoughtful of you to purchase the horn on Buchanan's behalf. I assume there arenae any romantic feelings between the two of you?"

Grace sighed as she lowered herself beside her sister. She had been rather heartless when she'd sent Frasier away on the pier, resolved to join her husband. His face had been so stricken, so resolute. He had thanked her for the gift and then bowed to her wishes. Any romance that had existed between them she had smote on the wharf beside the Thames. And now she would be in mourning for a year. The last thing she ought to think about is the handsome laird who lived in a hovel with no servants. "He is free to marry whomever he may choose."

Grace looked at the painting of Isidor above the parlor's marble hearth. But instead of the prince's pretty face, she envisioned Frasier's blue eyes, long dark hair when it was unbound, and strong jaw. Who was she fooling? Since the man had rescued her in the Highlands, she had thought of little else. She had even hung the marionette of the Highland lass on her bedpost.

"Well, I reckon Frasier Buchanan is a wee bit too rugged for the likes of you." Charity reached for a book resting on the low table. "Well, whatever you decide to do, I for one am happy to see you have come through all this adversity with what seems to me as a new perspective on life."

27

"Three wagon loads of furniture? Ye'll have all the gold spent afore the year's end!" Angus said as he rode up to the Dumbarton pier where Frasier, Davy, and Ramsey had unloaded his shipment of furniture from Glasgow and were preparing to haul it seventeen miles northward to Balmaha. The village was located on the shores of Loch Lomond where Frasier moored his new wherry which he used to transport everything to the castle.

It was already early November and Frasier hadn't even spent a quarter of his share of the gold. Of course, he'd given each family in the clan a portion for their own use. He'd had also purchased the Isle of Clairinsh from the crown after which he and a handful of hired masons as well as carpenters from the clan had repaired the castle including the addition of a new roof. Not surprisingly, Angus and Fiona had decided to stay in the Highlands where Angus was to oversee the livestock. His brother-in-law would be heading back to Druimliart as soon as they moved the new furniture into the castle.

Lena and her husband Davy had been elated to join Frasier, accepting the positions of housekeeper and butler even though they had no experience and knew little of what to expect when they entered into service. Nonetheless, Frasier had offered attractive wages and the young couple jumped at the chance to live in the castle. As did Ramsey who had proved himself to be a particularly good groundskeeper and had the gardens looking akin to a proper Scottish estate.

Frasier winked at Angus. "We've enough coin to last us the rest of our days." He climbed aboard the lead wagon and took up the reins. "Tell me, what are your plans with your share of the gold?"

Angus squinted his black eyes. "I'm no' letting it run through my fingers like water if that's what ye're asking."

Frasier snorted as he released the brake. The man was more likely to bury his portion and forget where he hid it than to spend a farthing.

"Buchanan!"

Recognizing the voice, Frasier immediately grabbed the lever and reengaged the brake. "Dunscaby? What the devil are you doing here?"

The duke gestured to his brother. "Gibb and I are just passing through on our way to the lodge to enjoy the shooting."

Frasier gave the sea captain a friendly nod.

Eyeing the wagonloads, Dunscaby whistled. "It looks as if ye've been busy. Last I heard, you'd purchased the Isle of Clairinsh. Dunna tell me ye've acquired another property as well?"

"Nay—rebuilt the old castle."

Gibb's horse sidestepped anxiously and he patted the fella's neck to calm the wee beasty. "I heard the place was in ruins."

"Aye, after three and seventy years the roof had caved in above the great hall, but we were able to salvage more than I'd hoped. That and we've been working like fiends to make the place livable afore winter sets in."

"I'm duly impressed." Dunscaby gestured to the flintlock rifle holstered on his saddle. "We'd be happy if you'd join us—shoot a nice stag before the snows come."

"Mayhap next year I'll have things sorted out enough to enjoy some sport."

"Verra well." Dunscaby cued his horse to walk on, but tugged the reins as if he had something more to say. "I'll have to stop by soon to see what you've done with the old fortress."

"I'd like that—you're welcome any time." Frasier nodded to Gibb. "All of you. Ah…" He bit down on his bottom lip. Not a day had passed when he hadn't thought of Grace. He couldn't simply let the duke ride away without asking. "How is the princess faring in Lithuania?"

A pinch formed between Dunscaby's eyebrows. "You havena ye heard?"

Oh, God, if that bastard hurt her in any way, Frasier would sail across the Baltic Sea and sever the man's ballocks. "Heard?" he asked all but growling.

"Isidor succumbed to consumption."

Frasier sat back, his jaw dropping. "She's a widow?"

"Aye, still in mourning," said Dunscaby.

Gibb moved his horse alongside the duke's. "She has another six months of it."

Six months? The prince must have died shortly after Grace left London. "If ye dunna mind me asking, is she still on the continent?"

"Nay," said Gibb. "She went there for a time with Charity but returned not long after the funeral."

"To...?"

The duke nodded toward the southeast. "She's at Newhailes helping my mother prepare Modesty and Kitty for their comings out."

Tugging up his riding gloves, Frasier bit his cheek to hide the maelstrom of emotions shooting from his heart to every fiber of his body. "I reckon she has her hands full, then."

"You're not wrong," said Gibb with a wink. "Though she's been a tad melancholy. Definitely no' the fiery Grace of late."

Frasier bid farewell to the two MacGalloway brothers and was about to release the brake again when Angus came marching up beside the wagon. "What the bleeding hell are ye doin'? Me and the lads will haul your finery to Clairinsh, ye numpty."

Still gripping the reins, he glanced back to his horse saddled and tied to the rear of his wagon. "There could be trouble along the road. I ought to see these things to the isle afore I go traipsing off like a lovesick whelp."

Davy was the next to abandon his wagon. "Och, Ramsey can drive my wagon and I'll drive this one. Ye'd best be on your way."

"But you heard His Grace," Frasier argued. After all wooing widows took careful planning. "The princess is still in mourning."

"Aye." Angus offered his hand and tugged the laird off his perch. "But she willna be forever. Stop acting like a bloody eejit afore the lot of us boot your arse into the Firth of Clyde!"

～

GRACE WALKED AROUND MODESTY, examining her sister's evening dress as the modiste worked to pin up the hem. "These sleeves deviate quite markedly from last Season's fashions. Is there too much puff, I'm wondering?"

"*Mais non, madame,*" said the modiste whom Mama had brought from Paris. "*Ce sont au top de la mode.*"

"I like them," said Modesty examining the cutaway sleeves in the mirror.

"*Nous verrons,*" Grace said, "we will see," to the modiste more than anything. Usually Paris fashions did very well in London, but there were only slight differences from one year to the next.

Nonetheless, Mama did not make mistakes when it came to ordering new gowns for her daughters. And though Grace had used a modiste who was located in London, she had always dressed in the height of style, which had helped her garner eleven proposals.

"Have you decided if you're going to chaperone our debut Season?" asked Kitty from her perch on the settee.

"I have decided that I am for it," Modesty added, twirling a red curl around her pointer finger. Evidently she had recovered from her fear of being introduced to polite society. "Especially since you will be wearing mourning whilst Kitty and I will be dressed fashionably in every color imaginable."

"Just do not wear orange," Grace whispered under her breath before she turned to Kitty. "I haven't yet made up my mind."

The housekeeper stepped into the withdrawing room and cleared her throat. "I beg your pardon, Princess, but a gentleman has come to call."

Kitty giggled and batted her eyelashes at Modesty. "*A gentleman.*"

"Scandalous," said her sister. "And with six more months of mourning yet to go."

"Hush." Grace plucked the calling card from the housekeeper's fingertips, read the man's name, and nearly swooned. She suddenly couldn't breathe, the room spun, her heart hammering.

"Shall I tell him you are unavailable, madam?"

"Oh, no." She quickly patted her hands over her hair. "Most certainly not."

Heavens, how did Frasier find out she was at Newhailes? Not that she was upset to have him know even though he had most likely come to tell her that he had found the woman of his dreams at long last— that he'd found a lass who loves his cottage at Druimliart and sees it as a huge step up from the one-room cottage she shared with her parents, sleeping on a dirt floor, no less.

Before Grace made it to the parlor, she'd reached the pinnacle of envy. What she wouldn't do to change places with the lass, drat it all! Why must everything in her life go up in flames?

Giles stood beside the door as if playing guard dog. "Shall I have the housemaid bring in a tea service, Your Highness?"

Stopping, she heaved a sigh. The first thing that came to mind was mead, but she doubted the wine cellar contained one single bottle. It was nearly time to dress for dinner and she had already imbibed in enough tea to make her eyeballs float. Why not enjoy an aperitif? "Honestly, I believe a bottle of ratafia is in order. Cook's ham and walnut finger sandwiches as well, if you please."

The butler bowed as he opened the door. "Straightaway, madam."

As soon as Frasier turned from the hearth and met her gaze, Grace was overcome with a renewed bout of swoon-inducing heart hammering. "My Laird. How lovely it is to see you." Managing to keep her voice serene and composed, she moved inside. How was it a man could be more beautiful than he was in her memory? His blue eyes more vivid. His jaw more masculine. Surely his shoulders were broader, his hose-clad calves more muscular.

Frasier's breath seemed to catch as his eyes brightened. "M'lady...*ah*...Princess." He crossed the floor, grasped her hand with trembling fingers, and kissed it. "Thank you for receiving me."

"Of course, you must know you are always welcome, Your Lairdship. But—"

"Hmm?"

How did he know he'd find her at Newhailes? "I'm afraid my brother is not at home."

"I didna come to see your brother."

"Oh?"

"Actually, it was the duke who told me..." Frasier glanced to the portrait of Grace's great grandfather, the fourteenth Duke of Dunscaby. "Well, he told me of your loss."

"I see." She fluffed the skirts of her drab mourning gown. Alas, he had paid a call to express his condolences. Of course, she had many such visits of late. "Please do not tell me that's what brought you all the way down from Druimliart."

He licked his lips, his gaze sweeping over her from head to toe, his expression one of a man who was starving and had been deprived of food for far too long. As he shook his head, Giles crossed the floor, carrying a tray containing two crystal glasses, a matching decanter of ruby liquid, and a plate of finger sandwiches Grace had requested.

"Shall I pour, Your Highness?" asked the butler as he set the tray on the low table.

"Please." She shifted her gaze to her guest. "Will you join me in some refreshment?"

"Thank you."

Together they sat on a settee much the same color as the drink. Grace picked up both glasses and handed one to Frasier.

"Ratafia?" he asked.

"Would you prefer something else?"

"Oh, no." He took the glass and waited for her to sip, then followed suit. "Mmm. 'Tis sweet."

"And delicious." She licked her lips. "So tell me, what have you been up to these past months whilst I've been thrust into the role of grieving widow?"

Frasier placed his glass on the table, stood, and started to pace. "There is so much to say, I hardly ken where to start."

"Then may I begin with an apology?"

"What? Why? You owe me no such thing."

She released a long, pent-up breath. "Regret is like a cancer that eats away at your soul. When it comes to you, I regret ever so much."

The highlander's expression brightened with the lifting of his eyebrows. "You do?"

"I only hope I am not too late."

He kneeled before her. "Too late for what, *mo leannan*?" he asked, his voice as breathless as hers.

Grace clapped her fingers to her cheeks to quell the fiery rush. Must she utter it? "I am sorry for so very much. Especially the way we last parted. I was rather curt when I sent you away and—"

"Och, nay. You had no choice but to proceed with your duty. I canna say how grateful I am to you for your gift." He grinned. Broadly. "There was far more to it than met the eye."

"Oh?"

He took her hands between his large palms. "As I said there is so verra much to say, but first of all I must tell you that within the horn and inside its box was hidden a fortune in gold."

Grace gasped. "Oh, my!"

"You are entitled to it as much as anyone."

She started to decline, but he silenced her with a subtle shake of his head. "Grace. Princess. Bonny lass. My heart beats only with my love for you. I never in all my days dreamed I would be in a position to offer for your hand, but now I would be the happiest man in the world if you would consider marrying me and sharing my fortune. I ken I'm no prince, but I—"

She tugged his knuckles to her lips and showered them with kisses. "I do not want a prince. I want a braw highlander who would risk his life to rescue me at the bottom of a ravine in the midst of a blizzard. I want a man who lives by a code of honor, who puts clan and kin before all else. I want you, Frasier Buchanan, and only you."

One of the glasses of ratafia clattered to the carpet as he surged forward and pulled her into his arms, his mouth meeting hers in a hungry maelstrom of passion. Their lips fused with an urgency which had been suppressed for days...for weeks...for months...for a lifetime.

As their kisses paused, Frasier touched Grace's forehead with his. "I hope ye dunna mind living in a castle on a wee isle in Loch Lomond."

28

S ince Martin was not presently in residence at Newhailes, Grace felt it was best for them both to speak to her mother at once. Feeling as giddy as she had been before she was introduced to Queen Charlotte, Grace's insides swarmed with the wings of butterflies as together they faced the dowager who received them in the upstairs lady's parlor.

Frasier held her hand firmly, almost too firmly, yet his grip was the only outward sign of his nervousness. "Your Grace," he began, bowing. "We have something of great import to discuss with you."

Mama cocked her head to one side. "The two of you?"

"Indeed," he said crisply, his breathing faster than usual. "I have asked Princess Grace to marry me."

"You?" Mama blurted as if the notion had never occurred to her.

Bouncing on her toes, Grace beamed and tugged Frasier's hand over her heart. "And I accepted."

Her mother's eyebrows angled outward as if she'd been taken by utter surprise. "Without discussing it with Martin first?"

"I am a widow," Grace explained even though her

mother had been a widow for far longer. "I am no longer subject to the same rigid rules as a maiden."

Mama's nostrils flared as she snapped open her fan. "I beg to differ. Martin must give his blessing."

Grace's temper chose this moment to send a fiery flash through her blood. "And we shall ask him," she sharply replied. "Since he is at the lodge, we thought you would like to be consulted first."

Mama closed her fan and lowered it to her lap as her lips pursed. "Buchanan, would you please allow me a moment alone with my daughter?"

"Of course."

Grace took a calming breath as she waited for Frasier to take his leave, then faced her mother, shoulders squared, a wall of armor at the ready.

Tilting up her chin, Mama heaved a heavy sigh. "Dearest, you cannot be serious. You are now a princess in control of a sizeable fortune. Is he aware you are worth forty thousand a year?"

After hearing Frasier's windfall, it hadn't quite seemed like the time to expound about hers. "I haven't found the opportunity to tell him as of yet."

"But you've been to Druimliart. You know how crude his living conditions are up there in the mountains. You of all my children are the last who would be able to tolerate such poverty. And even if you did use your money to build a suitable house, the cold would certainly sap you."

Grace glanced at the closed door and lowered her voice. "Since we are alone, it is incumbent upon me to tell you that His Lairdship has come into his own fortune and has restored his family's castle on the Isle of Clairinsh."

Mama's lips formed a perfect O. "How?"

"He acquired the Horn of Bannockburn at the Jacobite auction in London." Not wanting to explain she had used the pin money she'd been saving, she raced on. "As it turns out, the old relic had been stuffed full of gold coins and sealed with wax. Buchanan has no need of my fortune."

"But he's merely a Scottish laird. Last year you received a proposal from a duke which at the time was not lofty enough for you."

"Does it matter?" she asked, on the verge of shouting, but she held on to her wits and held forth, "A great deal has changed since my come out. Heavens, Mama, I never believed you to be a snob."

"I am not a snob!" Mama insisted.

"No?"

"I have only the utmost respect for Buchanan. After all, your father fostered him for two years. During that time he had many of the same opportunities as Martin. And you may recall I do invite him to most of our gatherings." This time Mama casually opened her fan and cooled her face. "Are you certain this is what you want? You never gave the man a second look until your ghastly accident in the Highlands. Surely with all that transpired, you were distraught."

"I was devastated."

"Well, I say, you are not the first young lady who has formed an attachment for her rescuer. It is only natural for you to become infatuated with—"

"This is not an infatuation. I assure you!" Grace pressed her fingers to her temples while she paced. "I have admired Buchanan ever since I can remember. Terribly so. Every time he was present at one of our affairs, I purposefully went out of my way to ignore him for fear of falling in love with the man. And now

I've gone and done so and absolutely nothing will change my mind!"

Mama continued to fan herself while she glanced out the window as if dreaming of a lost love. "A castle on an island did you say?"

"Yes. Frasier purchased his ancestral lands from the crown."

"Did he?" Mama chuckled. "Bless him for his role in preventing the kingdom from yet another bankruptcy." She leaned forward. "You do know I have always liked that boy."

Frasier was hardly a boy, but this was no time to argue. "He is a good man," Grace agreed.

"That is because your father gave him a solid foundation upon which to build his principles." Mama closed her fan and stood. "So, you'd best notify your brother straightaway."

"Frasier and I thought we might travel up to the lodge and meet him there."

"Together?" Mama asked, all dreaminess gone in a flicker.

"We shall bring along my lady's maid and a footman or two."

Mama slapped her fan in her palm as if she happened upon a good idea. "It would do Modesty and Kitty some good to accompany you as well."

Oh, dear, bringing the gaggling gossip twins was absolutely out of the question. "No, no, no! Have you lost your mind? I have spent the past four months with those two flibbertigibbets and I flatly refuse to take them into the Highlands where they might very well fall off a cliff and die. After all, Modesty already had such an incident when she traveled to Brixham with Charity."

"You can be so melodramatic. Modesty was only

eleven years of age. She's far more graceful now that she has finished growing."

"And you are far too optimistic at times." Grace shuffled forward and surrounded her mother in an embrace. "I love you dearly. But the two girls must remain here with you."

~

FRASIER WAS SHOWN to a guest room on the third floor of the manse, situated in a rear turret looking out over Newhailes' park-like grounds extending all the way to the Firth of Forth. The circular bedchamber was smaller than the one he'd been given in London but was neatly appointed with a Grecian-style bed which was topped by light green bed curtains, hanging from an ornate gilt crown affixed to the ceiling. The chintz fabric parted in two pieces which draped over both the bed's headboard and footboard.

He liked that the room was not symmetrical, the eye drawing to the arc of windows framed with the same green chintz as the bed curtains. There was a small fireplace with a cast-iron insert, a padded chair and writing table, and a washstand with a mirror on the wall above it.

Honestly, Frasier would have been content to sleep in the stables. He would have been content not to sleep at all. He was going to marry Grace MacGalloway, a woman he had admired ever since she had left the nursery. During his ride from Dunbarton to Newhailes, he'd scarcely allowed himself to dream that she might say yes.

A light tap came at the door. "Frasier? May I come in?"

He practically flew across the floor.

There, standing in the corridor was his love, wearing a lacy dressing gown, carrying a candle in a brass holder. He glanced beyond her into the corridor. "Is all well, *mo leannan*?"

She stepped inside and urged him to close the door, her expression a wee bit shy. "I am in mourning."

"Aye," he said, ever so glad her dressing gown wasn't also black.

"But I couldn't stay away."

He gulped as he traced his finger along the lace of her neckline. "Did anyone see you come up here?"

"No. I made certain of it."

He stood for a moment, gazing into her lovely blue eyes, his heart hammering so loudly he was sure it would soon start rattling the windows. "Grace," he whispered. "If ye remain here, I canna promise I willna make love to ye. Your scent, your captivating eyes, your mere presence makes me ravenous for ye."

"I was deprived of a bride's wedding night." A seductive smile spread across her lips as she slowly pulled open her satin sash. "But it has always been you who I've wanted. Will you please take me to bed this very moment?"

As he reached for her, the dressing gown dropped to the floor. His breath stopped. His mouth went dry. The woman was completely nude. Frasier was unable to draw a breath into his lungs as his gaze meandered over her creamy flesh, drawn first to the lush breasts tipped by a light shade of rose. Her tiny waist flared, gently arcing into womanly hips. At her apex, a nest of curls tempted him like a treasure waiting to be discovered. She was far more exquisite than his wildest imaginings.

"My God, woman," was all he managed to utter,

moaning, pulling her into his arms and sealing his lips over hers.

Grace's embrace was fierce as if she were holding on to him for dear life. "Show me what to do," she said, her breathing shallow as she rubbed her hips across his erection.

"Are you certain you dunna want to wait until our wedding night?"

"Six months?" She pressed her soft breasts against his chest, the only thing separating their skin, the thin linen of his shirt. "I'll go mad in that time!"

If she continued to caress him with her sublime, naked body, he'd be driven completely insane within a matter of minutes. He had dreamed of this moment—relived it over and over again in the darkness of night, but now that Grace was nude and in his arms without a moment of foreplay, he wasn't quite sure where to begin.

"Are you angry with me?" she asked, loosening her grip a tad.

"What?" He kissed her. "No. Never."

Casting caution aside, Frasier nuzzled into her neck as he lifted her and gently rested her atop the bed. With a few flicks of his fingers he shucked his clothes, staring at her face, at the direction of her gaze, at her gasp, at her interest in his cock. He stroked himself. "Do I frighten you, lass?"

"No," she whispered, reaching for him. "I want you. I want all of you."

He kneeled over her, kissing, nuzzling, skimming his fingers atop the sensitive skin on her breasts. She shuddered beneath him. "May I touch you?"

"Mmm-hmm."

With yet another surprise, she stroked him as he had just done. "Here?"

He chuckled, his rumble low and deep in his chest. Yes, he wanted her to touch him everywhere, but she was an innocent. He would first see to her pleasure. "If you touch me there, the party will be over afore it starts."

Grace squirmed beneath him. "But how do I make you feel as delicious as you make me?"

He nibbled kisses around her breasts. "Merely touching you makes me ravenous," he growled, shifting between her knees and nibbling all the way down to those lovely curls.

"But am I not supposed to—"

"Wheesht, *mo leannan*. Just lie back whilst I taste you."

With her sigh, he nudged her silken thighs open with his shoulders.

"Are you certain...?" she asked, her breath hitching.

"Quite," he said, slipping his finger along her parting—oh, so wet, oh, so ready for him. "Does that not feel good?"

Grace gasped. "Inexplicitly so."

"See? I ken what you want lass." As he licked her tiny button, he watched her face, watched as the focus of her eyes waned, replaced by an unfettered expression of ecstasy.

"Oh," she sighed, her voice quavering.

Frasier licked and sucked while working his finger in and out, then adding a second, then squeezing in a third, her body responding, adjusting.

"Oh, my," Grace cried, her hips swirling, her breath panting.

"Come for me," he growled, hastening the tempo, her thighs trembling against his ears.

"Yes. Yes. Oh, God, yes!" she cried, her body suddenly rigid as if balancing on the pinnacle of ecstasy.

Slowly, he eased the pressure, helping her to come back to earth. By the time Grace opened her eyes, he'd crawled up beside her. "Hello, bonny lass," he whispered.

"Hello, braw highlander," she said with as thick a brogue as he'd ever heard. "Dunna ye reckon 'tis my turn to bring ye a wee bit o' pleasure?"

29

"From where did your wee brogue arise all of the sudden?" Frasier asked, his voice bemused.

Grace buried her face in the curve of his neck and laughed. "Do you not believe I can affect a Scottish accent? I have seven siblings, none of whom attended Northbourne Seminary for Young Ladies, and all of whom speak with brogues nearly as thick as yours. She nudged his shoulder and rolled on top of him, kissing and giggling. "Now, m'laird. I shall pleasure you!"

Grace wanted to kiss every inch of his body and gave him no choice but to lie back and enjoy her ministrations as she attempted to replicated every delicious thing he had done to her. She had always admired Frasier's masculinity, but dear God, the man was potently virile. He had muscles where she'd never imagined them to be. He had white scars that puckered and demanded to be kissed. And he had freckles on his shoulders, each one delightfully kissable.

His chest was covered with a riot of dark hair, his nipples darker than hers, and smaller, tightening into tiny buds as she brushed her fingers over them. And when she swirled her tongue around them, he arched into her mouth and moaned with pleasure.

Grace grinned through her kisses. How delightful it was to gain such control over a man whose body abounded with power. Every kiss brought a new sound—a sigh, a low growl, a hum of bliss. Every kiss made her want him all the more.

She moved lower and circled her tongue in his deep naval, earning a guttural groan. Moving downward, Grace traced the line of dark, mahogany hair to the triangle of curls more riotous than those on his chest where, to her glee, his manhood did not rest, but stood as rigid as a bedpost. She studied it, tapping the velvety tip with her finger...and earning a most salacious moan.

She moved her hand downward and wrapped her fingers around the warm shaft. "May I kiss it?"

"Och, no lady as fine as you ought to—"

Grace licked him.

"Dear God!" he growled, his hips thrusting upward. "If ye keep that up, ye will bring me undone!"

She licked him again. "Is that not the objective, m'laird?"

"Aye," he croaked.

Suddenly, she propped herself up on her elbow. Grace knew enough about coupling between a man and a woman that the appendage she so desperately wanted to lick was what bridegrooms used to consummate marriages. "Bring you undone?" she asked, her mind whirring. "Does this mean I can bring you pleasure without copulation?"

He urged her up beside him. "Och, lass. Perhaps we are moving a bit too fast."

"Are we? Should I not have knocked upon your door?"

"No...I mean, yes, I am most definitely thrilled to have you in my arms. So much so, I never want to release ye. But we need to agree on how far to go. Ye must ken if we make love, you could conceive."

Goodness, her lack of experience in matters of the bedchamber robbed Grace of her usual aplomb. "Um... Now that we are to marry, does it matter?"

"We canna marry for six months. I reckon ye dunna wish to be six months along on your wedding day."

She swirled her fingers through the downy hair on his chest. "I suppose it would cause quite a scandal—though it is now five months and sixteen days."

"Sixteen, aye," he growled, kissing her. "The first time can be quite painful I've heard."

Grace glanced down to his erect manhood with no doubt of the discomfort something that size would cause. "Pain..."

"Only the first time."

No matter the sacrifice, she wanted him. "I have an idea."

"Oh?" he asked.

"Well...I do not think a woman should be caused pain on the happiest night of her life."

A deep rumble came from his chest as he nibbled her earlobe. "Nay?"

"Absolutely not." She turned her head and found his mouth. "Teach me how to pleasure you in every way. And by the time three months pass, we shall consummate our to-be-wedding day."

"Och you are so fine, bonny Grace." He smoothed his hand over her hair, his smile brimming with more joy than she'd ever seen. "As long as I am allowed to pleasure ye every bit as much, I believe we have arrived at an agreeable solution."

"Oh, this will be fun!" Grace said as she slid down the length of his body, stopping just before she wrapped her fingers around his member. "We will be occupied with non-copulating for two months?"

"Aye, lass. If we run out of ideas, we'll make them up as we go."

She grinned as she returned to the task at hand.

~

THEY SLEPT in each other's arms until the wee hours when Grace quietly slipped back to her own bedchamber, she'd thought it would be easy to avoid copulation, but the following three days proved her to be quite wrong.

Maddeningly so.

Rapturously so.

And slipping away from her family when she was absolutely consumed with desire required a great deal of ingenuity and scheming. How could a married woman possibly make it through an entire morning without spiriting above stairs for a rendezvous with her husband? Especially given the dreary weather in November.

When the household took their morning tea in the parlor, as Julia poured the duchess mentioned she would enjoy lemon cake. At the suggestion, Grace and Frasier nearly ran in their haste to spirit away, find the larder, manage to lock the door where he deftly lifted her skirts.

Thank heavens the following day when the ladies went to a luncheon Grace feigned a megrim as her excuse to remain behind. Since the housemaids were working above stairs, she and Frasier found the library's fainting couch to be quite cozy...

As was the carpet.

Though the table didn't offer much in the way of comfort. Fun, absolutely. And it was exactly the right height for Frasier to...

Oh, holy macaroons, the man could perform wickedly delightful things with his member between her legs.

The problem?

She desperately wanted his wicked tool buried inside her. She was ravenous for it. His cock (as he called it) was what she dreamed of at night. What she thought about as she dressed in the mornings. It was where her gaze drifted every time he entered a room —at least to the sporran covering his wicked treasure.

At last today they were setting out for the lodge to intercept Martin and ask for his blessing. Grace had insisted on taking two carriages to which Mama hadn't balked. After all, Grace was a princess and she was wealthy enough to buy two carriages if she so chose. One good thing about being the snootiest child in the family was that no one questioned her excesses. They expected them. Furthermore, no one knew exactly how much her time at Druimliart had changed her.

Little did her kin know she was thrilled to hear Frasier had employed Lena and Davy irrespective of their experience. In addition, Grace and her intended had agreed to pay top wages and ensure any servants they employed were comfortably housed and had at least one-and-a-half holidays per week—unheard of! Even Martin only granted a half-holiday per week and two whole days per month. *Pshaw!* And to think the duke was considered to be a most generous employer.

Once their goodbyes had been said and the lead carriage containing Grace and Frasier was underway, kissing, groping, fondling, occurred while Grace's bodice somehow fell off and her stays practically unlaced themselves. Though she ought to be bashful with her bare breasts in Frasier's mouth, she had never felt the necessity to cover up with him.

Fire raced through her blood as his tongue teased her nipple. "I want you so badly I've gone insane with desire," she said, sliding her hand beneath his kilt. He was already hard as steel.

"Ye drove me mad the first time you opened your eyes in my cottage. I looked into those fathomless blues and kent you were the only woman I would ever love." He flicked his tongue over her tender flesh. "I've hungered for you ever since."

She chuckled as she stroked him. "Were you ever hard like this?"

"More often than I care to admit."

"Truly?" She kissed his mouth. "Why did you not pursue me? Act on your desires?"

"Ye ken why. It wouldna have been right."

Goodness, she loved him. He had wanted her during all those lonely, tension-filled nights, but had acted the gentleman because it was the proper thing to do. She'd wanted him so much as well, but was the wedded princess—lost, afraid, in hiding, and on the verge of falling into an abyss of ruin.

He inched up her skirts and slowly slipping his hand beneath. "You are so fine to me, *mo leannan*."

"I want you to enter me," she whispered.

Frasier sat back, his hand stilling. "Are you certain? What if you conceive?"

Grace's shoulders fell. "Then I suppose Marty will go off and to challenge you to a duel. My dratted, overbearing brother."

"Not exactly how to begin a relationship when a man wishes to marry his closet ally's sister."

"No." She bit the corner of her mouth. "Such a co-nundrum."

He arched on eyebrow as if scheming. "There is one thing we could try."

"Oh?"

"Before I spill, I could 'interrupt' the act."

"Interrupt?"

"Spill outside your womb."

"As you have already been doing."

"Aye, though 'tisn't foolproof. You could still get with child."

Oh, this was most definitely tempting. "How likely?"

"Not certain. Angus and Fiona wanted to wait until their cottage was built afore a bairn came, so they interrupted."

"Did it work?"

"For a time, I reckon—though Angus said the bairn came a wee bit earlier than they'd planned."

"Well, my dear wicked Highland renegade..." Grace scooted closer and batted her eyelashes. "We only need a small amount of time."

Frasier nuzzled into her ear. "I dunna want to hurt ye, lass."

She slid her hand up his thigh, and brushed her thumb in the crease where the leg met the hip. "One moment of pain followed by a lifetime of pleasure."

"How did you become so wise?"

"They do not simply teach manners at North-bourne." Allowing that notion to settle for a moment, she pushed his sporran aside and bared him. Of course, her formal education hadn't contained a single mention of what happens between a husband and a wife other than a single sentence that read, "*A wife must submit to her husband.*" Nonetheless, Grace had heard enough gossip to know there was a great deal of pleasure to be enjoyed if one had the right partner, and she had no doubt she'd found hers.

"Aye?" He kissed the top of her breast. "Am I to believe 'tis a school for trollops?"

"Not exactly. I believe the trollop seminary is headed by a most robust laird I happen to be quite intimate with."

"A laird, aye?"

"Yes." Grace's breath sped as he slipped his hand beneath her skirts. "A very wicked laird who seduces widows."

"Mayhap one widow in particular."

"Mmm..."

Before he went any farther, Grace pressed her hands against his shoulders and slid her leg across his lap. "I do believe we arrived in this position at some point on the fainting couch in the library."

He grinned, his beautiful eyes shining as together their bodies swayed with the rocking of the carriage. "I'll never forget the fainting couch."

She kissed him deeply. "I won't forget a single moment."

He rocked his hips against her. "Are you certain you dunna care to wait?"

"Most certain," she said, lifting and capturing the tip of his member in the spot where his fingers had caressed her so many times in the past few days. Though she was as wet as she'd ever been, when she tried to ease downward, her body refused to cooperate. "I do not think it will fit."

His grasp tightened around her. "Does it hurt overmuch?"

Grace wiggled, trying to inch downward and feeling the stretch. "No."

"Well, lassie, just remember we're not in a race. We willna be stopping to change horses for a few hours yet. He grasped her hips and urged her to rock to and fro. "Easy now. You are in control. You can stop any time for any reason."

"But it should not be this difficult!" she groaned, losing patience.

Frasier chuckled. "I'm no' a wee lad."

"Neither are you as huge as a horse!" Grace dug her fingers into his shirt and bore down, the pain searing as if she'd ripped open her insides. Stars shot through her vision as she buried her head in his neck and bit down on her lip. She would not cry out. "Just a bit more," she squeaked, trying not to sound as if she were about to die.

"I think I'm buried to the hilt," he whispered, swirling his hand around her back. "Just breathe and wait until your body adjusts."

Closing her eyes, she did what he said until ever so slowly, he moved just a fraction. "Better?" he asked.

"Mmm-hmm."

"Would you like to stop?"

She looked him in the eye and shook her head. "May I move as well?"

"Aye," he croaked, his eyes growing darker.

She let him dictate a rhythmic tempo, moving her hips forward and back. "You will interrupt?"

"After you take your pleasure," he said, moving his thumb downward until it stroked the most sensitive place on her body. "Do you like this?"

"Yes." She increased the tempo with the thundering of her heart. Frasier touched her in exactly the right spot to send her into a ravenous tempest of desire no matter the pain, no matter the stretching.

While Grace cried out with her release, he

grabbed her hips and thrust three times before he lifted her and finished into his handkerchief.

As she slowly regained normal breathing, she reclined against the velvet back of the carriage's bench. "I do believe we have discovered my new favorite position."

30

Front Page News 7ᵗʰ May 1819: The Duke of Dunscaby is pleased to announce that his sister Princess Grace has joined in holy matrimony with Laird Frasier Buchanan of Clairinsh, wealthy landowner and Chieftain of Clan Buchanan...

Six months ago when the couple had traveled to the lodge to meet with the Duke of Dunscaby and ask for his blessing, he revealed that not only was it "about time," he also admitted to riding more than fifty miles out of his way to find Frasier in Dumbarton and ensure the laird received word that Grace had been widowed. Of course, after such an admission there had been no qualms as to the duke's blessing, especially since his duchess had expressed her concern over Grace's state of melancholy since the death of Prince Isidor. Furthermore, Julia was quite convinced the reason for the princess' sorrows had nothing to do with becoming a widow and everything to do with a certain laird whom Martin had discovered in a passionate embrace with his sister.

One year and one day after Grace was widowed, she married Frasier. Her second wedding was entirely different from her first. To her, the greatest difference was at long last she was marrying a man with whom she was utterly in love. Though spectators might have called the ceremony modest, it was the most sublime experience in which she had ever taken part.

They were married in the drawing room of Castle Buchanan before a small gathering of family members. Grace held a bouquet of dried heather, her only jewelry—a simple strand of pearls with matching earrings. Atop a shift of holland cloth, she wore a beautifully woven Arisaid in the MacGalloway tartan of dark blue and green, belted at her waist and pinned at the shoulder with her clan brooch. Biddle had styled her hair in a single braid adorned by a crown of heather entwined with white satin ribbon.

The groom wore a velvet coat in bottle-green atop a newly woven Buchanan kilt in the bold colors of red, green, yellow, and blue.

The house flowers had not come from a hothouse. They were clipped from Ramsey's garden and included lavender, daisies, and bluebells. The vicar from the kirk in Balmaha presided over the ceremony while Grace stared up into Frasier's striking blue eyes, reciting her vows with tears of happiness welling in her eyes.

Aside from their quest to sample every lovemaking position possible, they had actually found enough time out of the bedchamber to turn their new home into their own paradise. They combined their fortunes and decorated each room with an eye for comfort as well as style. They had traveled to Edinburgh on a quest to outfit their library with books of prose and poetry. Now the shelves were full and they had a globe marked with the places they planned to visit. Beside it was a black-and-white marble chessboard as well as Frasier's wooden cup with hazard dice (mind you, the challenges had grown quite deliciously wanton in the past six months).

It was late when the last of their guests departed the isle. As the door closed, leaving them alone, Frasier lifted his bride into his arms and started up the grand staircase. "I have never been so happy," he said, his ruggedly handsome face smiling down at her.

She laced her arms around his neck. "Nor have I. So happy, I never want this moment to end."

He stopped on the landing and kissed her. "Let us make a pact."

"What sort of pact?"

"That wherever we go, whatever we do, at least once a day we remind each other of how fortunate we are."

"I love that idea," she said as he continued up to their bedchamber which overlooked Loch Lomond and was furnished with a mahogany four-poster bed festooned with ivory bed curtains. "We are ever so lucky, are we not?"

He set her onto her feet and held her cheeks in his warm palms. "Exceedingly so."

She rose up and kissed him again, never growing tired will the thrill the touch of his lips instilled in her heart. "You must know I would have married you even if it meant living in Druimliart for the rest of our days."

He removed her crown of heather and dropped it onto a velvet armchair. "Truly?"

"Positively. When I am with you, nothing else matters. You are my home. Yes, we live in a castle with more than we need, but all of it is superfluous." She unbuttoned his coat and slid it from his shoulders, letting it fall to the floor. "Your arms are my elixir. If we lost everything on the morrow, my love for you would not falter."

He pulled out a note from inside his waistcoat. "Well, I dunna reckon we'll have to ever worry about being penniless, *mo leannan*."

"Oh?"

Frasier opened the letter and handed it to her. "Martin gave us your dower funds."

She read the exorbitant amount. "My heavens, I thought he'd paid this to Isidor."

"He confided that he had the note ready to give the prince afore ye left Carlton House, but circumstances..."

She chuckled. "Went awry." After placing the note into the writing table's top drawer, she returned to her husband's embrace.

Frasier's eyes were filled with love and contentment, his mouth curled in a satiated grin. "What would you like to do with all that coin? Buy a London town house, mayhap another estate?"

She tugged off his neckcloth. "I think we ought to save it for our children."

"I love that idea. And whoever said you were self-absorbed?" As soon as the question left his lips, his eyes popped wide. "Are you...?"

She released the top button of his shirt. "I don't think so."

He lifted her into his arms again and carried her to the bed setting her down on the soft feather mattress. "Well then, wife," he whispered in his alluring deep brogue. "That is something we must remedy."

AUTHOR'S NOTE

Thank you for reading *A Princess in Plaid*, book five in The MacGalloways series. Though these books are centered on the fictional MacGalloway family, they can be read in order or as stand-alone novels.

A word of note about Clan Buchanan. With the death of John Buchanan of that ilk in 1681, there were no male heirs and the line of the clan chiefs officially stopped. The clan continued on and supported the 1745 Jacobite rebellion. Francis Buchanan who was a contender to become the next clan chief, was the Armorer and Treasurer of the Jacobite Rebellion and was beheaded in a public execution along with other members of the Buchanan clan. In an attempt to crush the clan, the Act of Proscription was passed along with other legislation in an attempt to assimilate the Scottish Highlands, suppress the clan system, and prevent future rebellions. Clan Buchanan was particularly targeted, being declared outlaws. Fearing persecution and death, clan members laid low for the next three hundred years. In the 1970s when a group of Buchanans formed the Clan Buchanan Society of America, eventually becoming Clan Buchanan So-

ciety International. It wasn't until 1999 that Scottish
Parliament reconvened and John Michael Ballie-
Hamilton Buchanan of that Ilk and Arnprior was rec-
ognized as clan chief and given the Arms of
Buchanan.

THE MACGALLOWAY FAMILY TREE

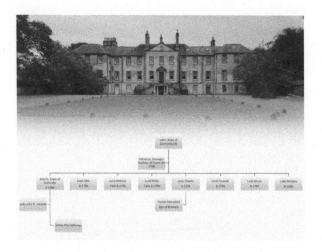

To view a larger version of this, click here.

In the Kingdom's Name
The Time Traveler's Destiny

Highland Dynasty
Knight in Highland Armor
A Highland Knight's Desire
A Highland Knight to Remember
Highland Knight of Rapture
Highland Knight of Dreams

Devilish Dukes
The Duke's Fallen Angel
The Duke's Untamed Desire
The Duke's Privateer
The Duke's Secret Longing

ICE
Hunt for Evil
Body Shot
Mach One

Blitzed

Defenseless
Unintentional
Tackled

Celtic Fire
Rescued by the Celtic Warrior
Deceived by the Celtic Spy

Lords of the Highlands series:

The Highland Duke
The Highland Commander
The Highland Guardian
The Highland Chieftain
The Highland Renegade
The Highland Earl
The Highland Rogue
The Highland Laird

The Chihuahua Affair
Virtue: A Cruise Dancer Romance
Boy Man Chief
Time Warriors

ABOUT THE AUTHOR

Known for her action-packed, passionate historical romances, Amy Jarecki has received reader and critical praise throughout her writing career. She won the prestigious 2018 RT Reviewers' Choice award for *The Highland Duke* and the 2016 RONE award from InD'tale Magazine for Best Time Travel for her novel *Rise of a Legend*. In addition, she hit Amazon's Top 100 Bestseller List, the Apple, Barnes & Noble, and Bookscan Bestseller lists, in addition to earning the designation as an Amazon All Star Author. Readers also chose her Scottish historical romance, *A Highland Knight's Desire*, as the winning title through Amazon's Kindle Scout Program. Amy holds an MBA from Heriot-Watt University in Edinburgh, Scotland and now resides in Southwest Utah with her husband where she writes immersive historical romances. Learn more on Amy's website. Or sign up to receive Amy's newsletter.